**THE WORST NAZIS NEVER WENT
INTO HIDING.
THEY ARE ALIVE AND ABOUT TO BUILD
A NEW MONSTER STATE ON THE
TIP OF AFRICA ...**

PROTÉGÉ

*THE FIRST WAS ERNST HARTMANN, AKA
JAMES LANGWAY MacKEE.* With an SS tattoo
on his inner arm and the IRS on his tail, he
faked his death to avoid detection—and taxes
on a $26,000,000 swindle. But even a headless
corpse without hands can be identified.

*THE SECOND WAS HANS PETER HIRSCH,
A BANKER FROM ZURICH, AN ASSASSIN.*
He's a killer with a .457 Magnum that could
knock out the eye of an elephant at 2,000 yards.
So murdering the President would be no problem.

THE THIRD WAS BARON HOVAGNY ...

THE FOURTH WAS STEENKAMP ...

THE FIFTH, SIXTH, SEVENTH, EIGHTH,
NINTH, TENTH ... AND ON TO NUMBER
TWENTY WERE ALL ALIVE, SINISTER
AND READY TO KILL FOR THE SAKE OF
THE MASTER RACE. NUMBERS TWENTY
AND TWENTY-ONE HAD ALREADY
JOINED ADMIRAL CANARIS ...

PROTÉGÉ
A PLOT TO TAKE OVER THE WORLD

PROTÉGÉ

Malcolm MacPherson

BANTAM BOOKS · TORONTO · NEW YORK · LONDON

PROTÉGÉ

*A Bantam Book / published by arrangement with
E. P. Dutton*

PRINTING HISTORY
*Dutton edition published June 1980
Bantam edition / June 1981*

To Barbara
with love,
for her support
and understanding.

HERMAN GOERING: The protégés of Wilhelm Canaris in Abwehr were the brightest and the youngest the Reich had to offer.

PROSECUTOR: Who are the protégés?

HERMAN GOERING: (No answer)

PROSECUTOR: Where are they?

HERMAN GOERING: (No answer)

—*From testimony given at the Nuremberg Trials, 1946*

1

His back against the morning light, a man was seated in a rattan chair on the veranda of the Kilimanjaro Hotel. A breath of wind off the sultry waters of the port ruffled the silver wisps of his hair. He listened to the lazy scratching of palm leaves, the Swahili chatter, the far-off diesel chug of dhows as they shuttled cargo from ship to shore. He saw natives on the quay laboring beneath jute sacks of Zanzibar cloves and coffee from the Highlands, and, in the street below, passing donkey carts with bells that chimed in the heavy tropical air.

In the early days, when this was called Tanganyika, he had found comfort and intense security within the confines of these now-familiar surroundings. The things he saw and heard were an exotic language telling him that past was past; he could do anything he wanted without fear or restraint. But it had been a rebirth within a lie. As the years passed, the world became a smaller place. The odds against him increased. He had thought that change was a word without meaning here but he had been wrong about that, too.

He took the cigarette from his lips and exhaled, once more checking the sequence for flaws. Yes, he thought finally, every part fit. He had planned well for his departure, the first time in twelve years that he had ventured beyond these frontiers. He butted out the stub end of the cigarette in the conch ashtray and looked up as a man in a blue blazer approached from across the terrace. When he came nearer, the man gave him a smile.

"Are we finally ready?" he asked in a genial voice.

"Yes, sir," the hotel manager replied. "Your car and driver are outside. If you'll follow me."

He stood up and pushed on the balls of his feet, stretching long legs. With remarkable china-blue eyes he glanced down to the canvas bag on the tiled floor. "Will you lend a hand?" he asked, then, "Be careful, though. It's heavier than it looks."

The manager shouldered the bag and they walked through the lobby to the ramp leading into Magazine Street. Nearby was the fort where the German colonials had stored their munitions. Now it was the mercantile center and teemed with hawkers and beggars.

An attendant stepped from the crowded sidewalk and opened the back door of a Land Rover, then kicked down a mounting platform. The man nodded thanks and swung into the seat, while his bag was thrown into the rear luggage space. The driver started the engine and, as they pulled into traffic, the manager saluted good-bye.

They took a familiar route from the port through narrow back streets. There had been a monsoon shower the night before and the pavement was guttered by congealed refuse and garbage; the houses and shops gave off steam in the rising heat. They came onto a main road of two lanes that led south to Kisarawe and far beyond, toward the Mozambique border, past warehouses, shipping offices, petrol stations, and over the last railroad bridge to the roundabout. Now there were fewer and fewer signs of civilization, where the bush began.

The man looked through the window at the cumulus. It meant clear weather. Those clouds, which drifted off the Indian Ocean and into the African interior, were like flags of the continent, for they existed only here, round and stately. The minute they left the western shores, they were buffeted by winds and broken up. Whenever he saw them, he felt a wave of nostalgia. Like a safe roof, they meant home.

Just beyond the Kiwalani Pond the Land Rover entered the stone gates of the airport. The man was a flyer and he had been here many times before to take his Cessna to Arusha. He ordered the driver to pull up across from the air freight offices. He got out and shaded his eyes, looking for the signboard. Then, hoisting the bag, he thanked the driver and walked toward a corrugated shed on the opposite side of the dirt road.

The pilot, in a dewlapped hat, hunched over his desk. Despite the early hour, even hungry geckos on the ceiling were too enervated to slither after insects. The pilot pushed back his hat and wiped a film of sweat from his neck. The papers he was rereading told his story. Soon he would have to relinquish ownership of his major asset, the sky-blue, twin-engine Partenavia that sat idle and mortgaged outside in the shade of the hangar. He was so far into debt that liquidation was his only salvation. He sighed, then turned at the unfamiliar sound of a footfall.

"I'm looking for Afro-Air," the man said, setting down the canvas bag. "Is this the place?"

"That's me," David Johnson said, rising from the desk. "I suppose you've come about the Partenavia." Sooner or later he expected some neat and tailored stranger to arrive and foreclose on him. Like this man.

"That I have," the man said.

"Well, she's out there," he said, pointing through the grimy glass toward the hangar. "If you've come to impound her, just do it and get it over with. Here are the keys." He turned back to the desk.

The man made a coughing noise. "You've got it wrong," he said. "I've come to charter the airplane, not impound it."

David Johnson looked over his shoulder distrustfully. If this guy was playing games, it was cruel. Nobody had rented the Partenavia now for more than a month. Christ, he thought, nobody had even inquired. He turned and looked at the man. "I . . . I guess I didn't hear you right," he said. "You want to charter?"

"Yes," he replied, unequivocally. "It'll be a day hop to Arusha and back."

"Excuse me, but why not use one of the other lines?"

"Because you need the business."

Johnson came forward, extending his hand. "I'm David Johnson, sir. And you're right about needing the work."

The man shook his hand firmly. "MacKee's mine. James MacKee. Glad to help you out."

Johnson looked at MacKee now with increased interest.

His eyes were like star sapphires, he thought. They bracketed a hawkish nose with heavy brows. There were lines around the mouth. By the look of his clothes he guessed he was a man of substance. What should he charge? thought Johnson. The rate for the Arusha run was usually around two thousand shillings.

"Do you know my rates?" Johnson asked.

MacKee shook his head. "I'll pay three thousand," he said, inwardly pleased by the pilot's sudden beaming reaction.

"That's a bit less than usual but I'll take it," Johnson remarked. Good, he thought to himself, he had himself a stay of execution. With this money the bank would hold off for a few weeks more. Maybe his luck was turning, he thought happily.

"I'll pilot her myself," MacKee said. "I should be back by late afternoon." He glanced at Johnson's thin neck and wrists and unconsciously touched the breast pocket of his safari suit.

"You're licensed?"

"Yes, of course."

"By—"

"The local TAA."

"That's fine, then," Johnson said. He went to the desk, where he found a standard flight plan, then handed it to MacKee. "Fill this out, the usual. You know where to file it?"

"Yes," MacKee said, uncapping a silver fountain pen.

"See you in the hangar." Johnson went to load the wing tanks and dust off the airplane.

MacKee made certain he was gone, then took out his wallet. He found the card he wanted and laid it on the counter top. On the form he printed the information in clear, bold letters, so there could be no mistake. His name: James Langway MacKee. Business affiliation: Chairman and Chief Executive Officer, Tanzanian Coffee Board. Before he filled in the space allotted for the license number, he checked the card. He printed the numbers and then, at the bottom of the form, the altitude, cruising speed, course, and ETA for his destination. Under the notation for passengers: NONE. Last of all, he signed his name with a flourish.

Now he went from the office in the direction of the flight center. He heard a roar overhead and paused on the path to admire the approach of the Lufthansa 747 on its daily run from South Africa to Frankfurt with stops in Dar es Salaam and Zurich. The jumbo reversed thrust and moved onto a taxiway.

In the air-conditioned flight center, MacKee watched as an African official read the flight form with routine interest. Finding everything in order, he stamped it with the TAA seal, then filed it and wished MacKee a safe journey. The process of filling out the form and filing it had taken nearly twenty minutes.

MacKee strolled to Afro-Air's hangar. He found the side entrance easily. Inside, he allowed his eyes to dilate and focus in the dim interior. Johnson saw him and crawled down from the port wing, tenderly running his hand along the aileron's surface. "Wish I could join you," he said. "I sure miss my wings, but I can't afford the fuel to take her up for a joyride." He shrugged off the thought. "Anyway, are you set?"

"All taken care of. The center has always been pretty efficient." He looked at the Partenavia, then at Johnson. He wore an expression of annoyance. "You could have saved me a lot of time telling me, you know."

"What?" Johnson asked, surprised.

"Look at her, she's a *twin,* for God's sake." His frustration was growing visibly.

"So? She was never a Gulfstream II."

"I'm not licensed to fly twin-engines, only single-props. . . . I mean, I can't fly her. I don't know how."

Johnson wondered how this man could have been so mistaken. Everybody knew he had a twin. All Partenavias were twins. "What can I say?" he asked. "I didn't mean to delude you, sir, but I sure as hell can't do anything about it now. You'll have to charter elsewhere, I guess."

MacKee folded his arms. He was silent for an instant, thinking. "Sorry if I barked at you. It isn't your fault. I should have known better."

"There's another charter service on the other side of the main terminal. They've got single-props." He hated to let this one go, but if the guy couldn't fly it, he couldn't.

"No, that won't do. There's no time. And I sent my driver away. How about you taking me to Arusha?"

It was just exactly what Johnson wanted to hear, but he held off his reply, knowing now that he had MacKee in a bind. "It'll cost you," he said.

MacKee didn't hesitate. "Another two thousand?"

"You're on, sir," Johnson said, the excitement showing in his voice, although he was baffled for the briefest instant by MacKee's generosity. He turned toward the hangar door. "Why don't you get aboard, I'll only be a minute. The flight report has to be changed."

"Is that so important? Like I said, I'm in a hurry."

"Those are the rules," Johnson said automatically.

"Do me a favor, just this once? I have to be in Arusha in an hour. I'll be late if you file. I might as well just cancel out."

Johnson felt the wad of bills in his pocket. "Well . . . I guess I can do it when we get back. Why not?"

MacKee gave him a friendly slap on the back, then followed him to the aircraft. "You're a good man," he said, handing up the canvas bag. "I won't forget it."

A few minutes later the engines coughed sluggishly and came to life. As the oil pressure and temperature reached their levels, Johnson set the parking brake and strapped a belt around the bag on the back seat. He went down his regs., then taxied to One-Right. After final magneto checks and RPM run-ups, Partenavia number 5YBBT bolted into the sky with Dar tower ordering a turn west and then north below the path of commercial jets at the outer marker. A while later, 5YBBT reached cruise elevation and became a speck on a clear horizon.

Inside the cockpit, Johnson concentrated on the instruments, trimming the aircraft before engaging the Bendix automatic pilot. MacKee was a good bloke, he thought. "This means a lot to me, sir," he said above the engine noise.

MacKee acknowledged the remark with a smile and

looked over his right shoulder out the window. The city of Dar es Salaam was just below and to the east. The waters of the crescent port were a brownish gray. He saw markers in the channel. It was narrow, but it was also deep. . . .

"Everything okay?" Johnson asked, seeing the worried expression on MacKee's face.

"Daydreaming," he answered.

"What's happening in Arusha?" the pilot asked, cheerfully, as he put aside a chart.

"Business and pleasure," MacKee replied, wanting to earn the pilot's confidence. "And listen, thanks again. If there's a question, let me know and I'll take care of it."

"It was nothing, really," Johnson said, warming to his passenger. "What line of work you in?"

"Coffee," he replied. "I'm meeting with the growers near Kilimanjaro."

Johnson whistled appreciatively. "That's a big business," he remarked. "Do you own your own land?"

"I did, near Arusha. But no longer."

"Got nationalized, huh? I'm sorry."

MacKee did not reply.

"I read where the government's taken over. They'll probably make a mess of it. Somebody said there's a lot of corruption already in the coffee trade. Now there'll be more."

"If they're like other Africans, the corruption will come easily. Running the business won't."

"Yeah, you're right. What about the pleasure side?"

"Oh, that," MacKee replied, mildly surprised by the question. "Some sport."

"Hunting?"

"No. . . ." He hesitated. "I wanted to arrange with the guides to take me up Kilimanjaro sometime this month. I'm an amateur climber."

Johnson looked at him. Kilimanjaro was the highest mountain in Africa and one of the toughest peaks in the world to conquer. Many advanced climbers had died trying. He was impressed. "No disrespect, sir, but you couldn't get me to climb Kilimanjaro. You go up, you go down. So what? That's how I feel about it. For myself, there's nothing like the strike of a black marlin. Have you ever tried?"

"Once or twice," MacKee replied. He pointed to the clock on the instrument panel. "Tell me, how far would you say?"

The pilot raised up in his seat for a clear view of the horizon. "Less than halfway. You'll be on the ground in about thirty minutes."

Just then the Partenavia rocked violently in a low-pressure pocket. MacKee tensed as the airplane hit bottom, then shot up again. The autopilot instantly checked the drift.

"Whoa," Johnson remarked. "That came out of nowhere."

"The Bendix worked nicely," MacKee said. "Is it special?"

"About as simple and normal as my budget allowed. But it's all we need, as you saw."

MacKee reached through the seat space and unzipped the canvas bag. By fishing around with his hand, he found what he wanted. He opened the lid of the tin box with his thumbnail. "Take one?" he asked casually.

Johnson hesitated, then reached into the tin. "I'm a gum junkie myself," he said. "So long as it clears the ears, though, it doesn't matter. Thanks."

MacKee made a show of choosing one. Out of the corner of his eye he saw Johnson trim the fuel mixture levers. He might be bankrupt, thought MacKee, but he was a good pilot. It was a pity really.

"Mind if I have another?" Johnson asked, reaching into the tin box. "My girl friend loves these. They're French, huh? Gelatin pastilles?"

"Yes," then quickly, "So you're a fisherman. Have you tried the trout streams in the Aberdares, in Kenya?"

"I hear they're great," Johnson said, rubbing his eyelids. He straightened in the seat.

"Is anything wrong?" MacKee asked solicitously.

"I didn't get much in the way of sleep last night," he explained. "A late dinner and too damned much brandy. There's nothing to worry about, though."

"I take it you're not married?" MacKee persisted, now concentrating on the time.

"My wife left me and went back to the States. I can't blame her, really. This isn't much of a life, not for a young woman with a career." But he missed her more than anything.

"I know what you mean."

"And you?"

"Unh-unh."

"Never married? I don't believe that. A good-looking guy like you?"

"That's the way it is."

"But lots of girl friends . . ."

"Some, but not many of them either. I've discovered it pays to be single-minded."

Johnson yawned loudly. He felt sluggish and saliva was forming thickly in his mouth. "Going back to fishing," he said. "My favorite haunt is off Lamu, you know, that island near the coast by the Somalia border. Some buddies and I fly up there every so often. Let me tell you, it's beautiful, like paradise."

"I've been to Petley's," MacKee said.

"You have? No kidding? Then you know."

"Yeah, a writer named Evelyn Waugh once called it the world's worst hotel. I didn't see much of the island."

Johnson reached for the nozzle in the ceiling and directed a flow of cool air onto the back of his neck. "Then he was wrong," he said. He felt awful. "The *most* goddamned exquisite little place on earth, Lamu is."

"Maybe so," MacKee whispered, knowing that the pilot should by now be almost beyond hearing.

"Mermaids are there." He stopped and swallowed hard, queasy and disoriented. What was it that MacKee had just said? "Not *real* mermaids, but tell that to the Arabs." He strained to focus on MacKee. He was a blur. "You know, dugongs, those sea cows that are extinct. Arabs made love to them, thinking they were, well, that they were mermaids."

"So I've heard."

"What?"

"I said . . ."

"And Queen Victoria's teeth, her *false* teeth, from the skulls of sailors, on the beach, in Lamu." Johnson patted the back of his neck. "Sailing . . . sailing dhows . . . and sharks from the Indian . . ."

MacKee's face was now masklike, cold. Johnson was turning gray.

"Mr. Mac . . . Help me, please!" Johnson's ashened face pushed toward MacKee's. His lips were swelling grotesquely, a bloated slash of purple across his face. "Help . . . me. I'm go . . ." He fell forward against the control column.

The Partenavia plunged on its starboard wing toward the ground. The altimeter spun behind the glass. Against the G force, MacKee managed to grab Johnson by the neck and pull his weight back. He wedged himself between the wheel and the pilot, finally righting the airplane. He wiped his mouth and breathed deeply, then switched in the autopilot. Moments later, satisfied with the trim and the heading, he reached over to Johnson. He lifted his eyelids with his thumb and forefinger. The pupils were wide and rolled upward. He pressed his pulse, trying both the arm and the neck. Then, to make certain, he placed his ear against his chest. There was nothing.

Number 5YBBT cruised on autopilot north at ten thousand feet above the dry scrubland of the Masai Steppe and, to the west, the village of Naberera. MacKee saw the landmarks, by now more familiar to him than any in the world. He twisted in his seat and struggled to pull the canvas bag onto his lap, spilling its contents in the footwell.

Again he verified the heading. Air speed was gobbling up precious minutes and he now needed every one. He drew back on the throttles. The Partenavia braked hard in midair, forcing him to lower flaps. At eighteen degrees, the plane settled at a slower ground speed. He hoped it would give him time.

The cramped interior space made movement difficult. But he made the most of what he had. The pilot's seat back lowered easily into a prone position. He straightened up Johnson's body as best he could, then got to work.

First he ripped open Johnson's shirt, emblazoned with the patch of Afro-Air. That had to go. Johnson's arms came easily out of the sleeves, but the pants were harder. He took scissors from the bundle of equipment and cut the trouser seams from ankle to hip. He then removed the halves, from top and from bottom.

Next he drew from the footwell an exact copy of his own safari suit. It was the same forest green, manufactured by Ahmed Bros., with his name and pattern number on the collar tag. He muttered as he strained to slip the legs of the suit over Johnson's shoes. On his knees, he pulled them up, then zipped the fly and cinched the belt, again like his own, with the gold double G's. Next came the shirt, which he buttoned effortlessly. When he was finished, he looked at his victim. Yes, he thought, it was going to work.

He checked his wristwatch. The switch had taken ten valuable minutes, more than he had thought. Now he definitely needed more time.

The Partenavia came around after he adjusted the heading knob on the Bendix. It arced in a wide circle and MacKee glanced at the terrain. To the east he saw the reassuring outline of Lake Pangani. He brought his attention back inside the cockpit and to the Bendix. If he was going to feather the starboard engine, he would need to compensate for the torque that would swing the airplane to starboard. He had to put on hard left rudder just to keep the airplane straight. And he would set the angle of descent at forty-five degrees.

Now he only had one thing left to do.

With calm deliberation he removed a brown oilpaper envelope from his breast pocket. Holding it in the sunlight, he saw the silhouette, then slid the Swedish steel sliver into his palm. The scalpel was perfectly honed.

MacKee rested the edge of the surgical instrument on Johnson's neck, then pressed down, slicing through the layers of flesh.

2

"Long-distance for you, sir." The secretary's nasal voice came through the desk intercom. "Shall I put it through?"

Hans Peter Hirsch neatly replaced the pen he was using in its holder. "Who is it, Marie?" he asked.

"The caller won't say, Mr. Hirsch. But he claims to know you."

Any other bank president would not have taken the call. But Hans Peter Hirsch was different. As head of the Commercial Credit Union, known in Zurich as CCU, he had clients who were pathological about secrecy and anonymity. Sometimes when calling they identified themselves by numbers, by proper nouns, or by codes. This caller wasn't offering anything at all, which meant he was a client. "Okay," he said, "Let's see who—" The connection was made in mid-sentence.

"It's Hartmann," the caller said, his voice distorted by the echo in the satellite transmission. Hans Peter Hirsch did not immediately reply. "Hello? Peter, are you there?" the caller insisted.

"Yes, of course. I'm listening, Ernst."

"Have you talked to them?"

"No," Peter Hirsch replied. He had been expecting this telephone call.

"I'll be there tomorrow evening. Set it for eight."

"Das lässt sich machen," Hirsch said.

"The Baron is coming too," Hartmann said. "We'll need rooms."

"You'll be our guest in Küssnacht."

"Our guest?"

"Yes, I have a surprise for you, Ernst."

"No surprises!"

"Don't worry, Ernst. I'm ready for anything. We *are* all ready. It is a great thing we are doing. I am sure it is a miracle."

"*Not* a miracle," Hartmann said, slightly annoyed. "Meticulous planning and hard work and timing. Miracles are made, they don't happen."

"Whatever you say, Ernst. Tomorrow at eight, then?"

"That's right," Ernst Hartmann said, and hung up.

Hans Peter Hirsch stared at the telephone receiver. Then, slowly, he smiled. Hartmann had always criticized him for talking too much, for his unbridled enthusiasm. Hans Peter was a dreamer, true. He leaned back in his chair and for a few minutes longer savored his thoughts. After all these years of secret dealings . . .

But he must get to work. He straightened up and flicked the intercom toggle, reading to his secretary a list of telephone numbers taken from the inside page of his personal book. Some were local, to the Schweizerische Volksbank. Another went to Vevey on Lake Leman, to ABF, the food conglomerate; then still more to a Basel pharmaceutical concern, a German town hall, an automobile manufacturer, and Italian and Austrian brokerage houses and banks. The total was sixteen.

The last Hirsch dialed himself. A number in Winterthur outside Zurich, it went through the switchboard of Switzerland's largest arms maker.

"Ruethli?" Hirsch asked.

"*Ja, bitte.*" Ruethli Gruetz owned the armament company.

"Hans Peter here," Hirsch said in Swiss-German. "We are on for tomorrow." He recited the time and location.

"Tomorrow we begin," he said, then hung up. Exultant, he glanced at his watch. Noon. Norah would be waiting.

She turned at the sound of the black Mercedes limousine as it entered the winding drive of the Hirsch estate in Küssnacht on the rim of Lake Zurich. Her mittened hands were freezing and a numb rosy nose made her look even more girlish. She had lost track of the time on her stroll by the shore. But despite the chill on her bones, she felt alive and purposeful as never before.

Seeing her, Hans Peter leaned across the seat to open the door.

"You must be crazy, in this cold," he said.

"Brrrrrr." Norah shivered in the sudden warmth of the car. She rubbed her cheeks, then covered the heater vent with her hands. "God, I didn't realize! My blood has thinned out. How do you stand it?"

Hans Peter looked at her with a rare glimpse of understanding. In many ways she was still the little girl he had once taken into his life and loved. But Norah was no little girl. She had straight blond hair, a faultless woman's figure, and colt legs. Her beauty was uncommon, everybody said so, they always had. Once that had made Hans Peter proud. He now saw her dark suntan. A few years ago it had reflected a life-style of winters in Gstaad and St. Moritz and long summers at his villa in Porto Cervo. But that freckled tan was not now the aid to beauty that it once had been.

In her he could see his Ruth. They had been married in the middle fifties when Norah was still an infant. He thought that he had loved her, but love had not been his initial motivation. What he needed for his business, especially in Zurich, was a wife. It made things easier. Ruth had assumed the role of hostess and together they had lived comfortably. Then came the accident.

Soon after Ruth died, the gulf widened between him and Norah. As her legal father, he had not been able to cope alone. She was too young and much too rambunctious. So he had sent her off to Montreux. Since her graduation, which he had not attended, Norah's life became a mystery which he hadn't cared to solve. But he knew the broad outlines. There had been casual affairs in Paris and London, a flirtation with drugs in Morocco, and a steady wanderlust. She had never settled with one man, though there had been no shortage of offers.

This visit was the first time in years that they had been together. Norah thought Zurich was a dull place and stayed away. Hans Peter's few friends and their sons were provincial, she said, which made this visit even more unexpected. In the week since she had arrived, they had circled one another cautiously, probing but respecting the other's privacy.

The car stopped near the broad front steps. In the cold, they did not notice the pale winter sun or the checkered patterns of vapor trails across the bleached blue sky. The garden at the side of the wooded estate was covered in a blanket of snow. A bright point of color, a Swiss flag fluttered on a pole near the edge of the pond.

They threw their heavy winter coats on a bench near the door, chatting as they climbed the stairs to a main sitting room, which was decorated through random acquisition more than by design. There was a zebra-skin rug, a large elephant tusk near the mantel, several Persian carpets, and African sculpture. The furniture was old and precious. On one table were photographs of Norah as a child, Ruth and Hans Peter, and several men whom Norah had never met. A wood fire crackled, giving off a comfortable warmth.

Norah fell onto a down-pillowed sofa covered in soft leather. Hans Peter went to the sideboard for a whiskey, then sat down in the Wassily across from the sofa. When he turned to her, he faced an impish grin.

"Did we make a fortune today?" she asked, wrinkling a button nose that had regained its tanned coloring in the warmth of the room.

In spite of himself, Hans Peter chuckled. "Not nearly enough, not nearly, to cover your bills." He looked her up and down, making the point. She had on expensive French jeans, a dark-maroon Saint Laurent blouse that hung loosely on her narrow shoulders. On her feet were soft, hand-sewn boots, which she tucked under her.

"There's only you and the little I earn," she said. "I'm grateful, really I am." The allowance he gave her permitted a few luxuries that she otherwise could not afford.

Looking at her now, Hans Peter wondered why none of the introductions he had made had ever worked. The men in the Zurich banking community had never turned her head. But at the age of twenty-five, he thought, she should be settling down. Like other women, she should be starting a family.

Indeed, he did not know in great detail what she did do. She had told him only that she worked as a secretary for a small import-export company based in Tel Aviv. He knew that her infatuation with Israel was temporary. It had to be, he thought. He hated the country and the people who populated it. Like her experiment with drugs, the stay in Israel would be of a short duration.

"What about a husband?" he asked. "Are you still turning down offers?"

"Nobody's asked lately," she said. Norah avoided marriage because the examples she had had were all horrible. Her real father had walked out on her mother when Norah was two. The last she had heard, he was writing poetry in Majorca. A year after their breakup Ruth had married Hans Peter, and that union, from what she could remember, had been completely loveless. She doubted seriously if Hans Peter ever cared for anything. But then she was not so certain about anything concerning Hans Peter anymore. Not if what Eli had told her was true.

She could only speculate about Hans Peter's true character. She had always thought of him as an ineffectual dreamer who had done well for himself through hard work and devotion to the bank. But none of that fit the puzzle that Eli had presented. Hans Peter associated with men who harbored dangerous ideas, and Eli had said that Hans Peter was the one among them who had fueled their fanaticism with a sort of mystic sense of superiority. She looked at him now and wondered how that could be. He was small and prim. His whole being seemed pinched. She wondered if Hans Peter wasn't the hapless victim of mistaken identity. It was as though she had entered a forest of mirrors. She wished he wouldn't go on about marriage. The subject was distasteful, but then, she thought, what else had they to talk about? It was a game they played whenever they were together. Their conversation was always cautious, never more so than now.

"Your problem, Norah," he was saying, "is that you won't give anybody a chance. You want the perfect man, and believe me, you're not going to find him. He doesn't exist."

"How would you know?"

"I know"—he paused—"because your mother was the same."

"Oh?" she asked, peeved. "And what would she have wanted for me?"

"Let me tell you what she *wouldn't* have wanted."

"I'm listening."

"She wouldn't have wanted you to marry one of those—" He stopped short.

"Go on, finish." She knew exactly where he was heading, and she could feel the anger rising.

"One of those people you live with. You know." If he had intended to goad her, he could not have had greater success.

"I already did," she said, impulsively.

"You what?"

She uncurled her legs and sat up straight. She needed to hurt him, to relieve some of her anger. "Got married," she said. "I married a country."

"You could not have been so foolish," he said.

"Yes, I became an Israeli citizen."

He said nothing, just stared at her for some time, then turned and started for the door.

"Come back here," she said. "Walking out isn't going to help either of us. Will you let me explain, please?"

There was nothing to explain, he thought, standing with his back to her. An Israeli citizen! So she had done the unthinkable; the dalliance in Israel had turned serious. A half-dozen memories came at once. Norah's real father was a practicing Jew. Not only did he believe fervently in the religion, but from what Ruth had told Hans Peter, he also believed in the cause of Zionism. Hans Peter couldn't understand how or why Norah had picked up that sort of thinking. She had never really known her father, and Hans Peter had tried to protect her from Judaism. She had not been told about her father's beliefs. But somehow, probably from Ruth, she had discovered the truth. It did not matter. He could not, would not accept it. He thought about tomorrow's meeting.

"You make it difficult for me, Norah," he heard himself saying. "But maybe you should leave." How could he trust her? And the others, what would they say if they knew? She could be an embarrassment. He could never allow that to happen.

Norah cursed her thoughtlessness. Maybe what Eli had told her really was true. She could not accept being thrown out of her own house for a moment of mindless anger. If she recanted, would he believe her? "I knew that would get to you," she said, an innocent smile on her face.

"I don't understand," he said, walking toward the sofa.

"Peter, come and sit down," she said, patting the cushion. "When you hurt someone, like you just did, it's normal to want to hurt back. Do you see?"

He nodded.

"Mother told me years ago about my being Jewish. She also told me what you thought about the religion. You were understanding when I went to Israel, and I thank you for it. I really do. It was not easy, I know. But it was something I had to do. Believe me, I would never give up my Swiss citizenship without talking to you first. With Mother dead, it is very important to me that you and I remain close—or as close as we can be."

"Then you didn't?"

"No, nothing has changed, nor will it unless you give your approval. Will you please believe that?"

He thought for a moment, wanting to believe her. Then he wondered, could he allow her in the house alone with Hartmann? He should have thought of that before. Because once he had left, they would be together, and that made him apprehensive. He wanted to do right by Norah, but she confused him. "Yes," he finally said. "I believe you. But that doesn't change my decision."

"Oh, Peter," she moaned.

"I'm going on a trip the day after tomorrow. . . ."

"Will you let me stay until then?"

"That's right, but only until then."

"You still don't trust me, do you?"

"To be perfectly honest, Norah, I don't. Neither do I understand you."

"About Israel, or marriage, or what?" She had her reprieve, if only a temporary one.

"Can't you see? That is a *bastard* country surrounded by enemies. There will be more trouble, peace treaties notwithstanding. And you'd end up stateless."

"If I wanted safety I would have stayed here. Peter, I had to find out what my feelings were. I still don't know, but please don't be angry with me for exploring one of the things that were given me at birth. It wasn't my fault, you know, that my father was Jewish."

"What is it you want?"

"I want something to believe in."

He nodded his head slowly. "Yes, we all need that . . . a goal we can live for. Just think before you act. Becoming a citizen of that nation won't help you."

She patted his hand. "Peter, if I made you angry I'm sorry. I truly am." She saw the confusion in his face. She had gotten herself out of an impossible situation. She vowed to choose her words more carefully in the coming hours.

After Hans Peter left to go back to his office, Norah clenched her fists, partly in anger at her stupidity, partly from the frustration she felt. She was no professional. They had recruited her because she was his stepdaughter and that was all. Well, she thought, she would find out what they wanted to know, then she would return to a life that was normal and safe, a life without nuance and lying and not knowing what was right and what was wrong.

She poured herself a cup of tea from the sideboard and, balancing the saucer in her palm, climbed the stairs. The animal wallpaper in her bedroom had bubbled with age. Giraffes, pandas, pigs, and cows were now a fading reminder of a lonely and loveless childhood. She gazed without feeling at the dolls, the lace-trimmed pillows, and torn posters. She had a real home, and she wished she were there now.

Hesitantly at first, she reached for the telephone beside the bed. Eli had told her not to call. But she yearned for the sound of a friendly voice, for the reassurance he would give, for him to tell her what she needed to hear. That she was missed.

The twelve-digit number answered on the first ring.

"Lime Tree Catering," a voice said.

She was switched through a series of interconnecting lines, finally to an office on the third floor of the Ministry of Defense.

"Eli Thre," the voice said.

3

Blizzards disrupted suburban routine in the warrens around Washington. The snowfall had gone far beyond that subtle turning point when what was fun became an annoyance. Gradually nerves were set on edge, except for those of schoolchildren with classes canceled and Ralph Crawford. He was stranded, which suited him fine.

He was reading a dog-eared copy of *Danger Is My Business,* about a British stunt man who had battled tigers in Bengal and sharks off the Great Barrier Reef. He looked at his watch, then closed the book. The hotel room had all the basics and nothing more. There was a black and white television set with rabbit ears, one chair at a desk, a bed that doubled as a sofa, and a bath with a rust ring around the drain. Just so long as he had a book, Ralph Crawford could be anywhere.

He needed this break. Ralph Crawford felt that home life was closing in on him, which was a sign to get away. Otherwise he and Marcia would pick at one another until somebody broke, and that wasn't healthy for the children or for them. But she was being unreasonable. She wanted more than their split-level life in Springfield, Virginia, even though she knew that he was doing the best he could. After the mortgage, food, and school bills were paid, they had almost nothing left but small change from his $400-a-month take-home.

"Women," he said to himself, rising and putting on his overshoes. Their logic was so different from men's. The other day, Marcia had commented on the shabbiness of his suits and the length of his hair, while only a month earlier his old suits and hair had been "professorial." She had read in the *Washingtonian* that short hair was in vogue and an unkempt look said that he no longer loved her. She also wanted to know where they would find the money to pay for the increased school fees, but hadn't he all along argued that country day schools were insane on his salary? Last in the litany had been the complaint that they never went out together in the evenings, but when they did go out, she wondered why they didn't spend more time at home with the boys.

So it was good for both of them to take time out, and the blizzard had been his excuse. It had been forecast and he might have made it home before the road got bad. But he had watched as the first tentative snowflakes fell outside his office window, secretly cheering them on. From then on during the day, as fellow workers left early, he had checked the buildup on the ground, then *finally* satisfied by the size of the drifts, he had made the call. He had no recourse, he told Marcia. Until the roads were cleared, he would be at the Harrington Hotel. That had been two days ago.

Now bent into the early morning wind, Crawford walked toward the Beagle Coffee Shop across from the Harrington. His haunt no matter what the weather, the Beagle was a convivial meeting place for FBI agents, wire service journalists, and men from the Justice Department, Internal Revenue Service, and Alcohol, Tobacco and Firearms Bureau. It served as a haven in which they escaped the heat of summer, the chill of winter, and, at all times of year, the dreariness of office routine.

He tugged at the laminated tag on his overcoat pocket. He hated the badge because it identified him for what he was, a middle-level tax investigator with the Office of the Chief Counsel at Internal Revenue, a job description with none of the glamour of FBI. He was at the bottom of the heap, a second-grade sleuth who never went beyond profit-and-loss statements and company reports. Not that everybody at IRS was the same. Some investigators put mobsters and racketeers behind bars and years back had started to fill the vacuum of international investigation left by the collapse of the CIA. But Crawford wasn't on their level.

Stamping slush from his galoshes, he opened the double doors. As always, the flare-up with Marcia had given him cause for assessment. He had no grand illusions: he was going nowhere at thirty-five. He was rail-thin and unathletic. Gogglelike glasses magnified curious eyes. The tag on his overcoat had him at five feet eleven inches, brown hair, one hundred and fifty pounds, male, and Cauc. He loved books and vodka martinis, which he preferred to drink alone. It wasn't much, but it was all he was.

The books were the most important. One pocket or another always bulged with a paperback, for his imagination took wing in reading, a necessary escape from the bloodlessness of work. Books were his ticket into other centuries and the souls and minds of men who had done what he never could. In those pages he became T. E. Lawrence; the seafarers of Conrad; Stanley on the Congo; Tipoo Tib, the Zanzibar slaver. Their exploits stayed with him through the boredom, blocking it out so he could become the lone man against nature, heathen tribes, and the great unknown. Books saved his sanity and earned him an eccentric's reputation.

He heard their voices now before he saw them. As usual, they were loafing. He hung up his coat and took an adjacent booth, listening with half an ear.

"Goddamned right you don't," the reporter named Sullivan was saying. He was the sort of journalist who pronounced on everything from aardvarks to zymosis. "But on the other hand—"

"—Middlemen," Sullivan's understudy at AP put in.

A waitress balanced three coffee cups, then put them down on their table, preempting their order by serving fresh mugs every fifteen minutes or so. Sullivan looked at her.

"You agree, Sally?" he asked.

Sally looked at him wanly. "Honey, your words are written in stone," she said.

Sullivan flattened his palm on the steaming mug. "What is a cup now, seventy-five?" He didn't wait for an answer. "The guy who picks the beans makes a penny, while the goddamned middleman sits on his ass and banks the profits."

The third reporter stirred from his reading of *The Washington Post*. "Wait a minute. There's something about that in here." He riffled to the Financial Section. "Yeah, here it is." He read from the article.

"Coffee magnate James MacKee died today when the private airplane which he was piloting crashed near the Tarangire National Park in Tanzania, two hundred miles from the Indian Ocean port of Dar es Salaam. MacKee, 58, Chairman of the Tanzanian Coffee Board, renounced his U.S. citizenship in 1975 after the Internal Revenue Service brought proceedings against him for alleged tax fraud involving an estimated $26 million. . . ."

"Excellent example," Sullivan said. "It's better that he's—"

An arm sliced over the back of the banquette between Sullivan and the other reporter, snatching the newspaper from his hands. "Give me that!"

Startled, Sullivan turned around to see. "Ralph," he said, noticing Crawford for the first time. "Jesus, you have the manners of an ape."

"Yeah," Crawford said, trying to find the item.

"If it's what we were just reading, try near the stock reports," Sullivan said.

Crawford held the newspaper close to his eyes. "Christ," he muttered.

Sullivan wondered why the histrionics. "What's the big deal, Ralph?" he asked.

Crawford slowly lowered the newspaper. "About five years' hard work, that's all," he said, thinking of the stacks of files back in his office.

"On MacKee?"

"We nearly had him, too. Jesus," he said, throwing the newspaper down. "Of all the crummy luck."

"I don't get it," Sullivan said. "Even though he's dead, the money's still there."

"The Service wants his money. But I wanted MacKee."

"Why the grudge?"

"It's a long story."

Sullivan liked long stories. "The newspaper says he renounced his American citizenship," he said.

"He owed Uncle Sam twenty-six million from when he was an American citizen," Crawford replied. He knew the facts on MacKee backwards and forwards. "Renouncing citizenship doesn't mean anything where we're concerned."

"What's the fraud, then? He didn't pay taxes?"

"That's the end of it," he said. "But it's more complicated than that. Do you want to know?"

"Sure."

"What he did essentially was defraud the world's coffee consumers. All of them. He made millions in 1973 when the coffee crop fell short—after the Brazilian freeze. Coffee's an integrated commodity. A shortfall here means a windfall there. MacKee was informed about the freeze and hurried out to buy tons of it on future through the New York Commodity Exchange. He raked in his profits but didn't pay taxes."

"What's so illegal about that? Not the taxes, but the other bit. The frost wasn't his doing, after all."

"Frost or no, commodities are a special gamble, like shooting craps with borrowed chips," Crawford continued. "You buy a crop in a certain quantity even before it's been planted. And you pray the price fluctuates before delivery comes due. But if you know the crop has failed and you horde, and then you don't pay taxes on the profits—you're our target."

Sullivan didn't understand at all: economics wasn't his strong suit. "So MacKee was a gambler," he said. "What else do you know about him?"

Crawford shrugged, wishing he could answer the question. "I never laid eyes on him," he admitted. "But it wouldn't be saying too much to call him a hustler in four different languages. When we indicted him, you know, he dumped his American citizenship."

"I get the picture," Sullivan said.

"Beyond that we don't know much, except that he was naturalized. He came here right after World War II, but he didn't stay long. Still, he kept his passport, for reasons I don't understand, till we went after him."

"He lived in Tanzania?"

"Yes. Tanzania's President—Nyerere—thought he ought to protect him at first—he was building up the coffee business and all that, and that's about Tanzania's only source of foreign exchange. But in the end Nyerere saw what MacKee had done, and promised to turn him over to us. We have no gripe with Nyerere. In fact, he's a pretty good man."

"It doesn't seem to me you've got much. I mean it's *confusing*." Sullivan's interest in the story was waning.

"Our cases are always confusing," Crawford said, sliding from the booth.

"Well, sorry he croaked on you. Anyway, you'll find somebody else to go after. You guys always do."

"Yeah," Crawford said. He made apologies for his earlier rudeness, then slogged across Constitution Avenue, cursing the day, the snow, Marcia, the IRS, and especially MacKee for having the temerity to die.

In room L-1505 Larry Calder was reading the *Post,* his feet resting on the corner of the desk. Remnants of a ham and egg sandwich lay in the folds of wax paper beside an empty in tray. He envied the whiz kids in the Administration and derived satisfaction from their ups and downs, as chronicled in the *Post*. As a civil servant he was safe from the buffeting of political winds, but he wished he could feel them blow just once in his life. What Calder did at IRS was light-years distant from any cutting edge. He was the liaison officer between the Service and international tax agencies. Some foreign countries cooperated down the line. Britain and France were the best, and he had cordial relations with his counterparts there. He coordinated the swapping of tax information and, from the American side, helped in the preparation of litigation. Recently most of the work had been corporate, and specific departments within IRS dealt directly with the foreign services, which left him with less and less to do. But when that rare important case did land on his desk, as today, he felt almost like one of the White House boys.

Miss de Rosser, his secretary, came to the door and coughed. He lowered the newspaper to his chin.

"Yes?" he asked.

"Ralph is here," she replied simply.

Calder swung his legs off the desk. Seeing him, he knew that Crawford had heard the bad news. "Tough, Ralph," he said. "I know how much you wanted him."

Crawford took a chair opposite the desk. "Yeah, thanks. What've you got?" He didn't feel like shooting the breeze.

"Word from on high, early this morning. All may not be lost."

That IRS had moved so fast took Crawford by surprise.

"They talked about your man. Frankly, they wanted to drop the case altogether, but fortunately for you, the boss outvoted the dissenting section heads."

"And how did they breathe life into our corpse?" Crawford asked without real interest.

"Don't be so negative," Calder cautioned. "The figures persuaded them. The investigation isn't going to cost them that much, and if they can get a piece of the twenty-six million, believe me, it'll be worth it."

"And Nyerere? What's *his* interest?"

"I don't see what you mean."

"Nyerere, the President. Why is it in his interest now to pursue the case? MacKee is dead, so why dig up a lot of dirt? It could be bad for him politically."

"Good point," Calder admitted. "But we are assuming that he'll still help out. It's a fair guess he will."

"Why?"

"Because he wants to stay on good terms with us. Southern Africa and all that."

"But why us?"

"Who else?"

"I would have thought the CIA was better equipped to make this kind of an investigation. It's a foreign country and I don't have to repeat, MacKee is dead."

"I think you know the answer to that. CIA doesn't know what its mandate is anymore. We do. And our revered director, the boss man who's keeping your case alive, likes to take up slack where he can."

"From the CIA, for God's sake?"

"Sneer if you want. At least in a small way the director sees IRS filling their role. He's anxious for us to explore investigations outside the U.S."

"I still don't see what the boss wants." More rummaging through ledgers, thought Crawford.

"Specifically, MacKee's estate. If one exists you're going to find it."

Crawford groaned. He should have been pleased, but he wasn't. There was a lot he didn't know, but from his investigation of MacKee to date he was certain of the implausibility of ever finding his estate. If one existed, nobody was going to trace it. Dummy Swiss companies, shelters, and fronts made the search a certain paper chase. He told Calder as much.

"Tell it to the boss," said Calder, who couldn't understand Crawford's attitude. "You're paid to follow his directives. And he's directing you to go after MacKee's estate."

"More queries to foreign governments?" How else were they going to get a lead on MacKee's cache?

"That kind of attitude's your big trouble, Ralph," Calder said, miffed. "Use your imagination for once."

"So tell me. How?" Calder was right, thought Crawford. But he couldn't help his feeling that the estate was irrelevant. He had wanted MacKee behind bars.

Calder thought he knew what Crawford was thinking. "Look at it this way," he said. "If you get the estate, you get a piece of MacKee."

"Okay," Crawford agreed. "How do I proceed?"

Calder had thought briefly of pulling Crawford off the case, but in the end decided against it. Nobody at IRS knew the details about MacKee better. And in the end, often in spite of himself, Crawford always did a good job. He sensed a fire that needed sparking in Crawford. "Join the IRS and see the world," Calder said.

"Meaning?"

"You're going to Africa. The Dark Continent's waiting for you."

Crawford smiled for the first time that day. The IRS *was* changing, he thought. It had the reputation of never sending its people anywhere. The travel budget was smaller than the yearly painting bill. Africe *meant* something. All the way to Africa. Either the boss was rewarding him for a well-prepared case or maybe there *was* a chance of finding MacKee's estate. He sat up in his chair, keeping his voice level. "That's great," he said. "I mean it. Really great. But there's one little problem."

"Only one?"

"What if I land there and find the door closed? And I'm not thinking about Nyerere, either."

"Listen, it stands to reason that MacKee had a wife, a relative, or someone he named in his will. It'll be probated. My guess is, finding the estate is going to be easier than you think. You can return a hero—a twenty-six-million-dollar man."

Some hero, thought Crawford. "You know how I read the case," he said seriously. "MacKee was important, I would guess, in more circles than just Africa. His network spread wherever growers raise coffee and wherever people buy it. And he was a criminal. I don't see him working alone. Now that he's dead the vultures will be closing in on the money he left behind. There'll be a mob converging on Tanzania; that's my guess."

"What are you trying to say?"

"Just this. Greedy people can play rough. We're not talking a few hundred dollars—it's a fortune. And those with access to it won't want us nosing around."

Calder didn't know how to reassure him. In fact he couldn't. Maybe it would get rough. But he trusted Crawford's judgment. "I said use your imagination," he said. "Don't let it run away with you."

"That's easy for you to say. Really. I'm being serious."

"I know you are," Calder agreed. "So let's leave it like this. If you so much as spot danger, get out. Quick. Don't play undercover games. That's an order."

"Believe me, I won't. Nothing's further from my mind."

"Good, then," Calder said, wanting to get Crawford moving. "When can you go?"

He had to get visas and shots, thought Crawford, and God only knew what objections Marcia would raise. "I can be . . . let's see," he said, getting up to look at the calendar behind Calder's desk. "I can probably be off the day after tomorrow."

Calder got to his feet and shook Crawford's hand. "Bring me home a souvenir," he said as Crawford went through the door. "And, Ralph, take care."

Crawford heard the familiar words of a Beatles song on the stereo as he came through the garage portico. When Marcia played that album it meant she was in a good mood. He saw her in the kitchen standing by the sink and snuck up, giving her a kiss on the back of the neck. Marcia turned and blinked.

"Ralph," she said, surprise and delight in her voice. "What on earth? I thought you were snowbound."

"I was, but I'm not anymore." Her genuine and happy response to his sudden appearance made him feel guilty for having hidden himself away in the Harrington Hotel. The boys, he saw through the kitchen window, were in the backyard making a snow castle.

"What happened?" she asked innocently. "Did they clear the roads?"

Crawford ignored the question; he was too excited about telling her. "Guess where I'm going, sweetheart?"

"Out to spend time with the boys—right now."

"No, really. I'm going to Africa. The office is sending me to Africa. Isn't that great?"

Her face dropped. "Then the roads weren't cleared?"

"I don't get you. I said Africa."

Her face flushed with anger as she wiped her hands on the cotton apron. "One thing at a time, Ralph. Let me get this straight. You drove home because of a trip to Africa. Then why were you *stuck* in Washington? That's what you said. Stuck!" She hated to catch him like this. It made her the one who started the arguments. He was the cause, not her, damnit.

"Listen, sweetheart, don't get angry. It's a critical assignment for me, and that changes everything. It didn't make sense taking risks on icy roads to come home for dinner. I'm sorry, but that's the way I see it." He went to the refrigerator for a beer. He flipped the tab, watching Marcia. "It has to do with MacKee. He's been killed."

Right now Marcia didn't want to hear another word about MacKee. She knew the details backwards, endless facts and figures that long ago had lost all meaning. MacKee fascinated Ralph, so she had always listened. While he talked about the trip, she faced the sink without replying or offering encouragement. She couldn't win.

He went into the living room. She hadn't asked any questions or even seemed to care that he was going to a bizarre and maybe dangerous corner of the world. No, that meant nothing. She cared only that he hadn't come home. He stood in front of the bookcase, searching the bindings. Most of the books were fiction, a lot of paperback thrillers, some biographies, and fewer histories. He spotted his prize possession, a first-edition copy of *Youth*. It had cost him almost a hundred and fifty dollars. He put his hand on another book, *The Face of Battle*. He had written its author, a man named John Keegan, who had even replied, thanking him for his interest. He found what he wanted on the lower shelf.

He took the atlas to the sofa and laid it on the coffee table. Turning to the index, he found the page numbers for Tanzania. It didn't have much, he thought, beginning to read.

"More than twice the size of California, Tanzania has a population of sixteen million. An underpopulated country; the topography is dominated by a hot, arid central plateau surrounded by the lake region in the west, temperate highlands in the north and south, and the coastal plains. Of its peaks, Mount Kilimanjaro is the highest in Africa."

He turned from the ledger to the map itself. He ran his hand over it, almost tenderly. The names kindled his imagination: Serengeti National Park, Lion Hill and Shifting Sands, the Masai Steppe, Ngorongoro Crater. The Olduvai Gorge. There were small crossed picks and shovels denoting the locations of garnet, ruby, and tourmaline mines.

On an impulse he got up again and went to the bookshelf for the encyclopedia he had bought the boys. Finding the letter *D*, he brought the volume back to the sofa and started to read.

"Twelve decades ago, Dar es Salaam was a staging point for explorations into the vast, uncharted interior of the continent by men like Rebmann and Krapf, the first whites ever to see Mount Kilimanjaro, and later Burton, Speke, Grant, and Henry Morton Stanley, who 'presumed' his greeting to David Livingstone on Tanzanian soil. In those days, the country was called Tanganyika. Kaiser Wilhelm counted Deutschostafrika as one of Germany's most important colonies. Since that time Tanzania's European roots have remained heavily Germanic."

Crawford stopped reading when he heard Marcia enter the living room. He looked up as she sat softly beside him on the sofa.

"It's time we had a talk," she said simply. She glanced down at the book. "Whenever we have troubles, you run to your books. Why?"

He didn't know what to reply. Because they didn't answer back? Because they didn't ask questions he couldn't answer? Because they pleased him? "I was looking up Africa," he replied.

"Then you were telling the truth about going there?"

"I'm afraid so. They want me there in two days."

"Two days? Oh, Ralph. It's just not possible." The timing was all wrong, she thought. The episode of his hiding out in Washington had been only one of many lately. As husband and wife, they were drawing further and further apart. She knew she was becoming a nag, but she couldn't help it. It was the only way she knew to defend herself and the boys. Within limits, Ralph was a good provider, husband, and, less often now, lover. More and more his mind was in the clouds. For her and the boys he wasn't there. She knew why, but the answer didn't help. He had never grown up and still couldn't accept responsibility for fatherhood and marriage. In the beginning his dreaminess had been charming, but now everything seemed to be passing them by. She had once seen an epitaph for an anonymous miner: "He lived, he died, so what?" And she wondered if that wouldn't be their final summation together. The road ahead for her stretched flat. But what did she want? How would she have it different? To start with, she wanted the security of knowing that Ralph was there, solid and trusting, behind her. She wanted him to start taking an equal share of the burden of parenting. The money didn't matter, it never had. That wasn't why she'd married him.

"What are we going to do, Ralph, you and me?" she asked. "We can't continue like this."

Crawford knew that, too. The less their home life measured up, the more he escaped into the realm of dreams. He was bogged down and with every month that passed his self-esteem diminished. He tapped the atlas. "This is a small chance," he said in a whisper, as though he feared admitting it to himself. "If it works out, they'll promote me, give *us* what we need to begin again."

She was frustrated by the answer. Marcia didn't know if she could trust him, or if this wasn't another excuse, another "maybe in the future" with no real meaning. There had been other new beginnings. "You've said that before," she remarked.

"Yes, I know, and I'm sorry."

"What's so different about this?"

"It's tough to explain."

"Well, try at least. You say that you're going to Africa, but beyond the fact of going there, what's so important about it?"

He cleared his throat. He didn't really know the answer. It was a feeling he had. "Can't you see, Marcia," he began. "I may never amount to anything important. I'm thirty-five, and I haven't exactly run up the promotional ladder at IRS. This . . . this Africa assignment says that my superiors think something of my work. They'll be looking at me, at how well I do. This is my chance to try."

"But Ralph, you are important to me, not the damned IRS."

"But it does matter to me."

"Isn't it that you're just sick of the boredom?"

"Of course there's that. But if I fail this time, then that part of my life, the Internal Revenue Service, the ambition, is dead. I *can* become a success as a father and husband. Right now I haven't succeeded at either."

"And IRS comes first?" There was hurt in her voice.

"How can I explain?" How could she understand that his work, no matter how routine and unrewarding, was a large part of him? It mattered. Right or wrong, success was integral to the view he had of himself. "It just is," he said.

"I can't argue with you, then," she said, her lip trembling.

"Please don't be hurt."

"It's difficult not to be, knowing that the boys and I take a backseat. For the moment we'll leave it like that. If you make me one promise."

"Anything."

"When you come home from Tasmania or wherever it is, *you are mine.* You will start to make an effort around here. But it must be genuine. I want you to think about that while you're gone. Will you?"

"Yes, of course, and I'll come home with conclusions."

"We'll start with a vacation. That will be our new beginning."

"It's a deal." He leaned over and kissed her on the mouth. "I promise." He meant it, too, this time he really did. He turned to the atlas, showing her the country. "And where I'm going is called *Tanzania*."

4

Due to foggy conditions and worse scheduling, three jumbo jets landed within an interval of ten minutes. Debarking Zurich passengers from LT 010, as a consequence, waited for immigration and customs clearances at the end of long and slow-moving lines. Uniformed officials tried to keep pace but couldn't be hurried from their thorough checks.

Two men stood quietly in the line. One was powerfully built, with thick arms, a high-ridged nose, muttonchop whiskers, and a full mouth that registered disapproval. Beside him was a thin, refined-looking man with hawkish blue eyes and brown wavy hair. The larger man had an almost loutish bearing and was dressed in a white linen suit with a paisley ascot at his throat. His wrists were loaded with a gold Rolex and a platinum elephant-hair bracelet, and he sported outsized lapis lazuli cuff links. His companion had on a neatly tailored charcoal pin-stripe, a blue shirt, and a conservative green print necktie. He wore no jewelry.

They now came up to the immigration counter and handed the official their passports. He looked at them, comparing the photographs, then turned to a large loose-leaf book. Once he had satisfied himself that these two had no records, he took the rectangular Swiss entry mark and stamped the first passport. Neither of the men said a word.

"Mr. Hartmann," he said to the thin man, passing the document without looking up. Ernst Hartmann took the passport. "And the Baron Hovagny." He glanced at the Baron. "Welcome to Switzerland."

They walked through the barrier and collected their suitcases, which were already on the carrousel, and then went to a limousine parked in front of the terminal. After they had boarded the black Mercedes 600 and started the drive through Zurich to Küssnacht, the Baron seemed to grow anxious. "I hope you can convince them there is no other way?" he asked.

"Convince them?" Hartmann appeared baffled. "They won't need convincing. They will be eager."

"What I meant is, they are all very comfortable. There is no threat to their safety, here in Switzerland. Why should they do this?"

"Their *safety,* as you call it, Herr Baron, will not be compromised by what we are doing. It may even be secured. Even if it were endangered, they *owe* their safety, their comfort, and most of all their prosperity to Protégé. They will do what I ask."

"You have not seen many of them for years. Years, Ernst. Comfort makes men lazy, it blunts ideals. These men are soft, Ernst. They haven't been in Africa, they no longer know what real conflict, what war is."

"We'll just have to see. We are at the point where we *must* do this thing. We have no choice."

"No, we still do have a choice," Baron Hovagny said. "We could stay underground. We don't *need* to come into the open." Hovagny was as anxious as Hartmann to take action, but he questioned the timetable Ernst had adopted —it was all to benefit himself. Hartmann was being selfish, that much he understood. Hartmann was in trouble. To come out into the open benefited Hartmann, because he had no other reasonable choice. But what about the others?

Hartmann looked out the front windscreen as the limousine slowed to enter a driveway. "We're here," he said. "This is where we begin." Then, almost as an afterthought: "If you have doubts, express them at the meeting."

The car stopped at the front steps and the driver came around to open their door. As they were getting out, Hans Peter came out of the house and greeted them effusively. "Ernst, Baron," he said, wrapping his arms around their shoulders. "It's been too long." It had been almost one year since he had last seen them in Dar es Salaam, when they had hunted and talked long into the night, when they had planned and weighed contingencies.

Hartmann smiled at Hans Peter. They had known one another since the forties, when Admiral Canaris had brought them together. The smile faded from his face and for an instant he looked seriously at Hans Peter. He seemed to have aged in the last year, to have shrunken. His features were more exaggerated now in their smallness: the pinched face, the small nose that seemed almost an afterthought, the narrow, inviting eyes. His black hair was trimmed close and flecked with gray.

As they walked up the steps and into the foyer, Hartmann thought about the indispensable banker. He had tried to bring him along. He had worked to develop Hans Peter, and he wondered whether he'd been successful. Hans Peter was still a dreamer, and in the early years his enthusiasm had been helpful in holding them together. But it had also been unbridled, dangerous. Hans Peter talked too much about things that none of them ever discussed. Until Hartmann had demanded that he come to Tanzania on a safari. The experience had helped to temper their host. The Baron and Hartmann had made him face the dangers of killing, and he had done well. He had had to be responsible for his own actions: you couldn't stop a charging rhino with a dream.

"It's wonderful you are here," Hans Peter was saying. "The others are waiting upstairs. Impatiently, I might add."

They deposited their heavy winter coats with the butler. Hans Peter led the way upstairs to the main drawing room, Hartmann following. Midway up the stairs he noticed a flash of yellow. He glanced into the ground-floor library. Norah was standing in the recesses of the room, her hair shimmering in a ray of setting sunlight. She looked straight at Hartmann, then turned her head as though she had not seen or recognized what she saw. Hartmann dropped one foot down on the next lower step.

Was this the surprise Hans Peter had promised him on the telephone? Norah? He hadn't seen her in . . . he couldn't remember how many years. But she had been just a girl then, a delightful, silly young girl with dreams of romance and love. "Wait a minute," he told the Baron and Hans Peter, who stopped and turned, curious at the cause of the delay. Hartmann went down to the library and peered in. "Norah?" he asked tentatively.

She turned from the window. A smile formed slowly on her lips as recognition dawned. "Is that you, Ernst?"

"None other, by God," he said heartily, walking over to where she was standing. They embraced, then he held her away from him, looking at her in silent wonder. "Where did the little girl go?" He was truly incredulous.

She was more stunning than any woman he could remember seeing.

"She went away, unfortunately, never to return. And you! What a handsome figure you cut, dear *Uncle* Ernst."

"That's right," he said. "You used to call me that."

Hans Peter came to the doorway. "Ernst, excuse me. The others are waiting." He consciously did not look at Norah.

Hartmann seemed hesitant and annoyed. If Norah was to be the surprise, why was Hans Peter so protective? "Did Hans Peter mention dinner?" he asked her.

She shook her head.

"Of course you are invited. You must come. I'll clear it with him," he stated, leaving her to make his way up the stairs.

The drawing-room drapes had been closed and the room was dim and shadowed by the small pools of light thrown by shaded lamps. A log fire crackled in the open hearth. There were sixteen chairs organized in a circle occupied by sixteen men in dark suits. They were all between forty-five and fifty, the age when men reach the height of their powers.

They rose and bowed with the tips of their chins as Hans Peter, the Baron, and Hartmann came into the room. Many of them had not seen Hartmann for the better part of their mature lives. They looked curiously at him, trim and athletic with a grave expression. Canaris had chosen well and with great prescience; Hartmann had turned out to be the man the Admiral had expected.

Hartmann, the First Member, took his place in the center of the circle of chairs. The others remained standing. "So we begin," he said almost in a whisper. "Baron, please?"

Hovagny went to the fireplace. His hands by his side, his head bowed, he began, *"As ek storm, volk my. As ek omdraii, skiet my. As ek sterwe, wreek my."* The others repeated the words solemnly.

Hartmann motioned for them to take their seats, then spent several moments composing himself. The pause, Hartmann knew, would give every man the opportunity to contemplate. Each knew what they had come to do. And they knew it would be done. How was the only question.

Protégé, the organization, consisted of twenty men. The original number had been twenty-one, but one member had died. None was ever to be replaced.

One member was not in attendance.

The basis of their belief was hate, a hate pure in its intensity. The object of their hate was Adolf Hitler, the man who had destroyed their dream.

The basis of their belief was devotion bordering on love. They were devoted to the cause of the race, racial superiority, to the flowering of a belief that had been the foundation of the Third Reich before Adolf Hitler in his madness had destroyed himself and their bold, conquering philosophy.

Their first leader had been Admiral Wilhelm Canaris. He had been executed by Hitler months before the end of the war. The reason for his execution, Hitler had said, was disloyalty, for he had learned that Canaris, the original First Member, had created the group and provided it with the funds needed to survive, grow, and occupy. Admiral Canaris, the leader of Abwehr I, the Nazi foreign intelligence network, who hated Hitler and loved the Master Race, had given birth to Protégé.

Admiral Canaris was a visionary who saw even beyond his death and planned—accurately—for the decades to come. A new form of national socialism would come, not under its old name, but as an invisible, cohesive ideology binding the vital parts of society, those that had not crumbled or given in to despair in the anarchy of postwar Europe. Those who still believed in the mission of Western culture, of white culture, and its need to rule, its destiny to dominate. One would not need a mass movement, merely a corps of totally loyal men. With the advances in technology and weaponry that were to come, thought Canaris, some nations would get stronger, but most would be weaker. If he could only create a core group of members that could act as his Protégé. It would take its time planning and growing, then one day it would have the power to rise from its place of hiding and take a country, occupy a land, which it would use as an example to the world of what national socialism might have been without the horrible excesses of Adolf Hitler.

Hitler had been mad, a demon who had overthrown an ideal for personal vengeance. Canaris had argued against the elimination of the Jews, but Hitler had not listened. Canaris had wanted the Jews transported from Europe and resettled in Tanzania, where they would work for the Reich. Canaris had argued to save the race, but when he failed, he planted the seed of Protégé and nourished it well with money stolen from Reich coffers and sent to a bank in Zurich. He had chosen well. Protégé had consisted of twenty-one young men who were devoted to him in Abwehr I. They were young, and he had taught them to believe in their absolute superiority. The First was Ernst Hartmann. The Second was Hans Peter Hirsch. The Third was Baron Hovagny. Along with the other members of Protégé they would bide their time, accumulating capital and gaining influence where they could until the moment when they had acquired the power to move.

Protégé had fled Germany shortly before the surrender. Most went to Switzerland. Hartmann and Hovagny had eventually settled in Tanzania, because they had had the idea that Canaris's deportation scheme might yet work one day in the former German colony.

They had used the fifty million Deutschmarks smuggled by Canaris into the CCU to acquire industries. They had gained total control of the businesses and split off a percentage of the profits for the Group. In Europe they went into armaments, processed foods, computer hardware, and transportation; abroad they bought up huge plantations in Africa and South America and cornered the market in sugar cane and coffee.

With the money they began to buy support. They sought out political movements, clubs and gangs, and religious organizations with odd beliefs—any group on the fringe that could not survive without them. Protégé never made clear just where the money came from, laundering it as they did through intermediaries and agents and always fixing on one corruptible member, a person they called the Target. That person was then given special treatment—"extras"—and encouraged to report back on the group's activities, its promising members and possible traitors. The bund or brigade or ad hoc revolutionary group in Spain, Italy, Canada, Latin America would know only that one member controlled their principal source of revenue, which rendered him invulnerable to attack. Meanwhile Protégé watched the Target for leadership, what "dominating" abilities he possessed, what he could do with finance. The successful Targets were then promoted to an intermediate organization below the group of twenty-one, called Prime Target. The unsuccessful Targets were eliminated, and their group's funding immediately disappeared.

Protégé had also supported influential men who had lost their power in mid-life through one crisis or another —if a corporation was bought out, the former president might need a job; if a revolutionary uprising forced a dictator from power, that dictator would need what Protégé had in abundance to give . . . secretly. Among this legion of the disgruntled were those fugitive Nazis who had escaped to other countries after the war. Protégé had provided them with funds to establish new lives and new identities. Contrary to popular belief, they were not banded together in an organization like Odessa. They knew only of a bank—the Commercial Credit Union—in Zurich.

"Gentlemen," Hartmann said. "We have come together, as the Admiral willed, because it is time for our dream to come true. The many variables mesh—*perfectly*." He reached up and smoothed his hair. "Now, what are they and why are they in perfect synchronization?" Hartmann had planned this speech just as carefully as he had his departure from Tanzania. He had no need to convince his Group, he knew they would follow him. But he had to be exact in his calculations: they were far from being fools. If they thought his timing was wrong, they would stop him.

"The first variable is Tanzania, our old colony. The country is weak militarily, after the protracted war with Uganda. A majority of the troops are still occupying that country. Tanzania itself has a weak infrastructure. President Nyerere has removed most of the old German settlers from positions of responsibility in his government in his attempts to foster socialism. These Germans will be invaluable to us." He looked at the Baron, who accepted the cue.

"Yes," he said, "the white settlers are on the verge of open revolt. Their lands have been expropriated, their jobs taken away. In a short time they will be forced to leave." He paused. "But they will never leave. They will join us," he said, grasping the arms of the chair.

Hartmann cut in, "The second variable is our own strength." He motioned to Hans Peter. "Will you please give us a rundown."

Hans Peter rose and stood beside Hartmann. He was smaller in stature, like a terrier beside a greyhound. He thought for an instant, licked his lips, then began. "Our accounts have reached the saturation point whereby, gentlemen, they can no longer be used in the customary ways. A rough estimate is in the region of ten *billion* dollars. If Protégé is to use that money profitably, I agree with Ernst, we must come into the open."

Ruethli Gruetz interrupted. Switzerland's largest manufacturer of arms, he had been a Gruppenkommandant under Canaris. "Please explain what you mean by 'profitably'?"

"Yes, yes, of course," Hans Peter stuttered. It was so simple and so brilliant a plan, he had thought they could make that deduction themselves. He cleared his throat. "Gentlemen, Tanzania is *under*populated. At the same time, it has *tremendous* mineral and agricultural resources. President Nyerere does not have the labor force to exploit those riches, and neither does he have finance. But we do. We shall therefore divide the land into five hundred plots averaging 64,000 acres from our estimate of 32 million arable acres. The major participants will receive one tract and the country will become a cornucopia. It will feed the hungry of Africa and Asia—*at a dear price.* There is power in food, and we will control that power."

Gruetz nodded, but still one piece of the puzzle was missing. "Where do *we* get labor?"

"I'll answer that," Hartmann interrupted. "Please," he said to Hans Peter, "take your seat." He waited an instant, then said, "A third variable is the country of South Africa."

"You propose to import labor from South Africa? Forced labor?" Gruetz asked softly.

Hartmann nodded and continued: "South Africa is *over*populated with blacks. And blacks are the cause of that country's troubles.

"Fellow Member Steenkamp, the one member who is missing today, as you well know, is Prime Minister of South Africa. But he is in a very difficult position." Steenkamp had been a devoted Abwehr I operative in South Africa during the war. "We need his manpower to build our state in Tanzania; he needs us to save South Africa as a bastion of white supremacy. With us, white South Africa has a future."

Hartmann went on now, rapidly. There had been a minimum of objections. They believed in him and his ability to do what he had promised. They were ready to commit themselves, no matter how daring the plan. The scale of their undertaking was enormous: but they were all giants, and this was the plan of giants. They had to create a state. It had to be Tanzania. If they agreed with that assumption, then the rest was purely mechanical.

"As a corollary—and it is a critical one, gentlemen— Prime Minister Steenkamp has pledged to support us *militarily,* so our strategy can be carried out swiftly, so very swiftly that the world will not be able to react. Remember, the variable of critical importance is South Africa. Steenkamp needs Protégé for his very survival; and we need him for the birth of our state. Let me emphasize this once again. We cannot *build* a modern state in Tanzania without labor. South Africa has workers, *forced labor* that it cannot tolerate on its soil any longer if the white government there is to rule. We also need an alliance with an established sovereign country. Look at the map, gentlemen. With Protégé in Tanzania and a secure white-dominated South Africa under Steenkamp, we will have seized the gateways here, here and there." He slapped the map with the back of his hand:

the Indian Ocean, the Cape, approaches from the South Atlantic. "In one bold stroke Protégé will have in its hands more power—*real* power, gentlemen—than the Reich ever did."

5

The sun had gone down. From her room Norah heard the men leaving the meeting. She lay against the bed headboard and tried to concentrate on what she guessed to be true, what was pure conjecture, and what connections she could plausibly make between the two. Her problem was that she could not be certain of *anything*. She half believed Eli, because he was what he was. He was paid to know those things. But what evidence had she found to substantiate his charges against her stepfather? None.

But that did not comfort her. Eli would not have sent her to Zurich without reason. Which meant that she should fear Hans Peter. And her own inexperience. An amateur, she could never know what mistakes she was making. And if she couldn't know, she was vulnerable. But vulnerable to what?

At first, when she was in Tel Aviv, she was flattered by the recruitment. Her interest was romantic: she wanted to prove herself to the people of Israel. It didn't make sense to her now, in this house and so close to Hans Peter. But it had then.

Until Israel, she had been spoiled and vacant; nothing had engaged her interest. Then she had made a snap decision. Israel had been attacked from Syria along the Golan Heights. They had assigned her with other foreign volunteers to a medical unit. What she saw, the suffering and dignity, had turned her head. These people were proud and *dedicated*. She had never seen the likes of it before. And it hypnotized her.

Then, later, when Eli Thre had approached her, she saw her chance to contribute in a unique way. She wished now that she had thought how difficult this service would be, before she had boarded the airplane to Zurich.

She had been working on the kibbutz in Kiryat Shemona, happily doing whatever she was told. The days had gone so quickly, and she had never felt more alive. One day, while she was visiting the small café in the center of the village, a voice called her name. She looked up and saw him, small and powerful, with a serious and sad expression. He had introduced himself as Eli Thre and said only that he represented the government. When he asked her to walk with him, she agreed.

At first he had tested her resolve, asking what she felt for Israel. It had been an intense exchange, and she had answered truthfully, sensing that he was probing for a deeper purpose.

He continued in a soft voice with his insistent questions for most of that afternoon. Slowly he revealed himself, as they sat on a stone wall overlooking a citrus orchard. As she listened, she smelled the clean, healthy air and heard the sounds of children playing.

Eli had begun by telling her a poignant detail from his past. As an infant he had been separated from his parents in the last days of the war. The American liberators took him to a camp for displaced persons, and when the camp's directors could neither locate his parents nor identify him by name, they called him Eli Thre. The "Eli" came from a displaced person who had watched over him. The "Thre" derived from the misspelling of the first number on his identification tag. In later years, before he emigrated to Israel, he researched his past and discovered that his real name was Martin Weiss, a Jew; but by then, he was known as Eli Thre. He never changed it, because it was by then more him than the original.

Then, having partly gained Norah's confidence, he had swung the conversation around to her, pointedly asking what he had come to learn.

"What do you know about your stepfather?" he asked.

"My stepfather?" She repeated, astonished. "How do you . . . ?"

He laid his hand gently on her arm and gave her a reassuring smile.

"He's a banker in Zurich. A very successful banker," she replied cautiously. "But I haven't seen him in ages. Why?"

"We know things about him, which is why we need you now."

"Need me?" She had laughed at the idea. His face remained serious. "Tell me what you mean?"

"This won't be easy and your first instinct will be disbelief. But please, listen to me anyway."

"I'm surprised you even know he exists," she said.

"We do know," Eli had said. "We have known for some time."

"What?" She suddenly felt suspect by association.

"Your stepfather's forebears started the Commercial Credit Union. It was a legitimate bank, among hundreds of others in Switzerland. Your stepfather took control when *his* father died just before the war. He was very young, very impressionable. His bank profited from the war. Most banks in Switzerland did. But your stepfather, Hans Peter, we *suspect,* went even further."

"I don't understand."

"Just listen to me," Eli Thre said. "As you know, last year the Israeli government tried and executed Dr. Josef Mengele."

"I remember," she said.

"Before we put him on trial, we interrogated him."

Again she interrupted. "Eli, who is 'we'? Who are you?"

"Give me time, and I'll tell you," he said, taking out a piece of paper. "I want you to read this. It's a transcript of Mengele's interrogation, where it concerns your stepfather. Or where we think it docs. Mengele was given truth drugs."

Norah took the page and started to read.

> THRE: You left Germany without funds.
> MENGELE: Yes.
> THRE: And yet you were able to protect yourself for years. How?

MENGELE: I can't answer.

THRE: How?

MENGELE: Funds.

THRE: What was the source of the funds?

MENGELE: I don't know.

THRE: Money supplied by Nazis?

MENGELE: I don't know.

THRE: [*To an attendant*] What does the polygraph say?

ATTENDANT: Positive. He doesn't know.

THRE: Was it a bank?

MENGELE: Yes.

THRE: The name of the bank?

MENGELE: Commercial Credit Union.

Norah slowly laid the piece of paper beside her on the wall without speaking. Mengele was one of the most celebrated war criminals, a horrible monster, the Angel of Death. He had identified her father's bank? "Maybe it isn't Hans Peter," she said hopefully. "He wouldn't get mixed up in something like this. He's much too impractical. Believe me." She was almost pleading.

"Maybe not," said Thre.

Norah remembered turning her head away. Tears had come to her eyes. Were they going to expel her from Israel because of Hans Peter? She didn't want to leave, ever. Now that she had discovered the only important thing in her life, it was being taken away. "And you want me to leave?" she whispered.

Eli Thre took her hand gently, which confused her even more. "We want you to make your home here," he said.

"Then why tell me these things?"

"We must find out about your stepfather. It is important, and I'll tell you why. If Dr. Mengele didn't know who was giving him the funds, then hundreds of other fascist criminals don't know either."

"So? I really don't understand you."

"There may be a small group of Nazi sympathizers. . . . No, they are not exactly Nazis, though they believe in the Nazi race doctrines. We have the sense that there is a group of extreme right-wing fanatics, a group of people, including your stepfather, about which practically nothing is known. They may have funded both right- and left-wing extremist organizations for some years now. And their base of operation is Switzerland. Otherwise the only common denominator among all the groups they fund—as well as the old Nazis, of course—is a virulent anti-Semitism. They have enormous resources. Our great fear is that this group—this thing that is almost totally anonymous—may be a great threat to Israel."

"Not the Arabs, surely."

"We don't know. There does not seem to be a clear connection. The first person we've located is your father, and if he's part of this group, then we must know. Once we know for certain, we can deal with him. We can eliminate him and the others who are with him. Norah, your stepfather may be a bigger threat to Israel even than Mengele. It's that serious."

"But you can't be sure."

"That's where you come in."

"You mean I should go to Zurich?"

"Yes."

Norah swung her bare legs off the bed and went to the dressing table. Expertly she put on makeup, then went to the closet and took out a mauve crepe de chine skirt and a ruffled eggshell silk blouse. Finally she adorned herself with simple gold jewelry. The ensemble expressed an elegance that money sometimes buys but only youth and good taste make effective.

Last of all she lit a cigarette and waited until she was summoned.

Minutes later, she heard her name being called. Before she could reach the door, Hans Peter came into her room.

"What is it, Peter?" she asked.

He closed the door behind him. "Ernst has insisted that you join us tonight. I told him that it would be better if you didn't, but he wouldn't hear of it. He insists."

"Great," she said in a cheerful voice.

"Listen to what I'm going to tell you. Ernst knows

nothing about your Israel experiment. I want it kept that way. You are not to mention anything about it, do you understand?"

"Of course, but why?"

"It is an *embarrassment.*" He couldn't add his other thought: if Hartmann knew of her affiliation with Israel, he would be furious with Hans Peter. Furious for having her in the house now. "If he asks you your plans, tell him you are leaving tomorrow—for London, where you're now working. Is that clear?"

It was perfectly clear. Hans Peter was frightened, and he was protecting something. It suited her needs perfectly not to tell Hartmann anything. "All right, Peter," she said.

Downstairs in the den, Hans Peter introduced Norah to the Baron and Ruethli Gruetz, the arms maker. Then she took Hartmann's hand. "I was so surprised to see you earlier," she said to him. "I still can't believe it."

"Neither can I," Hartmann replied. "I had quite a shock, too."

"How long has it been?"

Hartmann put his hand to his waist. "You were about that tall, and skinny as a sapling. And you had freckles."

"Twelve years ago, I'd guess." She figured on her fingers. "Was I such a late bloomer?"

"All good things take time," Hartmann said.

Norah blushed.

Hans Peter interrupted, "If we're to have a drink we'd better hurry." He signaled the butler, who passed glasses of champagne. "To us," Hans Peter said. He noticed that Hartmann's eyes did not leave Norah.

The Baur au Lac on Lake Zurich was the most opulent restaurant in Switzerland. The walls were hung with priceless Impressionist paintings; the tables were small and lit by candles. A string quartet in one corner played Bach. Waiters and table captains provided service that could be bettered nowhere in the world.

Norah and Ernst Hartmann sat alone. He had wanted

it that way, explaining that her stepfather and the other two men wanted to discuss business, while he wanted to discuss her.

Norah thought the arrangement odd, but she understood. Of course they were talking business, maybe even what Eli Thre had sent her to Zurich to discover.

Hartmann ordered a bottle of vintage Dom Pérignon, the best the restaurant had to serve. He felt like celebrating; the meeting had been a perfect success. The group had agreed to his plan. Most of them had volunteered to be among the advance group landing in Dar es Salaam. They had handed him carte blanche to carry out the strategy of his own devising. He was sure he would succeed. He looked over at the table to Hans Peter: there would be time for business later. But now he wanted the enjoyable company of a beautiful woman. Norah represented to him something he had nearly forgotten. He felt protective toward her, perhaps because he had known her as a young woman, a girl, really. She would not have cared, if she had known, about his past. Norah had accepted him as he was. She had even loved him, her Uncle Ernst: the thought raised a smile on his face. It had been a case of puppy love, exaggerated and obvious and even at times embarrassing.

The waiter hovered near their table. They had examined their *cartes*. Norah started with a crab soufflé; he took smoked salmon; for their main dish, she asked for a turbot with fennel and a special sorrel sauce and he decided on a steak au poivre vert.

Norah handed the menu back to the captain, then gave Hartmann her full attention. "Peter never writes," she said. "So I haven't kept up. But you look successful as ever."

"Africa has been good to me," he said. "I'm happy there. I'm glad it shows."

"So you still live in Tanzania?"

"I hope never to leave. And yourself?"

Norah had been ordered what to say. It wasn't difficult, for Hartmann had no way of knowing to catch her in a lie. "I'm living in London at the moment, in Knightsbridge, *actually*." She faked an English accent. She put her hand behind her head and grinned broadly. "I'm a model."

"You should be," he said admiringly. "What about boyfriends?"

"First Peter and now you. Boyfriends! Husbands! Is that all you men think about?"

"Then I take it there are none of either." Hartmann's interest in the answer was not avuncular.

"You take it correctly."

The waiter cleared the plates, while another served their entrées. Hartmann ordered a claret for himself and a Montrachet for Norah.

"Remember our trip?" Norah asked.

"How could I forget," he replied, laying down his fork.

It was the last time they had seen one another. She had been on Easter vacation from Montreux, and Ernst had invited her to meet him in South Africa. They had stayed at the Mount Nelson in Cape Town. She went on photographic safaris in the Kruger National Park, swam in the hotel pool, and ate ice cream sundaes with abandon. The two weeks had been memorable.

"Has South Africa changed, I mean, since we visited? You read so much about it nowadays."

"I wouldn't know."

"The whole world seems to be waiting for South Africa to fall, with that new Prime Minister—what's his name, Steenenkupf?"

"Steenkamp. Oh, I don't know. He's been around for a long time, though he was out of power there for a while, when the liberals came in. *That* resulted in chaos, but even I really wouldn't know. I don't get mixed up in politics."

Norah could not assess Hartmann. He had been a friend of her stepfather's for as long as she remembered. It was an African friendship, for Hartmann had never before visited them in Zurich. Uncle Ernst was in the coffee business and an enormous success. Beyond that she knew little.

She was confused about Hartmann, wanting to believe that he was one of Hans Peter's legitimate clients, not a member of the mysterious "group" Eli Thre had talked about. But what was his business in Zurich, and what did he have to do with all the other men who'd come to the meeting earlier that evening?

"Did your conference have to do with Africa?"

He looked up at her. "In a way, yes," he replied.

"Isn't it illegal to do business with South Africa? I thought there were strict embargoes."

Hartmann smiled. "That's what makes it profitable. . . . I'm going to Capetown tomorrow, you know."

"Oh. For long?"

"Oh, just until this venture I'm involved in gets off the ground. And how long are you planning to stay in Zurich?"

"I leave tomorrow as well."

"Shall we have lunch or dinner, whichever? When does your plane leave?"

"I haven't booked yet."

"Then let's make it dinner, an early one. My flight leaves in the late evening."

"It's a deal. But will you ask Peter first?"

"You think he would object?"

"It's just better that way, don't you think?"

Hartmann took the napkin from his lap and wiped his mouth, then, ordering coffee and a Monte Cristo for himself and an eau-de-vie for Norah, he excused himself. He got up from the table and went out of the restaurant toward the washroom.

Norah looked around. Except for Peter and his two friends, she recognized nobody in the room. The waiter came with the drinks and the cigar for Hartmann. She glanced at Hans Peter. Finally she decided to go over and say hello. It was a natural enough thing to do.

The men rose from their chairs. Hans Peter seemed upset by the interruption, but Norah guessed that she was imagining things. Finally Hans Peter spoke. "We were talking—talking about the hunt near Olduvai, weren't we, Baron? I was pretty foolish, I guess. When I missed the rhinoceros I thought I was a dead man."

"You nearly were," Hovagny said. "That rhino had you in *its* sights. You were green, then. Very green."

"I can't disagree." He turned to Gruetz. "Ernst and the Baron taught me how to hunt. I hadn't shot a grouse before."

"You always had it in you," Hovagny said. "The instinct just needed a little encouragement."

They continued talking for several minutes, until Hartmann returned from the washroom. "Are they boring you?" he asked Norah, grinning at the others.

"Dreadfully," she said, then giggled.

Hartmann spoke to Hans Peter. "We should get back."

Undressing in her room, Norah thought again of how foolish she was to have blabbered to her stepfather about Israel. But she wasn't used to secrecy and it seemed so natural to her now to be an Israeli. The remark had cost her time, but what did it matter now? Hans Peter was leaving and so was she. Her days as an agent of MOSSAD, the Israeli intelligence service, gladly, were drawing to a close.

She ran a bath and sat on the edge of the tub, thinking more about the telephone conversation she had had the previous day with Eli Thre. His voice had been reassuring, but other than that, there had been nothing specific. He had merely reiterated the same orders: watch and listen.

Well, she thought, she had followed those orders exactly. She had watched; she had listened. And she had seen nothing and heard even less.

She got out of the tub and dried herself, splashing herself generously with toilet water, then put on a flannel nightgown and pulled back the covers on the bed. Turning off the light, she tried to sleep, but sleep would not come. She threw back the covers and turned on the light. Then she sat, trying to think what she could do in the little time that remained.

The downstairs library was a small room decorated to a man's taste. Red and blue morocco book spines gave the walls a somber appearance. A fire crackled. There were zebra skins on the floor and rock-hyrax blankets on the sofa. African hunting scenes were portrayed in the paintings and fertility statues stared from the tabletops and mantel. A Lizst concerto was playing softly in the background.

The men were seated around a heavy wooden table methodically examining pages of names, cable addresses, and locations. They were culling the list for a final count of two hundred and fifty who, because of their specific skills, would be invaluable in Tanzania. The choices they made were critical, so they took their time in choosing. Only Hartmann and Hovagny had ever met any of the people named on the lists.

"Niki Baer," Hartmann said. He followed the information on the page across a line with his forefinger. "SS Gauleiter in Bohemia. Sought by MOSSAD for propaganda work and extracurricular activities during the war. Now mayor of Leipzig, owner of a glass factory. Good with words."

The Baron looked at Hartmann. "What'll he do?"

"Propaganda. Baer worked with radio and knows its uses. He can handle public announcements from the Voice of Tanzania."

Hans Peter noted Baer's name and phone contact.

"Bill Herrick," Hartmann read on. "One of the leaders of the Manchester Klan. Pretty good on the streets and he knows how to handle blacks. Bring him and four or five lieutenants. We'll need the security."

Hans Peter made the notation.

Hartmann silently eliminated several names. Then, "Luigi Renato. Italian fascist. Maybe he sings. I don't know, we'll find something for him to do."

They had been at the work for more than an hour. Hans Peter yawned. Hartmann looked at him, then over at the Baron. Their faces were drawn and they would be useless in Tanzania tomorrow unless they got some sleep. "We've pushed ourselves hard enough," he said. "You two turn in. I'll finish this. It won't take long."

Hans Peter tried to object, but Hartmann would not listen. "You have an early flight. Now I insist," he said. "Go to bed."

Hans Peter and the Baron started toward the door. Hartmann remembered what he had promised Norah and called Hans Peter back. "I'm told Norah is leaving tomorrow?"

Hans Peter was wary. What had she told Hartmann? Had she mentioned Israel? "That's right," he said. "She's going home."

"She's beautiful, you know, Peter. You are very lucky."

Hans Peter sighed with relief. So she had said nothing. "Thank you," he said.

"I asked her to have dinner with me tomorrow before I leave. She wanted me to ask you. A woman with old-world manners, I guess. You raised her well."

Hans Peter couldn't refuse without making Hartmann suspicious, and he thought it better to leave well enough alone. "If that's what you want, Ernst, I have no objection."

"I didn't think you would." He turned back to the table and the lists of names. Hans Peter went upstairs to his bedroom. Within minutes he was asleep.

Hartmann worked on the lists for a half hour longer. Progress was maddeningly slow. But he had to get it right. He leaned back into the sofa and checked his wristwatch. Late, he thought. And he had to figure on yet another hour's work. But his mind was fuzzy, and he wondered if he was thinking clearly. Now he caught himself dozing. His chin fell against his chest. He stood up and shook his head. A cold shower was what he needed. Yes, he thought, heading for his bedroom, a cold shower.

Norah jumped at the sound of a closing door. Her nerves on edge, she still couldn't sleep. An hour or so ago she had heard the Baron and Peter say good night in the hall. She guessed that the closing door now was Hartmann going to bed.

She went into the bathroom. She had to get some sleep, even if it meant taking a Librium, which she was normally reluctant to do. Pills made her sluggish in the morning, and tomorrow she had to be at her best. She went to her makeup bag and searched for the bottle of pills. It was not there. She wondered where else she might have packed it. No, if it wasn't in the small bag she had left it in Tel Aviv. "Dammit," she said to herself.

She threw herself back onto the bed.

Lying there, she thought about Hartmann again. Perhaps the impression he had made on her at dinner was what prevented her from sleeping. She couldn't tell. Should she suspect him? She didn't know. Eli Thre had told her nothing about Hartmann. MOSSAD had trained her in the business of stealth. But they had not been able to alter old habits. She was not a suspicious person; the need to believe in people's goodness had always put her in trouble, especially with men.

On impulse, almost angrily, she got up from bed and opened the door leading onto the hallway. If she didn't have a Librium, she thought, going down the corridor, she would get a shot of brandy. A large shot.

Except for the rattle of window frames in the winter wind the house was silent. She reached the backstairs, which she had used as a child, when she would sneak down to the kitchen for a glass of milk. Milk, she thought. How times had changed: now she was searching for grown-up's milk, a swig of sleep-inducing Hennessy.

She passed through the door separating the kitchen from the library. The firelight cast eerie moving shadows on the walls. She went over to the sideboard and unscrewed the cap from the cognac bottle, then, thinking how unladylike it was, she tipped the bottle to her lips. She coughed as the amber liquid burned her throat.

She put the bottle back and went over to turn out the light, thinking how lazy and careless their butler still was. Looking down at the table, she noticed the pages and bent down to see what they were. Minutes of their business meeting, she surmised, raising a page to the light.

They were names with addresses and numbers and some unrecognizable order of rank.

But what did they mean? Were they . . . could these be the . . . "group" that her stepfather's bank had funded? It didn't seem possible that they would be listed like this, right in front of her, so easy, so clear and complete.

There was a noise upstairs and her mind went blank.

Movement on the landing: she cocked her head. Was

somebody coming downstairs or was it Hartmann going to bed? She listened carefully. Then she heard the sharp sound of a door closing and feet, bare feet, padding on the stairs.

She panicked and threw the pages back on the table, then ran into the kitchen and pressed herself against the wall. The room was dark and cool.

She heard it all so distinctly it was as if she could see into the library. Footsteps. Tapping of paper on the wood table. Breathing. A mutter.

"What the—" It was Hartmann.

She heard the riffle of paper.

He must know that she had seen the lists. She smelled it all over herself: the toilet water.

6

Foreigners called them rock spiders because they were not easily shaken. They were farmers, ranchers and miners, police and army, Dutch in their ancestry, xenophobic, and bound together by a stern Calvinist faith. They were the proud inheritors of the Voortrekker tradition; their forefathers had fought the Zulus, then the English, and won decisively by forming up their covered wagons in the laager, a fortified position that had become a defense of the mind, as impregnable now as the circled wagons once were. These people had withstood pounding from the forces of reason, and their thinking had not altered. Only Johannes Balthazar Steenkamp had the power to make them change and he was beloved because he never did, and never would.

Standing there, Steenkamp looked the full measure of the Boer, as much the creation of the Afrikaaners' society as South Africa's gold and diamonds were the unique products of the Cape's geological eons. Stout, with massive shoulders and thick peasant arms, he still carried the suggestion of a powerful man despite sickness, age, and his temporary fall from power. They had tried to stomp him out, to get rid of him, almost as if he were an embarrassment. But the liberal fools had failed. A momentary scandal in the newspapers, an attempt to "liberalize" the laws on apartheid—hadn't he always told them that there could be no halfway measures, not in South Africa, not in *his* South Africa? One crack in the wall and the whole edifice would crumble.

Now their "experiment" was finished. It had been a miserable failure. Some of the blacks were content for a while, but then they had demanded more. First it was universal education, then universal suffrage. There was talk of labor unions and black socialism. It had not lasted long. When the whites realized what was in store for them, they quickly turned back to the man they could trust to restore their power. The Boers had always been with him, but in the reelection he had won over 75 percent of the English population as well.

Still, the situation remained precarious, and the dramatic turn back to the Right had endangered South Africa's standing with the rest of the Western world. London and Washington had severed relations upon learning of Steenkamp's first decree: the compulsory resettlement of 100,000 blacks into the countryside.

Steenkamp was back in power, but his health had not improved. Now he was in his early seventies, his skin was flaccid. He had a bloated face and drooping, weary eyes that watered incessantly. The burst capillaries of his cheeks showed even from beneath the pancake of powder. The glare of television lights reflected off a thin sheen on his forehead and jowls.

Like a fundamentalist minister, he had talked for almost an hour without really saying anything, but he had no need for substance. The faces in the audience were enraptured. They drew private conclusions from the small silences between his words. He had them hanging, as he knew he would. He leaned into the microphone, his voice now heavy with sarcasm.

"They say we are the villains, the oppressors, while our blacks are the righteous and oppressed." He flexed his shoulders and scanned the room with quick black eyes. "They say we should get out of South Africa. The blacks must govern."

Several farmers shouted, "No—no."

"That's right." His voice was a hiss. "Their thinking is not just false. It is dangerous."

Those words suffused their minds, tranquilizing areas of doubt and concern. Johannes Steenkamp, the Prime Minister of their South Africa, their tribal chief, was standing behind what they believed. He would not desert them in this, their hour of need. Many of them leaned forward in their seats.

There was much he wanted to say. But words were failing, as was his health. He couldn't concentrate, so anxious was he to begin with deeds what he had failed to do with words. He had trouble even thinking, and he wondered somewhere in the darkness of his mind if the pressure of events wasn't edging him toward madness.

The "Operation" would begin soon, he thought, sliding a finger across his upper lip, feeling the nervousness. These people in the audience were the key. He needed their support. But there was another reason why he was addressing them. He needed to gloat. He—Johannes Balthazar Steenkamp, the greatest leader South Africa had ever known—he would provide the solution. He would leave a legacy of permanent peace, of permanent *white supremacy,* of a white South Africa.

He now spoke with a demagogue's fervor.

"We will not watch our beloved homeland be destroyed by ignorant talk in the United Nations, by ignorant and pompous world *leaders,* by the infiltration of communists, by intimidation. No!" The word bounced off the back wall. "The failure of others leaves us now with no choice. I repeat, we have no choice but to rely on ourselves, as we have always done."

There was cheering and the stamping of boots as he turned to the row of local dignitaries behind the lectern. One came forward with a glass of water. Then, as Steenkamp drank, the politician held out his arms to bring order to the hall.

"In our best democratic tradition—" the politician said. Nobody listened.

"Please. Can we have quiet, please. I know the Prime Minister appreciates your support."

Five minutes later they were silent, and the man began again.

"In our best democratic tradition here in Nigel, Prime Minister Steenkamp has agreed to answer questions. Use the microphones in the aisles." He stepped back slightly, as a round-shouldered Boer farmer shuffled from his seat to the aisle and grasped the microphone. His voice was thin and reedy.

"May I say first, Mr. Steenkamp, that your words soothe our hearts. You are one of us!"

There was more applause. The farmer became confident.

"The world points an accusing finger at us," he said, his voice deepening. "And we are bloody sick of it. What have we done wrong? Nothing, that's what. This is *our* country. The kaffirs are our people." He raised a thick fist. "We built South Africa with our hands—"

The politician bent into the microphone. "Please, no speeches. If you have a—"

"—question? Yes, I do," the farmer said. "How much longer can we go it alone? Can we hold out?"

Steenkamp shaded his eyes. "In white South Africa, we whites rule," he said. "We can handle our blacks." He wished what he said was true, but if something dramatic did not happen, if the "Operation" did not begin, then defeat could come in a matter of weeks. His breathing quickened. "If our enemies want to bring us to our knees, I warn them now. Let them guess again. I cannot say what my plans are. But let me assure you, a solution to our problem, our *black* problem"—he spat the words out—"has been found. You and your children, and your grandchildren, will thank me for what I am about to do."

He stopped, thinking that he might have gone too far. Hartmann would not want him to tip their hand, and he could be angry when he wanted to. But what did it matter, he thought, walking from the hall. They were at the brink. Now nothing could stop what they were about to do.

The orange and white Bell Jet Ranger moments later left a shrinking circle of sun-reddened faces below on the helipad. Quickly gaining altitude and speed, the prime ministerial chopper passed on an easterly course over a dreary horizon of manmade hills and valleys, abandoned mine shafts and knolls of slag, then less than an hour later through the sawtoothed ridges surrounding the capital city of Lesotho.

Lesotho alone could provide what Steenkamp needed. That necessity galled him, for South Africa engulfed Lesotho on all sides. By Steenkamp's thinking, Lesotho should never have been granted independence. He disapproved of Lesotho's laws and morality, for the tiny country had become a haven in which white South Africans escaped puritanical blue laws. Almost anything went in Lesotho and Steenkamp wished it otherwise.

He pushed that thought out of his mind as the helicopter lightly set down outside the Lesothan palace. Mesawa Loba, the Prime Minister of Lesotho, extended a pudgy hand and led him at a waddling gait into a private sitting room on the second floor. Alone except for a uniformed guard, they took chairs beside a cavernous fireplace. Outside the dormer windows Lesothan peasants on ponies passed in red woolen serapes and conical straw hats, but neither man appreciated local quaintness.

Despite himself, Steenkamp did not hesitate. "Before we start, I would appreciate a refreshment," he said.

Loba nodded, reaching into a veneered cabinet for a bottle of Stellenbosch and two tumblers. He had known what Steenkamp wanted. He saw it in his eyes. But he had waited for Steenkamp to beg. That was what Loba craved. "If I remember correctly, this is your drink," he said, teasing the Prime Minister, who replied by pouring. The cognac renewed him and numbed the pain. He leaned back with an audible sigh.

"We share many secrets," Steenkamp said finally.

That was true, Loba thought, piqued that Steenkamp had, as usual, assumed *his* role as host. In each of their several meetings, Steenkamp always started the discussions, laid down the rules, and initiated the bargaining. But this visit, arranged in haste, made Loba more wary. It made no sense that Steenkamp would visit in a time of such crisis for South Africa. He wanted something, and that signaled trouble to Loba, who knew that Lesotho had nothing left to give.

Mesawa Loba was the epitome of African venality. Moonfaced, with bulging red-rimmed eyes, he was so corpulent that simple breathing made him perspire. His greed was equally large. He had filled personal accounts in Switzerland by playing his country off against South Africa. Commissions and kickbacks were the common fare. The United Nations had been a gourmet meal, supplying Lesotho with aid after Loba charged that South Africa had barricaded its borders. Nothing of the sort had happened, but the UN didn't know that. And now Loba, made rich beyond even *his* dreams, could not be bought. What Loba wanted now was influence.

Steenkamp took another swallow, broaching with flattery. "As a nation we are grateful for the help you gave in the past," he said in a flat, unfeeling voice. "While other countries condemn us, you are restrained. Despite their efforts to destroy South Africa, you hold your counsel."

Loba took the bait. "I hope we can continue to help," he said.

"You've already done more than I could reasonably expect. But since you ask, there is something." He waited, but there was only silence. "Well . . . what I need is critical to the survival of South Africa. If you agree, I will be forever in your debt, Chief Loba."

Loba raised a hand to his mouth and coughed. Steenkamp was leading to something important. The thought seduced Loba, anxious now to hear what Steenkamp wanted. "I don't see what I have of *critical* importance."

"Let me tell you, then," Steenkamp said. "I propose an agreement. For Lesothan contract labor in South Africa's mines."

Loba shook his head. His people would rebel. It was dangerous, unhealthy, and it paid nothing. No matter what he did they would refuse—they had before.

"To anticipate your question, our blacks are being removed from the mines."

"But if *your* people won't work there?"

"You don't understand," Steenkamp said, wanting to reveal only enough to secure Loba's cooperation. He had to conceal his real intent. "Our blacks are a burden. They sabotage the machinery, they strike for better pay and hold dangerous demonstrations against conditions. With them gone, the Lesothans will become the mines' single work force."

Loba tugged at the button straining in the hole of his jacket. "They won't do it," he said with finality.

Steenkamp wondered if Loba really thought that. "They'll do exactly what you tell them," he said. But he could not be certain.

"Will there be better pay and guarantees of conditions?"

"I can't say," Steenkamp replied. "Maybe in the future, but for the moment, things will remain as they are."

"What if they won't?"

"Then you'll force them," Steenkamp said. "Remember, Loba, *you* have no choice."

Loba didn't need to be told. However much Steenkamp now needed Loba, Loba was still controlled by Steenkamp. Without Steenkamp, Loba would never have become the new nation's first Prime Minister. The election results had been overturned by the supervising Bureau of State Security, when it arrested the true winners on trumped-up charges and installed him as Prime Minister. He owed everything to Steenkamp and that debt was being called in. Still, what could he do? The people had seen relatives and friends killed in the mines. They would do some things for him, but definitely not this. Unless . . . he thought. "Monshoe is the only way," he said.

"I hoped you'd reach that conclusion," Steenkamp said. "He'll do your bidding."

"That's not guaranteed," Loba cautioned. Monshoe commanded the affection and confidence of the Lesothans. They would do *anything* he asked. And Loba hated him for that. "What if he refuses?"

Steenkamp smiled wanly. "Then use force," he said.

For the first time, Loba sipped the brandy, wondering how he could influence Monshoe. He was in London and would ignore his appeals. But there was one way, he thought, rubbing the smooth amulet in his pocket. Even Monshoe, the enlightened one, could not ignore a higher power.

"There is still no guarantee," Loba said.

"But I need a guarantee."

"He is a stubborn young fool." This was getting them nowhere. For every objection, Steenkamp had a counter-proposal. Loba would do what he could. If he failed, he would face the consequences. "All right, Mr. Steenkamp, I *will* try," he said.

Steenkamp nodded.

There was a moment of silence. This was to be a negotiation, Loba thought, but from where he sat it was one-sided. He had received nothing from Steenkamp, and the prospect of Monshoe's cooperation with the South Africans made him greedy.

"Your proposal is less than generous," he said.

Steenkamp laughed. "But it's all I am offering," he said.

"And nothing more?" Loba feigned an offended tone. "If I might suggest—"

"—You'll get a sweetener. One rand per month per worker, out of their wages."

Loba's expressions of gratitude were interrupted by the sound of the door opening. A military officer in flight coveralls of the South African Air Force came abruptly over and whispered in Steenkamp's ear. Seeing his eyes flicker, Loba knew that something was wrong. Steenkamp got to his feet, talking to the officer in Afrikaans. Then he turned to Loba.

"There's trouble in Soweto," he said, extending his hand. "I appreciate what you're doing, and keep me informed on Monshoe."

Loba watched as the Prime Minister's back disappeared through the door.

Seconds later, Steenkamp was trotting across the palace lawn toward the waiting jet commander. He bent to avoid the rotor downdraft as the officer slid back the side loading panel, securing it after him and mounting the cockpit. The helicopter lifted off as though it were under fire.

As they sped northward, Steenkamp issued commands into a headset and listened intently to reports from the ground. What they told him was bad, and he wondered if his speech, only hours before, had not triggered the riot.

"What about casualties?" he asked.

"Twenty dead on our side and three times that wounded," the officer in charge, a general, replied, from the mobile headquarters on the ground.

"They're armed?" Steenkamp was incredulous.

"Yes, sir. They hit us without warning."

"But can you contain them?"

"They're moving past us into Johannesburg."

"Then issue this order," Steenkamp said. "Your men are to shoot *on sight* any one of them found outside the township."

"But my standing orders, sir—"

"To hell with them," Steenkamp yelled, his anger rising. "I said kill them."

A second's hesitation, then the voice responded. "Our pleasure, sir."

The helicopter approached Soweto Township from the south. But even from ten miles away the billowing black smoke could be clearly seen. The field commander at Soweto said that the blacks had used fires as a diversion. They had switched tactics, knowing that police and army strategists were expecting rioting within Soweto. The Standard Operating Procedure was to cordon off the black township. Nobody cared what blacks did to their own homes, just so long as they didn't destroy the all-white suburbs. The difference this time, Steenkamp was told, was their calculation. The blacks had started the fires and waited as the Army sealed off the entrances to the township. Then they charged through, shooting *white* soldiers as they ran toward the city. Steenkamp received reports now that bands of marauding blacks were firing on private homes. This was nothing at all like the riots a decade earlier. This was civil war.

The chopper skimmed the road on its approach, the skids all but grazing the treetops. Steenkamp pressed his face against the Plexiglas window. What he saw sickened him.

Cars and buses had been overturned and were in flames. Soldiers were removing the bodies of white children from a bus that had been riddled by gunfire. Some of them were being put into ambulances. The housing projects near the city were engulfed in smoke. Helicopters buzzed around the perimeter of Soweto and bright yellow flashes came sporadically from their gunports. Tanks and armored personnel carriers moved across the road and into the fields near the Soweto fences, trying to contain a situation that was already well out of hand.

The helicopter slowed and then hovered. Steenkamp went to the other window to find out why. Below and twenty yards distant he saw soldiers on a grassy knoll. They were carrying automatic weapons and were in full battle dress. An officer held a microphone to his mouth, his foot resting on the side of a communications Jeep.

Then for the first time Steenkamp noticed the blacks on their bellies, their faces pressed into the turf, hands bound tightly at their backs. Several soldiers stood over them, pointing weapons at their necks.

"Put me down there," Steenkamp ordered the pilot.

The helicopter swung in a wide arc and came over the road, blowing sand and dirt onto the soldiers, who crouched and turned their faces away. When the skids touched the ground, Steenkamp waited for the rotors to slow. The pilot came through his compartment to open the sliding doors.

"Hurry it up," Steenkamp demanded. "I don't have all day."

"Yes, *sir.*" The officer grabbed the handle and swung back the door.

The veins in Steenkamp's neck bulged. The pilot saw his anger and wondered what it meant. He extended his arm, like a doorman, and helped the Prime Minister to the ground. The soldiers at first didn't recognize him, but as he got closer, they snapped to attention and saluted. Steenkamp stared at the blacks.

"Who are they?" he asked.

"The last to get out, sir," the young officer replied, his arms rigidly at his sides. He looked to be in his teens. "They had rifles, over there." He pointed to a cache of automatic weapons. "Excuse me, sir, but these bloody kaffirs got one of my men." His voice was choked with anger.

Steenkamp saw the soldier lying nearby on a stretcher, a bandage covering his chest. He went over and peered into his face, bending down and gently brushing matted hair from his forehead. "You'll be all right, son," he said. "I'll get you out of here." He ordered the officer to put him aboard his helicopter. "And give me that," he said, reaching for the officer's holstered pistol.

The feel of the gun, its balance and weight, were familiar in his hand. He switched off the safety and went up to the blacks. He raised one of their chins with the stubby barrel and stared into a face distorted by fear. The man saw the pistol and began to tremble.

"Azania," he said in a clear voice.

Steenkamp knew the word, the black nationalists' rallying cry, the name for a black-ruled South Africa. This kaffir was what the world wanted to run his country. This man and millions like him were tearing his South Africa to pieces. They were destroying what white men had worked and bled and died for. Well, it wouldn't be, he thought, staring into the black man's eyes. "Azania?" he whispered. "Not while I hold this."

He pointed the gun at the man's forehead and pulled the trigger. The pistol exploded, disintegrating the back of the man's skull. The dead black slumped grotesquely on his side as Steenkamp returned the pistol to the officer, speaking in an even voice. "No more arrests," he said. "Do you get that, Lieutenant? From now on, they start to pay."

7

"What do you make of it?"

It was an hour before the morning security briefing with the President, and Admiral Winfield Cowles, the director of the CIA, wanted to know what to report. South Africa had become the main foreign policy preoccupation for the first-term President. As such he would certainly want a rundown from Cowles on Prime Minister Steenkamp's hard-line speech and, equally, the meaning of the outbreak of riots in Soweto.

Stanley Andrews looked at the newspapers in his hands, then back at Cowles. "What can you expect from Steenkamp?" he asked. "The President hasn't only pushed him to the wall. He lifted him off the ground and beat him with a club. Whatever the President has in mind, Steenkamp will never give power to the blacks."

"The President doesn't agree," Cowles said. "Something will crack. And the President is banking it'll be Steenkamp."

"I'm not so certain," said Andrews, who, as the chief African analyst at the CIA, knew better than anyone in Washington how unpredictable the continent's politics were. Andrews was cynical, though, and he didn't much care. The Administration and Congress had jumped aboard the southern African bandwagon, but Americans didn't give a damn about anything in Africa except the elephant herds. Most American whites thought all Africa was white South Africa; all black Americans thought Africa was *Roots*. The other evening Andrews had asked his dinner partner where Chad was. The young woman thought "he" was "on tour." What the hell, Andrews thought, Chad was only the third-largest nation in black Africa. It made him laugh.

"Look where Steenkamp is now," he said to Cowles. "And he hasn't budged an inch."

They both knew, as did the President, that White South Africa was cut off and desperate. Rhodesia's white population had fled after the "black truce" was signed between moderate and radical black liberation movements. The United Nations had wrenched independence for Namibia, which was now ruled by the militant wing of SWAPO. Until Steenkamp's reelection, South Africa had been slowly progressing toward a more equal society—under extreme pressure, it was true, from its Western allies. That "interference" had been one of the principal themes of Steenkamp's election campaign. That and an undisguised hatred of the kaffirs. Since the election and Steenkamp's reestablishment of strict apartheid, the country had been virtually abandoned by the civilized world. It was isolated economically. Western nations had closed ranks with embargoes and sanctions. No industrialized nation and no private corporation bought from or gave credits to South Africa.

The worldwide strangulation of the country had one purpose: to force Prime Minister Johannes Balthazar Steenkamp to dismantle apartheid and give equal representation under the law to South Africa's eighteen million blacks. But Steenkamp held out; he survived.

"I don't know how much longer," Admiral Cowles was saying. "The stuff in Steenkamp's speech was portentous, but what are the specifics?"

"I can only guess," Andrews said.

"And?"

"He may be going to precipitate something politically on a scale we haven't seen before," Andrews said. "Maybe he'll go to the Soviets."

"Never," Cowles said emphatically.

"Then maybe he'll unsheath his nukes."

Preposterous though it sounded, the possibility was real. South Africa had a nuclear capacity. But use of the bombs was tantamount to suicide.

"How can we know for certain?" Cowles asked.

"We can't."

For the better part of six months now there had been

no foreign agents in South Africa. The Bureau of State Security had closed off as a source and nobody else, not even the British Intelligence Service and MOSSAD, had gone in. The CIA received less intelligence on South Africa than did the foreign editor of *The New York Times*.

"So there's *nothing* more we can do?" Cowles wondered how that would be received by the President.

"Just wait and see."

"And ask our brothers? Maybe they picked up something."

"We already have background information," Andrews said. "But it's not all that pertinent or new."

"Show me," Cowles said, wanting something hard to give the President.

"Actually two things—one old, one less old. The Brits profiled Steenkamp. He's sick with a cancer of some sort and he doses it with cognac. They figure he's deranged, with delusions of grandeur, irrational hatreds, and the like. In other words, he's dangerous. You don't need more proof than these press reports."

Cowles had been stunned by the *Post*'s account of Steenkamp's killing a man in cold blood. He nodded solemnly. "And the other item?"

"MOSSAD sent us a query the other day. They're worried about this deep group—"

"Neo-Nazis again? When will they ever let go of that?"

"They don't know exactly what they're onto. Except they consider it a real threat."

"That's all we need," said the CIA director sarcastically. "An unknown anti-Semitic terrorist group which hasn't done anything. And that's a threat?"

"Well, they did get a line from Mengele before they strung him up. It seems that a person, or maybe even a group, is financing the old Nazi network. Mengele said as much."

"Mengele was just a tired old man. I'm not going to get excited about a German old-age club. Anyway, what's the connection with South Africa? As I recall, that's what we were talking about."

"MOSSAD thinks this deep group has something to do

with Steenkamp. They wanted help from us, but I told them we didn't know. They've planted an agent somewhere on the Continent I think. . . . You never know," Andrews said. "Steenkamp needs help. He might just hook up with fanatics."

Cowles rolled his eyes at him. "We don't have enough problems?" he asked sardonically. "Forget ghosts, please. Stay on Steenkamp."

Andrews agreed. "The way things are, even old Nazis wouldn't want to touch South Africa."

8

The Covent Garden underground station smelled of mildew and human staleness. The sounds of pattering feet and English-accented talk reverberated off the vaulted ceiling as commuters jostled for position on the platform. Men in dark suits carrying brollies read the evening news beside secretaries and clerks. A punk rocker with cockatoo hair, a pin in his cheek, bright makeup, and a beertab necklace stared defiantly at those he passed. Few paid him much mind.

The young black man found the punk amusing, as he stepped back to let him pass. Where he came from, faces were often painted with bright colors. The punk's face even resembled an African mask used by the black man's tribe to celebrate the birth of a child. He followed him with intelligent eyes. Seeing a businessman frown at the punk, he reflected on his own appearance. The shabby clothes he wore hung like a coat on a nail from his angular, spare frame, and his tumbleweed afro often drew the approbation of proper Englishmen, just as the punk was doing now.

Students at the London School of Economics knew him as David, the solitary and bookish African. They would have been surprised to learn that his name was prefixed with a title, King, because a king did not dress in army surplus clothing or survive on an allowance of $8,000 a year. But young David knew something they didn't. In Africa, royalty was superfluous, even in the constitutional monarchy of Lesotho.

In these days, a king was a figurehead, a splash of gilt and an object of pomp to entertain the citizenry on days of national celebration. But King Monshoe of Lesotho was peculiar for representing something more. After his father died, he had inherited both the throne and the deep affection of the Lesothan people, who defended and followed him, because they sensed that he was their best hope for a prosperous and peaceful future.

David was so self-absorbed now as a train entered the station that he did not notice another black man standing by the tile wall who had watched the young black royal since the moment he had walked onto the platform. He was a singular figure with tribal cheek scars, gray hair, and gnarled hands. With a quick, spidery movement, he followed Monshoe into the train.

David Monshoe took hold of the strap and thought more about an occurrence earlier that day, when he had been reading in the LSE library. He had heard a sound like the rustling of leaves and turned to see the Lesothan ambassador. The man bowed and unctuously intoned the customary but archaic Lesothan royal homage. This was embarrassing, for the rituals meant nothing to Monshoe. And he mistrusted the ambassador, a thin shadow on the diplomatic scene who rarely emerged from the shabby embassy on Great Portland Street. The envoy never entertained, never accepted invitations, never, as far as David could tell, represented Lesotho, except in the daily ritual of hanging out the national flag. During his years in London, David had seen him twice.

David was curt and impersonal. The ambassador's courtly bow had drawn curious glances from fellow students, and David wanted him gone. "Say what you have to, then get out," he said.

The ambassador did not change his expression. He was like a tape recorder, David thought, mechanical and unimaginative.

"Your Prime Minister sends greetings," the ambassador said in a smooth voice. "He asks about your health and progress in school and wishes you good fortune in both things. He has asked me, as well, to convey a formal request. He believes the time to be propitious for you to return and lead your people in their Independence Day celebrations."

Inwardly David laughed. Unless he could be used to further Chief Loba's political career, he would never be asked home. Loba despised him, feared the time when David would wrest his power from him. "Reply with these exact words," David said with a hint of mischief. "King David II, the Lesothan sovereign, tells Prime Minister Loba to go to hell."

The ambassador spun on his heel and walked from the library.

Now David bent to read the station sign. "Piccadilly." Only three stops to go before Knightsbridge. He massaged the top of his right knee. The cold London winters cramped his leg and accentuated his permanent limp. Except in weather like this he barely noticed his prosthetic leg, but whenever he did, enmity returned. It had happened after the death of his father, when David became Loba's ward. He had gashed his lower leg one day while playing alone in the rocks near the palace. Loba had not sent for a doctor, explaining that pain helped forge men. David's leg soon became gangrenous. When a doctor was finally summoned, there was nothing to be done but amputate. He had learned to live with the false leg, which now was almost a natural part of him, but he could never learn to forgive Loba's callousness.

As the train accelerated from the station, David heard a soft tapping sound. It came from a small hand drum played by the scarred black man's long, hoary fingernails. The sound made some passengers uneasy at its far-off rhythm and at the man's entranced, unfocused expression. But it frightened David for the images it evoked. When he looked into the old man's eyes he felt a chill.

David knew that this was the drum that opened the eye of Death. It was a myth that every Lesothan believed, that Death was a giant covered with long, silky hair who took a boy to be his servant in the beginning when there was famine on earth. In payment for the servitude of his brothers and sisters, Death fed the boy delicious food. meat he had eaten was their flesh. Angry villagers killed One day, to his horror, he saw their bones and knew the the giant by setting fire to his hair, in which they later found a charred packet of magical medicines. They sprinkled some powder on the bones and the brothers and sisters miraculously sprang to life. But the foolish young man put a pinch on Death's eye. From then on, the sound of the drum disturbed his slumber, and every time Death opened and shut his eye, a person died.

The train screeched to a halt, but the tapping continued as David stared into the old shaman's face. Against all reason he knew that he had to get away, that the man was after him for a purpose he couldn't know. With quickening breath, he squeezed past others in the crowded car and darted out the instant the doors mechanically opened.

The old man walked from the train with hands buried in his overcoat pockets, as though guided by a force. He saw only an inner beacon directing him to King David Monshoe.

From a vantage point on the moving escalator stairs, David watched the old man on the platform and then started to run, turning every couple of steps to gauge the distance gained. He saw too late the woman carrying her baby and a collapsible carriage and toppled into them. His leg buckled and he fell on the sharp surface of the stairs.

"Idiot," she screamed. "You've hurt my baby."

But David did not hear. Holding his leg, he rushed to the top of the escalator and froze with the decision now whether to take another underground train or run into the street. It didn't matter which. He had to get away from whatever evil the old man intended. He made his decision when he spotted a train with its doors open. Half limping and half running, he approached the nearest car. A few more steps and he would be rid of what stalked him. But just as he prepared for a final push, the doors closed and the train went off, leaving him frightened and alone.

He glanced in both directions at the sound of laughter. A group of schoolchildren skipped down the platform. He took a seat near the wall and tried to conceal himself among the commuters. A few minutes later, a distant rumbling in the tunnel and the flash of yellow headlights brought him to his feet again. He breathed easier now that another train approached. He inched to the side of the track, waiting.

The touch was soft, as though one of the children had nudged him. He spun around: there in front of him was the grinning death's head of the shaman, who whispered in Basotho, then pressed an object in his hand. Immobilized by fear, David watched the old man retreat down the platform. He bumped into passengers and stumbled once, nearly falling. People tried to get out of his way but seconds later, as he neared the center of the platform, the old man fell. His spindly legs flayed in the air as he sank down the narrow track wall. Warning screams were drowned out by the noise of the oncoming train, then cold steel wheels cut into the shaman again and again with blunt and lethal edges.

Without looking, David jammed the object in his pocket and walked unsteadily toward the exit. When he got to the top of the stairs, he saw paramedics hurrying down, but he knew their efforts were useless. Outside on the street he hailed a taxi, which took him to Lowndes Square. He had barely entered his apartment when he rushed to the bathroom and emptied his stomach in a catharsis of relief.

An hour later, after he showered and put on clean clothes, he went into the living room and sprawled on the sofa. African sculpture, masks, and votives stared down on him from tables and walls. For many collectors they were expensive ornaments. But they always hinted to him of something foreboding and presently aware, as though their spirit had not died, even so far from the dark heart that gave them birth. They represented the millennia of

African mystery, and despite his education, David still could not uproot himself from belief. For each sculpture in the room with an evil purpose, he had carefully collected another with the power to protect, like the Bapende animal mask over the couch.

For those reasons, he was in no hurry to investigate the shaman's gift.

The old man was an agent of Prime Minister Loba. That much David knew. When the ambassador had failed, he cabled Loba, who sent the witch doctor to the deadly appointment. What he had whispered, *"O lo Velo,"* held little mystery for David. It was the priest's command for men to return to the kraal and ready themselves for battle. One order was diplomatic, the other religious. David resolved to submit to neither. Yet, rather than do nothing, he would find out what he could, although he suspected the reasons why Loba had done this. He needed him, or he and Steenkamp did, to force the Lesothans to do something they feared. David alone had that power to persuade, and he would use it only for the common good.

The decision buoyed his spirit, and he felt now that whatever the shaman had put into his hand could not shake his resolve. The thought was soothing as he went to the closet and took the object from the coat.

The sight of it shocked him. The medicine packet was beautiful and horrible at once, with intricate hemp weave and three leopard claws sewn on the bottom. The size of a man's fist, it was designed to contain a substance of magical power. David placed the pouch on the table and got a knife, which he ran along its curved seam. Fine white dust spilled out as he held the pouch in trembling hands. He lifted the lid. The legendary powder that opened Death's eye was inside.

Now King David Monshoe II had no choice.

9

Radical change had swept Tanzania, but at the German Settlers' Club history, like a fly in amber, was suspended in time. Even a fresh coat of cerise paint could not conceal the decay within. The club harbored German colonial hangers-on who centered their existence on the Bavarian bar with its backgammon and billiard tables, a turkish bath attended by servile but sullen blacks, and a restaurant for *members only* that featured Wiener schnitzel on Fridays. The Settlers' Club was home for those who had lost touch with their native Germany and were equally removed from an independent, modern Tanzania.

The Teutonic ambiance was why Hans Peter Hirsch stayed there. He liked the quaint in places and people, and this trait was abundant in the Bavarian bar where he and Baron Hovagny were relaxing after their long flight from Zurich.

They had checked in an hour earlier and were shown to their rooms in the Military Wing. Hans Peter had unpacked, bathed, and shooed away noisome swallows nesting in the eaves, before rejoining Hovagny on the bar veranda, where they now shared a liter bottle of Tusker. Hans Peter hummed a madrigal and surveyed the Baron, one of the first people he had met in Dar es Salaam.

Theirs was a curious friendship. Outwardly they had nothing in common. Hovagny was large, with a brusque manner, crude tongue, and a streak of meanness he didn't try to conceal. He knew Africa like no one else. That knowledge had made him self-sufficient and, for most of his days, a loner. He had hunted through Kenya and Uganda and on every game block of Tanzania, and he understood the habits of animals as spinsters know the peculiarities of their household pets. He was incapable of

76

tolerating weakness in others and drove people as hard as he drove himself.

Once Hirsch had seen the Baron take aim at a Cape buffalo. He had snapped the big rifle to his shoulder. Because he hadn't positioned the rifle securely, when he fired the scope lashed back with the recoil, concussing him. Most people would have fallen to the ground, but not the Baron, who had aimed again, angrily this time, and killed the charging animal. He had then turned to Hirsch, blood streaming down his face. He said merely, "Now let's get you a buffalo," and walked onward.

From the start, the Baron had joked about Hirsch's ignorance of nature generally and Africa in particular.

"Do you wonder why your flight was late?" he had asked back then, when he first picked up Hans Peter at the airport. Hans Peter remembered asking why. "I shot a bush buck off the runway so your plane could land," the Baron had told him. In those days Hans Peter believed what he said. They drove a battered Land Rover into Dar and the Baron filled his head with wonder. "The game is migrating now, so it's abundant," he said. "But it still isn't like in the old days, when we shot five lions before noon and during that same afternoon the other lions ate five coolies in revenge."

Hans Peter returned again and again after that. He didn't know why, nor did he think about it. But if he had thought, he would have answered in one word: Romance.

Most of Hans Peter's youth and early manhood, right up to middle age, had been devoted to his work, for the bank and for Protégé. Therefore, not to do a complete job of manipulating its finances was unthinkable. He dreamed of Protégé's greatness. And he dreamed of other things, envisioning himself to be like other men, men like Hartmann and the Baron, men of action and quick decisions. They endured hardships, even when there was no need.

Then Africa happened to him.

The Baron said he had contracted the fever. "Africa gets in your veins and, like malaria, stays forever," he had told him. And he was right. He had learned how to control fear and taste the triumph of a kill. He also learned to savor the sense of his blood running thin and warm on the hunt. But he remained controlled. He could never be quite so expressive as the Baron, or quite so calculating as Hartmann.

Together they had roamed East Africa as if it were their private domain. Hans Peter learned to know himself on those starry nights, in those sunny days. He transformed himself from a banker to a passionate and concentrated adventurer. And he saw in both disciplines similar requirements for success. On the hunt he had to track his prey, then commit himself to fire in that critical moment. The animal would kill him, or he it; in business he would defeat his competitor or be defeated.

The thought now that soon—very soon—this whole country would be Protégé's private domain made him draw a breath. He signaled to Michael, the Masai barman. *"Rafiki,* another Tusker, *haraka sana,"* he said. He then reached for his briefcase and took out the document that Hartmann had given him. He handed it to the Baron. "This was the source of the idea—it's just a little piece of paper, but it's all there."

The Baron held it up to the sunlight. *"Das Tanganyika Projekt,"* he read. Now it was memorabilia only, and he admired the ornate seal on its cover. It was bound with faded blue ribbon and the bronzed letters were oxidized.

GEHEIME REICHSSACHE

15 August 1940
Abwehr I
Kurfürstendamm 116
Berlin

Code DIII/2173 Top Secret

To The Führer:

Our coming victory rewards Germany with the duty to answer, once and for all, the Jewish question. The details herein are for the resettlement of four million as a vanguard in the former colony called Tanganyika. We have singled out that country for its German heritage. By locating the Jews there, they will be prevented from further tainting any non-negro ethnic group.

The long-term goal: All Jews out of Europe.

Unless the League of Nations cedes its protectorate (Tanganyika) to the Reich, we recommend its being taken by force (Chapter Two): A commando force of 300 SS troops will suffice for the elimination of the League's garrison.

The Jews will be transported by ship from ports in Germany and France (Chapters Three to Seven). The Jews will be deprived of German citizenship. Henceforth, and once they have been resettled, they will become citizens of the Reich Protectorate of Tanganyika. This approach has several advantages.

1. They will remain in the Reich's control.

2. They can be held as ransom for the silence of their fellow Jews in America and Allied countries.

3. The Reich Propaganda Ministry under Goebbels can argue that our Führer has created a culturally, economically, and administratively private state for the Jews. Thus, Tanganyika will seem as a gift.

A Reich governor (SS) will command our forces in Tanganyika. He will be directly responsible to the Führer for the Jews' security.

The long-term benefit to the Reich: Jews confined in Tanganyika will provide the Reich with their labor. They will create a German satellite farm. The Jewish labor will exploit Tanganyika's enormous mineral and agricultural wealth. Within one decade, Tanganyika will become a major source of food for the Greater German Nation.

Heil Hitler,

Wilhelm Canaris
Ernst Hartmann
(Abwehr I)

The Baron smiled, impressed. "It says four million Jews," he remarked to Hirsch. "What was the total?"

"Twelve to fifteen million. But Hitler rejected it finally for Himmler's solution."

"And how many blacks?" Hovagny asked.

"Around fourteen million. The first shipment should be about one-tenth that. They're arriving in stages from Capetown."

"This country will absorb them with ease. There's a lot of room to spare."

"We will set them to work immediately," Hirsch said. "Put them in temporary camps along the rail lines. They'll build their own permanent shelters."

"And security?"

"The South Africans are lending a hand. Remember, we will control Tanzania's Army."

"It's like a military campaign." He tapped the document. Human masses had been shifted from place to place throughout history, Hovagny recalled. Negro slaves across the Atlantic to the Americas, red Indians in the United States, Moslems in India, Indonesians, Chinese. . . .

The Baron got up and went to the Land Rover parked a few yards off the end of the terrace. He returned carrying a leather case, which he placed beside Hans Peter. "I'll be going soon."

"What do you want done?"

The Baron put the case on the table and unlatched and opened it. Inside was a Holland and Holland .457 magnum, double-bore rifle.

"What a beauty," Hirsch said admiringly.

"Yes indeed," the Baron remarked.

"Five hundred grains?"

"That's right. A standard elephant load." The baron took a velvet pouch from the case. "This is a Zeiss 9X, the best scope money can buy. You owned one once, I think."

"It sure reduced the guesswork," Hans Peter said.

"By nine magnifications."

"And you want it mounted?"

The Baron took out a notepad and printed a name and address, then handed it to Hirsch.

"It's an armorer in Dar I've used," he said. "They have a rifle expert named Gabby. Ask for him. Tell him the scope is for a target at a range of about five hundred yards."

"Right," Hirsch replied, putting the paper with the address in his briefcase. "Now let's get to work."

On the other side of town, Ralph Crawford felt as though he had just landed on an alien planet. He stripped off his tweed coat and slung it over his shoulder. Dar es Salaam, he thought, was a swamp, and he was the only one who seemed to mind. From where he was standing in front of the Kilimanjaro Hotel he saw local residents walking past at a pace that suggested a much cooler climate. They wore loose-sleeved shirts or no shirts at all, light cotton dresses and trousers, and hats to keep the pounding sun from broiling their brains. Their voices sounded strange with the jabbering singsong of their language. To his right, in the open-air café under a towering almond tree, people lazily drank tea and soft drinks and conversed with surprising animation. The natives were different colors and sizes, and mostly they seemed friendly.

He had landed a few hours earlier and checked into the hotel. He had tried to sleep, but he was washed out from jet lag and the noise from the street kept him awake, so he finally decided to go exploring.

Across Magazine Street from the hotel, he saw a taxi rank. He raised his arm and watched with amusement as several drivers dashed to their cars from the lawn where they had been lying. It was like a Le Mans start, he thought. The first off the grid was a cream Peugeot. Its engine throbbed and bluish fumes bellowed from underneath as it bucked to his side of the street. The driver, a black man with crooked teeth and a nose that seemed to have been squashed on his face as an afterthought, jumped out and opened the door.

"Snake Park, *bwana?*" he asked cheerily.

"What?" Crawford made the connection slowly: The snake park was probably a tourist attraction. "No." He shook his head for emphasis. "Ministry of Revenue. You understand?" He wasn't certain if Africans spoke English.

"Fifty shillings," the driver said enigmatically.

Crawford computed the rate of exchange. "That's nearly ten dollars," he said. "Where is it, anyway?"

"Just up the road. You'll be there in a jiffy." With a peremptory wag the driver waved him into the taxi. "If it's so close, I'll walk," Crawford retorted and started down the street.

The cabbie followed at a trot. "You win, mister," he said. "Ten shillings."

Pleased by his little triumph, Crawford returned to the taxi. The sprung seat and collapsed shock absorbers signaled bumps in the road with bone-shattering clarity as they passed two roundabouts and the post and telegraph office before coasting to a stop at the entrance to a new building. He told the driver to wait and went up the steps, patting his coat pocket. The letter was in there, the one written by Mr. Charles Wyanga, chief counsel of Tanzania's revenue department, containing a promise to cooperate with the IRS.

Crawford found the office number on the directory and took an elevator to the fourth floor. A man in a uniform passed him with a tray of tea as he went down the long corridor, checking the door numbers. Finally, at the very end of the hall, he found what he was looking for.

A secretary was putting on her makeup. Crawford coughed to get her attention. She looked up with a smile and asked what he wanted.

"I think he'll see you," she said, taking his calling card and disappearing into the inner office. After several minutes, Crawford wondered what was taking her so long. Finally she came out again, looking more disheveled than when she had gone in; he guessed Mr. Wyanga was a ladies' man.

"He will see you now," she said, returning to her desk and the makeup kit.

The office was cluttered with stacks of computer print-

outs and reports. Behind a large wooden desk sat a black
man with a chiseled, handsome face. He was dressed in a
shirt and necktie and his suit jacket was tailored impec-
cably. He got up and extended his hand, which Crawford
took, introducing himself.

"Welcome to Tanzania," Wyanga said, pointing to a
chair opposite. "Can I get you tea or coffee?"

"Neither, thanks," Crawford said. "You're very kind to
see me on such short notice, Mr. Wyanga."

Wyanga waved his hand. "It's my pleasure," he said,
sounding sincere. "I have your letters. Now I can put a
face on your signatures. I'm happy to help."

Crawford was uncertain where to start. He looked
around the office. "Who is that?" he asked, pointing to a
portrait on the wall.

"Our President, Julius Nyerere."

"A very refined-looking man," Crawford said. Nyerere
was thin-faced, with large, curious eyes and speckled gray
hair.

"That's kind of you to say."

"He looks younger than I thought."

"He isn't very old, you know." He leaned forward.
"But you haven't come to discuss our President. I assume
it's about James MacKee?"

"Yes, exactly," Crawford said.

"A nasty business, that, nasty. Tragic, too. He did
much for Tanzania, but we didn't know until recently
how much he had done for himself. In the end, he took
much more than he gave. But he did begin our largest
export business. He taught us how to grow coffee but, as
you probably know, controlled the levers of sale himself."

"How was that?"

"Well, all the growers sold their beans to him. He got
even more from a contraband network flowing from
Uganda, Kenya, and countries to our west. Then he held
the stocks and released only the right amount to maintain
a price that we discovered to be artificially high. He kept
the profit and gave none of it back to the growers or to
the government."

"What was the extent of his empire?"

"Enormous and complete. As far as we can tell, he had the major share of coffee production in Africa. And we have heard rumors that he had gone into South America. To make a comparison, what King Khalid is to oil, he was to coffee. And even more so, because he ran the cartel."

"Then what went wrong?"

"Our President was thankful to Mr. MacKee for starting the export business, but he had grown too large for his own good. It was as if he ran an independent state within a state. President Nyerere made the decision that, after all, the coffee is Tanzanian, and the people should benefit. He nationalized the industry."

"But you must excuse me, if the President was so grateful to MacKee, why didn't he protect him?"

"Because he had damaged our country's reputation. Nyerere hated that. You Americans wanted him and we had no further use for him."

"Now that he's dead, we hope to prosecute his estate, which still owes *us* taxes from the 1973 frost fraud."

"That's some time ago now. A regrettable business."

"To start with, I'd hoped to get a listing of his local assets," Crawford said. "Perhaps they will lead us to his executor. I'm assuming they're being liquidated."

"That aspect is out of my hands. We don't have a death tax in Tanzania, so what he did with his last will and testament is none of our affair."

"But could you find out for me?"

"I think so. Let me see," Wyanga said, swiveling his chair to a side table.

Crawford watched as he dialed the telephone. When the number connected, Wyanga spoke rapidly in Swahili. Some of the words had English roots, so Crawford guessed that he was getting nowhere. Finally, he hung up.

"They have nothing. The Ministry of Finance," he added helpfully. "But don't despair," he said, dialing a further number.

Again he spoke in Swahili. After a minute's conversation, he raised his eyebrows in Crawford's direction and reached for a pencil. "Here we are," he said, once he had put down the receiver. "But I think your trip . . . well, to put it mildly, could have been avoided. I'm sorry."

The disappointment showed on Crawford's face. "I don't understand," he said. "Why?"

"I just talked with a colleague at the Central Bank," Wyanga explained. "MacKee had fifteen million shillings, about one and a half million dollars, in liquid assets. They don't know the sum for stocks, land, and the like."

"So?"

"They were transferred two days ago."

"Where?"

"Zurich, I fear," Wyanga said. "The Central Bank had instructions. In the event of his death, his liquid wealth was to be transferred immediately."

"And the name of the bank?"

"The Commercial Credit Union. The bank president has been named executor of MacKee's will. He's the man you must see."

"Do you know his name?"

Wyanga went to the bookshelf behind his desk and took out a directory. He needed only a minute to find CCU's entry. "Hans Peter Hirsch. Here are the particulars." He gave Crawford the Central Bank clearance number and the address of the CCU. The names meant nothing to Crawford.

"Then you'll fly to Zurich?" Wyanga asked, his voice sympathetic.

Damnit, Crawford thought. This was the worst possible luck. Learning what he just had, he could have prevented the Africa trip simply by making a telephone call from Washington, and then gone directly to Zurich. It made him mad: All this for nothing. "No," he said.

Wyanga raised an eyebrow. "But what can you do here?" he asked.

"I don't know. I just don't know," Crawford said, frowning. "But I *am* here, so I might as well make the most of it. If we finally do prosecute his estate we're going to need details of his holdings in Tanzania. It may help."

"Well, I wish you luck," Wyanga said, showing him to the door. "If I can help further, don't hesitate to ask."

Now where to begin, Crawford wondered as he came out into the oppressive heat of the late morning. His one solid lead, Wyanga, had *not* panned out, at least so far as Tanzania was concerned. Sure, he could go directly to Zurich. He kicked at a pebble on the steps of the building. But he was steamed up about Africa and he wasn't going to leave after one day. If necessary, he would make excuses.

He walked toward the waiting taxicab, thinking that he had virtually nothing on MacKee that was not financial. He didn't have a recent photograph, a profile, or knowledge of his friends and enemies. Zero. The IRS was brilliant at gathering *data*. It had whole computer rooms filled with nothing but facts and figures. Within nanoseconds the computer could tell him the deductions made last year by any of the millions of tax-paying American citizens; the digital power was prodigious. But try to put a face on those financial entries, or a history. Flesh and figures did not mix.

And so he decided to begin at the end.

10

The Dar es Salaam morgue, a squat structure not far from Wyanga's office, was painted cadaver-gray. Yellow interior walls sweated condensation on a sign, "Corpse Inquiries," while translucent, flesh-colored lizards moved along the ceiling attacking flies. From deeper inside, the pungency of formaldehyde made Crawford wish for a mint to kill the sickly taste on his tongue. His stomach churned when he compared this morgue with another one, the FBI forensic laboratory, which he visited soon after he began at Revenue. That had been brightly lighted, surgically clean and orderly.

But for the echo of his own voice, no sound answered his tentative call. He tried several more times, finally deciding that the morgue was empty of the living and maybe even of the dead. He thought of returning sometime in the afternoon but dismissed the thought. He was here, so he might as well get it over with.

A door was open at the far end of the central corridor. He hesitated for a second, then went in. The room had one ventilating fan and bowl-shaped lamps over each of four slab tables. Beside them on service racks were chipped porcelain instrument pans. There were greenish strips of mildew in the corners. Crawford heard the throbbing of a compressor outside.

He knew what he had to do. The wall opposite the windows was constructed of twenty squares, like filing cabinets, with handles, locks, and frames for identification cards. Somebody had scribbled on several of the cards. Crawford tried without luck to decipher the code. He pulled at the handle of a random cabinet and the shelf slid out with surprising ease. Refrigerated air instantly dissipated in the sweltering heat of the room. Staring up at him with unseeing eyes was the placid face of a dead African. Crawford pushed the shelf back with the guilty thought that he had invaded the dead man's sanctity.

"What, no vacancy in the hotels?"

The voice startled Crawford, who turned to see a tall, thin black man wearing a spattered surgical gown and the mischievous expression of one so used to dealing with the dead that he found greater than normal amusement in the predicaments of the living.

"I . . . I didn't mean to . . ." Crawford stammered.

"No need for apologies," the man said, introducing himself as Dr. David Mfu, assistant medical examiner at the Julius Nyerere General Hospital. "The girl out front is sick today. She's always sick. I can't blame her, working here and all. And I was over at the hospital. Maybe I should have locked the door." He smiled and touched a shelf handle. "These folks aren't going anywhere."

Crawford told him who he was and why he had come.

"An interesting case, that," Mfu said simply.

"Then he's here?"

"Nobody claimed the body, so the state will bury him in time. I said it was an interesting case because MacKee was a big deal around here. I would have thought that friends would have buried him." Mfu walked past Crawford. "Anyway, I suppose you want a look." He pulled out a shelf and swept back the sheet covering the cadaver.

"Jesus," Crawford whispered to himself when he saw. Then, to Mfu: "This isn't MacKee!" He was going to be sick. *"This isn't even human."*

Crawford averted his eyes. His stomach was churning again. A truncated cadaver lay on the shelf. Head and hands were missing, and it was a sickly white. Blue rims of flesh contrasted at the points of severance. The torso itself had wounds. One of them gouged so deep that Crawford thought he had seen a protruding rib. The violence of the impact, Crawford guessed in wonderment! He had not seen many corpses in his life, but this wasn't even a corpse. It was the end product of an abattoir.

"I should have warned you," Mfu said, seeing Crawford's expression. "I'm so used to it, I sometimes forget."

Crawford accepted the apology with a thin smile. "How can you know *what* that is?" he asked uncertainly, "let alone *who* it is?"

"I can't," Mfu's answer was simple and final. "Without teeth and fingerprints we have nothing positive. We don't even know MacKee's blood type."

"But *you* said it was MacKee."

"I took the authorities' word. They said MacKee was piloting the airplane. It crashed. One body was found. Ergo, MacKee."

"But you can't be sure?"

"Around here we don't waste time investigating what doesn't exist, like you Americans," Mfu said. "No offense intended. It's just the way we do things."

Crawford ignored the remark. "Where *are* the head and hands, then?" He looked at the other drawers containing bodies.

"Unhappily, they were never found."

"How can that be? They found the torso, so why not the identifying parts? Doesn't that seem odd?"

"I see what you're saying," Mfu remarked. He offered

Crawford his own rationale. "But as you can tell, the impact was tremendously violent. Maybe animals carried off the parts. That I can't say." He paused and raised a long finger to his cheek. "But now that you bring it up, Mr. Crawford, it was pretty selective trauma at that, if you make certain assumptions, which I did not. Let's have another look."

Mfu leaned over the body. He lifted the arm and inspected the stub, then ran his finger around the flap of skin at the rim of the corpse's neck. "Hhhmmmmmm," he said. In a cabinet near the autopsy slab he found a magnifying glass. He looked at the raw ends through the oval. "You might be onto something."

"Can you explain?" Crawford asked, bending over the shelf, curiosity conquering squeamishness.

"Sure, if you'll look through this," Mfu said, handing Crawford the glass. "See how clean the cut is?"

Crawford grunted a reply. It *was* clean, but so what?

"It could have been made by a scalpel. Or a very sharp knife."

"Is there any way to tell?"

"I think so, if the tissue hasn't decomposed." Concentrating and mumbling to himself, Mfu snipped a sliver of skin off the flap with surgical scissors, then inserted it into a glass slide, which he clamped on the platform of a microscope. He looked through the eyepiece, then stepped aside for Crawford to see.

"Notice the brown beads?" he asked.

Crawford saw the tiny bubbles that shone on the skin's surface. He couldn't guess what they were. He turned to Mfu. "So?"

"Oil. A thin film of preservative oil. It's just possible it smeared off a scalpel."

"Then you'll admit the possibility, no matter how vague. That may not be MacKee," Crawford said.

"No, I won't," Mfu replied. "First I'd need to do lab tests and compare results to oil compositions used on scalpels. If that checked out I still wouldn't have a positive answer."

"But of course you would."

"You can jump to conclusions, Mr. Crawford. I won't.

Even if there was foul play, this still might be MacKee. In order to *know* who it is we'd have to do tissue tests for age and forensic recompositions for body weight and size. And that's just a beginning."

"Then let's get going," Crawford said, misunderstanding Mfu's meaning.

"I wish it were that easy," he said. "It may be hard for you to understand, coming from America and all, but we don't have the equipment, at least not to test tissue sections. They'll have to be sent to Europe."

"So it'll take a while?"

"Longer."

"Then, if you don't mind, I *will* jump to conclusions," Crawford said. He wanted to be convinced. It was a small thread on which to base an investigation, and maybe he was wrong, but it was reason enough to keep him where he wanted to be: in Africa; and the missing head had a mystery that delighted his imagination.

"What conclusion?" Mfu felt that he might have overstepped his bounds by showing Crawford what he had.

"That this chunk of hamburger isn't MacKee." Crawford suddenly made a move to leave. "Let me know, Doctor," he said, going through the door. "And thanks for your help."

Outside a few minutes later he inhaled a deep breath of fresh air and caught a glint of sunlight reflecting off a gold-capped tooth. The grinning taxi driver stirred from his lounging position on the Peugeot's hood and slid off to open the door.

"Where to now, bwana?"

"I don't really know," Crawford replied, climbing into the backseat. "Give me a minute." The torso was a surprise. He had not anticipated the possibility that MacKee was still alive. But it made sense. The IRS was in hot pursuit and the Tanzanians were about to extradite him. What better motive for faking a death? But he had to be certain. Once he knew what he suspected he would hunt MacKee, the man; not MacKee, the estate. He looked at the driver's face in the rearview mirror. "Do you know where the airport is?" he asked.

The African answered by kicking over the starter and

engaging the gears. As they drove, the breeze through the open windows cooled Crawford's face. For the first time, he saw patches of the African countryside. The road was peopled by antlike lines of natives carrying heavy loads of firewood and produce. The soil beneath their feet was an ocher color, which meant fertility. As far as his eye could see there was lush vegetable green. He half expected to spot African animals, but the only four-footed creatures they passed were mangy dogs and untethered cattle grazing near the shoulder of the road. What impressed him most was the sky—cobalt and patterned with cream-puff clouds, and stretching down to the horizon.

The driver said nothing until they reached the airport environs. His passenger didn't have suitcases, but Europeans, as he called all whiteskins, were sometimes strange. "Which airline?" he asked simply.

"I don't know." Crawford came out of his reverie. "One of the charters. For small airplanes."

The driver stopped at the edge of a sidewalk leading to the operations office of Safari-Air, explaining that most fares who booked with air charter firms asked to be driven here. Crawford went inside and saw the back of a person in a khaki uniform. When she turned to face him, his whole body tingled; the sensation was disorienting.

"Can I help?" She saw his predicament. It wasn't the first time men had stared openly at her. "I'm Farita Blake."

"I'm bowled over," he said, and smiled. It was not the sort of thing he was used to saying.

"Now what kind of a name is that? Bowled over . . ."

Lord, she was chatty. "It's not a name," he said. "It's a feeling. My name, though, is Ralph Crawford."

She was the office manager at Safari-Air, she said. An African, she had anglicized her surname to Blake. She was also a fully qualified commercial pilot, she bragged slightly, asking if he wanted to charter.

By now Crawford was regaining his composure. "First," he said, "can you help me find something at the airport?"

"Sure," she replied happily.

He explained briefly what he wanted.

"I know who owned the airplane," she said. "Does that help?"

"Can I talk with him?"

"Afraid not," she replied. "Afro-Air—that was his charter business—was literally a fly-by-night affair. When that charter fellow—what was the name you mentioned? MacKee?—well, when he crashed, Dave Johnson ran for it." She paused to see that he understood. "Dave was a great guy, but money was a mystery he couldn't solve."

"Okay, but don't pilots file reports?"

"You mean flight plans?"

"That's it."

"We must have them before takeoff. MacKee's will be at the center."

Farita agreed to show him. As she locked the office door, Crawford told the taxi driver to return in four hours. When she finally joined him, Crawford couldn't stop looking at her. She was tall and slim with loose hips, a thin waist, and perfect breasts. She wore fitted khaki trousers with patch pockets front and back and an oversize man's khaki shirt that billowed at her waist.

In the air-conditioned center, Farita glanced at the flight form, then handed it to Crawford. "Does that tell you anything?" she asked. "It doesn't me."

"Maybe," he replied, looking at the form. "So MacKee was going to Arusha? Did he crash near there?"

"I know the spot," Farita said. "It's close to a dirt airstrip the rangers use, about thirty minutes south of Arusha."

"I see," he said, asking questions in the hope that something would click. "The Partenavia. What type of airplane was it?"

She told him.

He found the name of the aircraft on the form, just where it should have been. The flight report was all regulation; it showed nothing irregular. "This is a dead end," he said. He wondered what the next step might be. He had a thought. Why the hell not? "Why not fly out there?" he asked aloud.

"Okay by me—that's how I earn my living," she replied. "But we'll have to get moving. There's not much daylight left."

Fifteen minutes later they were airborne, with Farita in command of the four-seater Cessna 170. Her mastery of the instruments and controls fascinated Crawford. He loosened the safety belt enough to turn toward her. "Are you Tanzanian?" he asked tentatively.

"Born and bred," she replied, glancing at him with that dazzling smile. "My family comes from near Arusha. I was raised beneath the snows of Kilimanjaro. Do you know it?"

"The novel or the mountain?"

"Very funny." She laughed inside. "I know your country too."

"School?"

She shook her head. "I was a stewardess. Before I learned the front end of these machines, I flew the galleys with British Airways. Americans are my favorite people."

"That's kind to say." He wondered if she would join him for dinner.

She said nothing more until they had reduced altitude and were on approach to the rangers' strip. She turned the frequency dial on the VHF radio and raised the microphone to her mouth, asking for somebody called Crile.

They landed a few minutes later and parked the airplane off the washboard strip on a smooth section of grass. In the distance they saw a dust cloud moving in their direction. Just as they were climbing from the cockpit, a pickup truck stopped at the tail of the airplane.

The young man who got out had long, blond hair tied in the back with a string. He wore patched jeans and logger's shirt. Around his waist was a belt with a shiny silver buckle: in the center of it was a silver dollar. He came over and hugged Farita, looking at her fondly, then introduced himself as Loukie, a volunteer game ranger. He had been a full-time student at the University of California until he decided that one day's experience in Africa was worth one year in class. He had saved enough money for a ticket to Tanzania, and now lived off what he could earn and the generosity of doting parents.

All three piled into the cab of the pickup, Farita in the middle. They drove for several miles on a road that was nothing more than a track. Every few hundred yards they detoured into the bush to avoid cavernous ruts.

"It's only a few more miles, Mr. Crawford," Loukie said, gripping the steering wheel tightly.

Finally they stopped and walked a hundred yards past several man-sized anthills. The brush was chest-high, but they easily threaded their way through. The terrain was identical to that in New Mexico or Arizona, Crawford thought. He didn't know why, but he had expected Africa to be jungle.

"There it is," Loukie said, pointing.

The wreckage of the Partenavia was a frightening tangle of metal and fabric. It had been picked over, as clean as a jackal's bone, by scavengers. Crawford looked inside at what had been the cockpit. The seat had been torn out and there was a hole where the instruments had been. He stepped back, hands on his hips, and turned to Loukie. "Who discovered the crash?" he asked.

"One of the Sambaas from around here. But he's long gone by now."

"They're nomad herdsmen," Farita said. "By the looks of this they're scavengers, too."

"Did anybody question him, this Sambaa?"

Loukie shook his head. "He led us here, then vanished," he said. "Sambaas are like that."

"Can we talk to his tribesmen?"

"Maybe. They shelter in a dry wash near here," Loukie said. He knew the region well.

Farita partly rolled up her sleeve. "No time now," she said, checking her watch. It would be dark soon. "The risk isn't worth it, unless you don't mind our staying the night with Loukie." She left the decision with Crawford.

Loukie tried to influence him. He liked company. "Mr. Crawford, Sambaas move in the morning when it's cool, like the animals, and in the evenings. If you stay, we might find your man."

Nothing compelled him to return, Crawford thought,

except for the taxi driver, whom he would compensate for his trouble. A night in the African bush would be memorable.

They returned to the pickup and drove back in the direction of the airstrip. Loukie explained that he lived in a tented camp. Seeing the question on Crawford's face, he described his home. A tented camp in Africa was unlike a similar campsite in America. A canvas tent, as large as a small living room, covered a wooden floor and comfortable furniture. There was even a separate tent to shower in.

"Is it safe?" Crawford asked. "Can the animals get in?"

"There's not much cause to worry. Sometimes they get curious, like people do." He looked at Farita. "Remember the time with the buffalo?"

Farita giggled, then described the incident to Crawford. She had been at Loukie's; evening was falling. She had stayed inside her tent while the others gathered for dinner. She had decided to join the others after all and extinguished the gas lamp. The night was pitch-dark when she walked out of her tent. Suddenly she bumped full-face into what seemed like a tree trunk. She heard a loud snorting noise, and when her eyes focused, she saw the "tree" was a bull buffalo. Fast as her legs would carry her, she fled. The buffalo wandered off, unperturbed by the chance encounter.

She told the story well and soon Crawford was laughing at the absurdity of it. "Could you have been hurt?" he asked, finally.

Farita and Loukie smiled at one another.

"I'll put it this way," Loukie said. "The biggest man-killer in Africa is the hippopotamus. Buffalo come second. Thank God it was dark."

They continued slowly along the road. Loukie bent under the dashboard and put a tape on. It was a *Brandenburg* concerto, which seemed suitably majestic for the panorama before Crawford, who watched birds with long, kitelike tails, hawks, and ones with dazzling feathers. He wished he could identify them. Then he saw something large move against a tree. "Look at that," he said, pointing at what he guessed was the rear end of a rhino not more than twenty yards away.

"*Kifaru*," Farita said. "With a calf."

"What is *kifaru?*" he asked.

Farita smiled. "What looks like an armored tank and has two horns?"

"*Kifaru,* of course," Crawford replied, smiling. He hadn't noticed the baby at first, but now he saw it running beside its mother. It was fifteen times smaller but an exact replica of the adult and buff-gray. He wondered how Farita had spotted the young rhino so easily and he guessed African eyes had a special way of seeing.

"Let's track them," Loukie asked. "It'll be fun."

Rhino were becoming a rare sight, their numbers thinned to near-extinction by poachers who killed for the horn, which was ground into powder and sold in the Orient as an aphrodisiac.

"Sure," Farita said, pushing Crawford out the door. He had seen dangerous animals before in zoos and always from the other side of strong iron bars, so he didn't jump at the idea of being near a murderous rhino on its own turf. But Loukie didn't seem worried. Still, Crawford took Farita's hand.

They stalked from bush to bush in an Indian file, following the rhino prints in the dry ocher dirt. They were the size of soup plates and pushed deeply into the soil. They came upon a tree and hid behind its trunk. From there they now saw the rhinos clearly. The adult was magnificent: a primitive and fearsome giant that used its nose and some celestial map imprinted on its genes for guidance across vast distances. If it barely saw, Crawford could not tell. Cow and calf walked ahead of them in complete silence.

Crawford blinked, and when he refocused his eyes they were gone. "Where are they?" he whispered to Loukie.

"They slipped behind those bushes," he said, pointing to a clump of brush.

Crawford was amazed that beasts so large could move with the stealth of ghosts.

"They know we're here," said Loukie, standing up straight. He told Crawford what was happening. The nervous cow, smelling them, he guessed, was now trying to circle *them*. It made the hair tingle on Crawford's neck.

"Let's see what she does," Farita said, setting off toward a mongongo tree.

Crawford followed warily. He wasn't going back to the pickup alone. He couldn't see beyond Farita's back as the bush closed in on them. Thorns the length of a finger pulled at his coat and, once, painfully punctured his skin. They had lost the rhinos, and he prayed the rhinos had lost them, too, as they continued through the bush and finally into a clearing. They were on the edge of a dry wash, and from where they were they saw smoke billowing from small fires in the distance.

"There are your Sambaas, Mr. Crawford," said Loukie, truly surprised.

The nomad *manyatta* was a circle of small woven huts covered with animal skins. Goats and cows were corralled in pens, and children who were chasing pet dogs in the powdered dirt stopped and stared as the three intruders approached.

The more primitive tribesmen were, the greater was their suspicion. Strangers meant interference. Some came to study them; some to take their children away to school; and some came to steal. But rare was the stranger who brought good tidings.

True to their natures, the Sambaas elders neither greeted them nor seemed to take notice of their arrival. They sat in the dirt and did not look up, even when Loukie addressed them in their own language. When they did not respond to his questions, Loukie turned to Crawford. "These people are scared," he said.

Finally, after many minutes, the oldest of the male Sambaas gave an evasive answer in a few short sentences.

Loukie translated. "The old boy tells me that your man has taken off, like I suspected. Maybe it's true, maybe not, but one thing's certain. They don't want us snooping around." Loukie turned to the old man and asked more questions.

Farita and Crawford wandered through the *manyatta*

looking at the Sambaas' pathetic huts, the mean tools of their lives, and an odd assortment of scavenged bits and pieces. "How do they survive?" Crawford asked.

Farita shrugged. "Our President tried to give them better. He promised water and electricity and schools. But their ways die hard."

Crawford had heard about the famous nomad Masai tribe and asked if they lived like this, too.

"They're the same type," she said almost sadly, "like the tragedies." She glanced toward Loukie squatting near the old man. "If they weren't so damned proud, they could have been a great people."

Crawford bent to his knee by the side of a hut, looking at the crudely sewn skins, insulated between the skins and the wood frame by shreds of animal pelts and scraps of cloth.

"Better leave that," Farita warned. "They may look harmless, but believe me, if threatened there's no stopping them." She smiled at him and started back to Loukie.

"Nobody else saw the airplane when it went down, or so he says," Loukie reported. "My guess is they're nervous because they took some scrap from the wreckage. But that's none of our business now."

The tribesman had said all he was going to say. There was no point in lingering. Following the same track, they returned to the pickup.

The minute they were out of sight, the old Sambaa got slowly to his feet and went to his hut, the one beside which Crawford had knelt. From between the goatskin outer covering and the inside frame he pulled out the bright Day-Glo nylon parachute that days ago he had found near the crash.

He unfolded the parachute. Wrapped in it were the desiccated hands and severed head of the pilot, David Johnson.

11

A hundred miles from the *manyatta* in a dwelling far different from the Sambaas' huts, Baron Hovagny ran his fingers through his hair, organizing his thoughts. Two hundred carefully selected white settlers from all over Tanzania had come to his Mount Kilimanjaro home. They were gathered to receive their final assignments, and they now milled in the regal splendor of the damask-draped reception room of Tembo, the Baron's formidable ranch.

What all these expatriate European settlers had in common was the love of "their" Tanzania. They had cleared the land, built homes and farms, cultivated crops, and raised families all on this African soil. Many of them had achieved prominence in the Tanzanian civil and military administrations starting when the nation was young and in need of their expertise.

The Baron was now demanding that same expertise in the service of a greater goal. The Baron knew how these men were being retired from their military and police commands. They were being pushed aside to make room for Africans. The Baron was also fully aware of how they were being kicked off their land through mass expropriation and how their businesses were being bought up from under them. Africanization was almost complete; and these men were equally complete in their hatred of the black man. It was that hatred which Protégé intended to exploit.

In his formal remarks, Hovagny had told them only what they needed to know. Then, reading from a roster, he split them into groups of thirty, each with a different assignment during and after the coup, without revealing the names of the captains whom he, Hartmann, and Hans Peter had selected in Zurich. Once that was done, he

. . . mong the ten groups to outline logistics, effec-
. . . ness, and timing.

"Dant, yours is the easiest," he said to Dant Steinforth, including Steinforth's group with a sweep of his eyes. There were seven coasters in the Tanzanian Navy, armed with mortars. The small ships rarely patrolled and were easy targets, especially for Steinforth, who had served as chief adviser to the African admiral. "Like everybody else, you'll move on the message beamed on the Voice of Tanzania that Nyerere is dead."

Steinforth nodded, knowing the Baron was repeating himself only for emphasis. "Five boats are at the Dar base, the others at Tanga," he said. "We're only to incapacitate them?"

"Correct," Hovagny answered. "Under no condition destroy them. We'll need those boats later."

"It's as good as done."

Another three groups—roads, transport, and medical —also had assignments that were necessary but mechanical. Hovagny talked to them quickly before giving more intense scrutiny to the military and police aspects and communication.

"What's your strategy, Willi?" He wanted Willi Hoder and his men to repeat it. Hoder worked at the Voice of Tanzania as its electronics specialist. During the war he had designed transmitters for Goebbels's propaganda ministry.

"When word comes in that Nyerere is dead," he said stiffly, "my first group will seize the transmitters at the Lunga station. With control of communication, we'll broadcast the death, issue instructions to the army bases, and keep the people calm, until you get back to Dar."

"Do you foresee any problems?"

"None. The transmitters are unguarded, as you know."

"And the second?"

"That group will hear the same VOT signal and take the satellite ground station, again unguarded but manned. With that in our control, we blunt external communication. And the country is cut off."

"Good," Hovagny said and walked to the far end of the room where Robert Conroy was talking to his men.

He listened until he was satisfied that their plans were complete to clear shipping from the ports at Dar es Salaam and Tanga. "When our ship arrives from its embarkation point, Robert, we're going to need all the room, lots of it, particularly in Dar," the Baron said. "Remember, nothing gets scuttled. That's critical. Absolutely nothing. Coordinate with Steinforth on the naval craft."

He called for the groups with military assignments to come together. Their four leaders still held command positions in the Air Force, the 18,000-man Army, and the police. For that, their participation was indispensable.

"We have one major problem," Hovagny said. They knew what it was. "Has there been a change in that?"

"The General Service Unit will remain loyal to Nyerere," said Colonel Max Fortgang, a military adviser to President Nyerere. "They're our real opposition, and it may be significant. You know how well they are trained."

"Yes, and I also know how their ranks were thinned in Uganda," Hovagny said. The GSU had borne the brunt of the fighting in the protracted but successful campaign against Idi Amin. The GSU troops were exhausted to a dangerous degree.

"Here's what we've decided. They will be inside the barracks at Gatundu. Not on maneuvers—"

"Then you seal them off at Gatundu?"

"Right, but they will still resist."

Hovagny didn't like the sound of it. "How effectively?" he asked.

"Enough to create a danger," Fortgang replied, running a hand along the top of his gray brush cut. "We'll contain them with our loyals, but loyals are no match for GSU."

"Can we use the Air Force?"

Claus Deutschle interrupted. Chief of Air Force maintenance, he would see that the Tanzanian F-5s were grounded on the day. "I can put up one of the Fives for tests, armed, sir," he said. "The timing must be precise, and it'll have a single strike at the barracks. If it works, we're safe. If not, our loyals will have to hold."

"Okay, then, that's it," Hovagny said, still unsatisfied. But their trump, which he would throw personally, was certain to cause adequate confusion. It offered them the slight edge they needed. Now that he had finished with the groups, he called them together.

"Some of you asked about our real ability to bring this off," he said. "I can assure you, we have that ability, so put your fears aside. For one thing, Tanzania is defended poorly and, at that, against external invaders, not an internal putsch. We possess the element of total surprise. And I might remind some of you what this means." He gave them figures on the numbers of coups d'etat in Africa in the last ten years. Most had been successful. He followed with a description of the ease with which these had been executed by outsiders. The Comoro Islands had been taken by *thirty* armed mercenaries. Equatorial Guinea once nearly fell to *twelve* Europeans led by a journalist. "I think the preparedness of our force gives us an edge that virtually ensures success. Just remember, your land will be returned in tenfold measure, and the country that now rejects us will soon be ours."

12

Admiral Thomas Voerwerk raised Zeiss field glasses to his eyes, searching the darkness for silhouettes. As they finally came within the binoculars' field, the admiral, who had lived with ships for two decades, had trouble comprehending their size.

"Put your men at ease," he ordered, lowering the binoculars.

The army lieutenant accompanying him on the Swakopmund quay repeated the command to his squad of battle-toughened South African marines, who laid their equipment and rifles in neat stacks.

"It'll be a while before the launch arrives," Voerwerk added helpfully.

The admiral of the South African Navy, Voerwerk had

been sent to Swakopmund by the Prime Minister, who personally told him why and precisely what he was to do. This mission was far removed from normal military duty, but as Steenkamp had said, it was of vital importance to the survival of the nation. It made good sense to Voerwerk, who would not have questioned the order anyway. With the sanctions, there were no oil imports. But Steenkamp somehow had found a source and a means of transport. The admiral was doing his duty, as part of a nation-saving plan.

From beyond the darkness he heard the sound of a marine engine and had the lieutenant tell his men to hitch up. A white launch with brass fittings and admiral's burgee came abreast of the pier. Navy NCO's leaped from the gunwales and lashed its bows, while the admiral and marines quietly loaded aboard. Voerwerk again looked toward the far reaches of the harbor where the ships lay in a gently rolling sea, and again, as he caught the glare of superstructure lights, he wondered if his eyes weren't deceiving him.

They pushed off the quay and with diesel rumbling went toward the hulks, which loomed larger with every mile of sea the launch covered. Three constructions of welded steel and planking, they were ultra-large cargo carriers—ULCC's—the largest ships afloat. As he steadied himself against the launch's sway, Voerwerk reviewed what he had learned that afternoon.

ULCC's were conceived first in Japanese shipyards as new leviathans, each with a capacity of 750,000 tons, to carry crude oil from the Arabian Gulf, West Africa, and South America to refineries in the industrialized world. Their bulk reduced costs dramatically and made shipowners like Ravi Tikkoo, C. Y. Tung, Getty, Niarchos, and Ludwig rich beyond even their bloated dreams.

But the concept did not account for the 1973 oil embargo, which bumped up oil costs and reduced demand, glutting ULCC's. Too valuable to scrap, they were mothballed in Norwegian fjords and, many of them, along the coast of Africa, waiting for that day when they would again have a purpose.

Some few mourned their passing, but not the public.

ULCC's were ponderous, single-engine ships requiring three miles to come to a full stop, a dangerous fact that caused controversy. In the first of several incidents, *Torrey Canyon* had gone aground in the Scilly Islands, spilling its tons of black cargo along Britain's scenic southern coast. In the years when they had plied the seas, few shorelines escaped a similar fate, and at the ULCC's demise, ecologists cheered.

Ravi Tikkoo, the Indian shipping tycoon, owned the largest fleet of the largest and most advanced ULCC's ever built. Now three of his tankers lay at anchor in Swakopmund, a berth he had chosen for its proximity to the Gulf.

A year earlier they had been converted for an experiment that was to become a legend in shipping circles and a derisive joke at Lloyd's. If the world did not want his ships for *oil,* Tikkoo had reasoned, they would transport other commodities, including *mutton.*

Workers welded the holds, forging a maze of cages capable of holding millions of live sheep. Each cage was secure and designed to keep the animals alive. Then Tikkoo contracted with the Saudi government for his ULCC's, like giant arks, to bring the sheep from Darwin in Australia to the port at Jidda.

One ship, the *Bronze Maru,* had picked up the sheep. Three million of them were herded from distant ranches in Australia to the loading point, where they were held in outdoor pens until all were assembled. Once the animals were aboard, *Bronze Maru* steamed across the Indian Ocean and into the Arabian Sea. Sheep that died were jettisoned.

The plan was brilliant, but the economics went wrong. The cost of handling and transport made mutton more expensive in Saudi Arabia even than oil. The disgruntled Saudis scrapped further development of the plan and instead put their money into hauling an iceberg up from Antarctica. The ULCC was returned to its anchor at Swakopmund, where it had remained ever since.

Voerwerk ordered the launch captain to make for the center ULCC, the *Bronze Maru,* which floated in the

Atlantic darkness with its plimsoll line 150 feet above the surface. *Bronze Maru* was 750,000 tons, 1,640 feet from bow to stern with a beam the length of a football field. So enormous was she that while she was at sea the rotation of the earth affected her navigation. She drifted clockwise in the Northern Hemisphere and in the opposite direction south of the equator.

With 7 million feet of steel plating held in place by 700 miles of riveting sectioned in five giant holds, *Bronze,* when loaded with crude, represented the compressed thermal energy of a hydrogen bomb.

On *Bronze*'s deck now, Captain Karl Koch stood in sneakered feet lamenting his ship's idle fate, as he flipped switches on the panel of now-silent computers and electronics needed once to navigate and load the *Bronze*. To bolster his flagging spirits and to keep the crewmen occupied, he maintained her in perfect repair. But Koch was a ship-sitter who knew as well as anybody that *Bronze* wasn't going anywhere. He wrinkled his nose unpleasantly, smelling the ammoniac stench of dried sheep dung, which permeated the holds below and everything else on board even twelve months after the sheep fiasco, then turned to his second officer, who was wearing a Tikkoo Company baseball hat and coveralls and had just come onto the bridge from below.

"It's a launch, sir," the man in coveralls said. "What should I tell them?"

"We have no orders," Koch replied. "Tell them to go away."

"But, sir, they're flying an admiral's pennant. It looks official."

Koch told him to have them come aboard after all, thinking that they might be inspectors, the boring little men of the South African Merchant Marine who were always looking for faults. He went to the "off limits" door and closed it. The room behind contained sensitive satellite equipment, and Koch especially didn't want them snooping there. For the Darwin-Jidda run, *Bronze* had been outfitted with InTelSat IVa inertial navigational gear, an amazing device in Koch's eyes, which had the capability of steering the ship from one point to another without human interference, like an airplane on automatic pilot.

Getting aboard *Bronze* from the launch required more than dexterity. It demanded courage, Voerwerk thought, waiting for a swell to raise the launch to the lowest level of the Jacob's ladder. He jumped as the launch swung back with the sea, and held tight to the rope rail, then waited while the marines, weighted down by their gear, did the same. They climbed to the deck, where they were met with a suspicious look from the seaman in the baseball cap, who demanded to know why they had come aboard.

"Merely a courtesy call," Voerwerk said pleasantly.

"With rifles?" he asked, pointing to the marines.

"Oh, those," Voerwerk said. "I'm taking these men back with me to Capetown." He feigned innocence. "Their lieutenant wanted to have a look, too, so I said to come along. Hope you don't mind." Voerwerk wanted to carry out his assignment without trouble, which meant considerable duplicity. Steenkamp had told him what he could expect.

"I don't mind, but Captain Koch will," the second said, waving Voerwerk and the lieutenant to the ship's stern, where they entered an elevator that brought them to the highest point on the six-story superstructure. When the door opened, they were met by Koch.

"Nothing like this in *my* Navy," Voerwerk said affably, introducing himself and the Marine officer.

Despite Tikkoo's standing orders against visitors, Koch welcomed them, cautiously at first, then with enthusiasm. They rarely had anyone aboard except the inspectors, and the cheerful admiral was both admiring and knowledgeable.

"I have to confess, Captain, I've wanted to tour a supertanker for years," Voerwerk said, half in truth. "*Bronze* makes my stuff look puny."

"*Bronze* makes all other ships look puny," Koch said, swelling with pride. "But you're not in Swakopmund to visit *Bronze*."

"It would be worth the trip, believe me. But no, we're

not." He explained, making part of it up as he went. He was on an inspection tour of the Treaty base leased by the South African Navy. Seeing the tankers at anchor, he wanted a closer look.

An ex-Navy man, Koch understood. "What can I show you, Admiral?" he asked.

"This is so different from what I'm used to, I don't know where to begin. Why don't you lead the way, and the lieutenant and I will ask as we go along. Maybe we can start right where we are."

Koch went to the consoles of instruments, giving them a rundown on electronics and standard navigation, then an overall description of the ship's dimensions and capacities, ending with the thirty-man crew complement.

Voerwerk seemed genuinely surprised. "You mean you can manage with that few?" he asked, wondering if Koch hadn't mistaken mothball for operational crews.

"More than manage," Koch said. "With thirty men we can take *Bronze* anywhere." He went on to explain. "In fact, *humans* are not really necessary, if you see what I mean. *Bronze* is automated, a design feature to minimize labor costs, you understand. The crew goes along just in case something breaks down. Otherwise, computers plot course and supervise loading."

"That's fascinating," Voerwerk said. "But I don't completely understand."

Koch pointed to the "off limits" door. "Our plots come in from satellites stationed above the Indian, Atlantic, and Pacific oceans. No sextants and stargazing on the *Bronze,* I can assure you. The link—a mini ground station—is behind that door." Koch approached the elevator. "Now, if you'll follow me, we'll go below."

Even in the elevator, Voerwerk was all questions. He had to be prepared for the grilling Steenkamp had told him to expect when he returned. "How fast will she go?" he asked.

"Oh, let's see. Fully loaded, about fourteen knots."

"Something of a turtle, then, eh? *Cutty Sark* made seventeen."

Koch did not like the comparison, thinking the admiral stupid for stacking a clipper ship against a supertanker.

"*Cutty* wasn't hauling 750,000 tons, either," he remarked simply.

They got out of the elevator and went through a hatch leading to a ladder on the inside of the hull.

"You maintain her in excellent shape," Voerwerk exclaimed. "My officers should do as well. How sea-ready is she?"

"If Mr. Tikkoo ordered, we could sail inside three hours. I make a point of it, because the day he tells us to move, we'll be gone like a shot. Believe me, harbor duty is the worst."

"I can sympathize," Voerwerk said. "I've been strapped to a desk for ten years, so I know the feeling."

Koch, wondering at the silence of the Marine officer with Voerwerk, engaged a switch on the bulkhead.

"This is another design renovation," he said. "Mr. Tikkoo invented it as well." Koch liked his boss. Tikkoo did things that others could never even envision. Koch pointed to a watertight hydraulic door, which opened to the sea below. "Most ULCC's, of course, don't have these," he continued. "Mr. Tikkoo had it cut into the hull, though. This was how we loaded the sheep." He told them about the ill-fated experiment.

The Prime Minister had said the tanker was for *crude oil*. Perhaps there had been a mistake, Voerwerk thought nervously.

"How long would you need to reconvert?" he asked.

"To tear out those cages? The better part of a year, I'd say," Koch replied. "Not that Mr. Tikkoo plans to use them again. I don't see why he didn't reconvert the moment we got back from Jidda."

Steenkamp must know what he was doing, Voerwerk thought. He had said *crude*, but maybe he planned to move livestock. Voerwerk didn't know. No matter who was mistaken about what, he was going to need answers. "It's hard to imagine, sheep, I mean," he said.

"Believe me, it wasn't *Bronze*'s proudest moment. We scrubbed out the holds for six months before we could breathe."

"They died, the sheep?"

Koch grimaced, thinking of just how many had died.

"It wasn't our fault," he said. "They went from the heat. It got like an oven down there across the Arabian Sea. Admiral, let me tell you. It was like nothing else. They say other ships followed our course just by the carcasses we threw overboard." He laughed. "There was a *school* of sharks to our stern all the way from Darwin up the Red Sea. We weren't especially appreciated in Jidda for that, either."

They went deep within the ship, along a catwalk above a gunmetal steam turbine and boiler. The machinery gleamed in the dim light. Koch's voice echoed in the quiet emptiness. "One engine, on shaft, one screw, one hundred thousand horsepower," he said, explaining quickly.

"And what if it breaks down?" Voerwerk asked.

"Knock on wood," Koch said. "It hasn't happened."

"But say it does?"

"We drift, quite simply, like a log and hope to Christ somebody takes us off."

"You'd abandon her?" Voerwerk asked. The merchant marine had a different code of seagoing ethics.

"In a gale, hell yes. Otherwise we radio for tugs to keep us off land, then work like dogs to fix what's wrong," he said, wanting now to end the tour. He craved a cocktail and asked the guests if they'd join him on the bridge.

Voerwerk hadn't seen it all yet, and he was a thorough man. The drink could wait, but he doubted Koch would ask, once he discovered their purpose. "What about the cargo holds?" Voerwerk asked. "Can we have a look?"

Koch figured that he should finish what he'd begun, even though he disliked the holds, because of the smell, and the bad memories they evoked. "Sure, if you want, but it's not a pleasant sight," he said, telling them about the hold as they went.

"I see what you mean," Voerwerk said, when they finally arrived in the number five, sternmost, hold. Bathed in a blue light, the hold was a nightmare, a madman's vision, Voerwerk thought, and he'd seen a lot of awful things in his life. He had no words for it, looking up and around them at thousands and thousands of pens. But as with other things that suggested horror and held no threat, he was fascinated. "Mechanically, how does it work?" he asked.

"Like everything else Mr. Tikkee does, it's simple and automated," he explained. The wire floors were spaced to allow animal waste to drop on curved pans, which were hosed down automatically by spike jets of water. Along the front of the countless rows, troughs for feeding liquid slops were fitted with self-cleaning devices. Tufts of wool were still stuck to the edges of the wire.

Voerwerk felt a chill. He shook his head. "What a *bizarre* scheme," he said, now fully understanding what he hadn't from Koch's earlier description. Nobody in his right mind would believe this without actually seeing it, he thought, conjuring the image of what the hold must have looked like with row upon row of animals cramped in pens, dying, bleating in a unison of horror.

Voerwerk wanted out, into the fresh air, and finally away, but that couldn't be, he thought with desire nearly defeating duty. No, he had been charged with the task of sailing *Bronze* on Steenkamp's schedule. He glanced at the lieutenant and nodded to him knowingly, then turned to Koch, clearing his throat. "Captain, under the Emergency Acts of the Government of South Africa, I must tell you that my men and I have just commandeered your ship. You will comply with—"

"What the . . . ?" Koch said.

"—with my orders and instruct your crews to do the same."

The Marine lieutenant watched Koch, who made no move to resist, as Voerwerk led them back to the bridge. Never before had he felt such foreboding.

13

Norah gazed at the beetles mounted in a glass case on the library wall. The horn on the male curved back from its head, belligerent and threatening, while the smaller female, appearing benign, had no need for aggressive ornaments. Norah remembered watching, when she had visited in South Africa, as the defenseless male beetle faced a predator, which the female circled. Suddenly she attacked, digging her stinger into its skin, then retreated, as the poison from the gland in her bowels acted fatally on its brain. The lesson was not lost on Norah, who wondered if she had it in her to be as lethal.

She liked to imagine herself capable, but she knew that was an illusion. She had nothing to inject into her enemies, and even if she had, could she bring herself to do it? There were women who did, but deep down inside she wasn't one of them. She had been raised in a cocoon of luxury in which aggressions were never acted out, if ever they were entertained. Her reaction to the previous night had been an overwhelming desire to escape. Even now she could not take the offensive, but, feeling almost like a naughty child, she waited passively for a punishment she feared might come.

What held her back, though, was the idea she represented. That idea, that country could not be allowed to fail. The thought of Israel brought to her images, of the whisper of a breeze through cedars and scented olive trees, the throaty voice of Eli Thre in conversation with men not afraid to laugh or, in times of trouble, to cry, of women and children bound to a country and a land by a history that had no beginning and would have no end, and finally, of the stars shining with the light of *shechinah*. She had taken all of that from Israel, and she had given back love. Now she had to give more.

For the first time she had something concrete to seize on. There actually was a list of names and addresses, and Hartmann had it, although she was not yet prepared to believe in his guilt. Her mind reached out for the pleasant memory of Eli Thre. She thought of him more as dangers surrounded her. He was her beacon of security despite the distance separating them, a solid, flesh-and-blood memory to which she was drawn.

Some administrators within MOSSAD had argued to veto her mission to Zurich on the grounds that she was inexperienced. She might compromise their strategy. She wouldn't have minded if they had. Yet others had wondered where her allegiances lay, with her stepfather or her new country. If the former, they wouldn't have her in Israel. The latter could be proved by what she might accomplish in Zurich. Eli had been in the middle. He had told her of his fears for her safety, while admitting that she alone might do what the entire MOSSAD apparatus could not. In the end, he had chosen the side of MOSSAD.

"Norah!" she heard a voice say now. Startled, she turned to see Hartmann. "I wondered where you were," he said.

"I didn't want to be a nuisance to you. So I stayed in my room most of the day. And I went for a walk."

"Have you packed?"

She nodded. "And booked a flight. It leaves for London at ten."

"Then we'll go out together. I leave at ten-thirty."

"Perfect," she said. He looked more somber somehow, and she wondered if he had literally smelled her presence last night in the library. She watched him now for any sign of change.

He went to the sideboard and poured from an open bottle of Soave. He felt tired and in need of companionship, somebody to talk with, the sound of a voice. He had worked hard during the day, but now what he had to do in Zurich was finished. After much searching he had located a pirate transponder, for which he had paid ten thousand dollars. And he had contracted with Aeroteck for the Boeing 707. They had wanted a fortune, but he had not complained. And he had finally finished culling the list for the men to make up the 250. Now he just wanted to relax, but first he had to be certain.

"Norah?" he asked, sitting down beside her. "Did you come downstairs late last night?"

So he did suspect, she thought, quickly weighing the advantages of a lie. This was her stepfather's home, after all; so why shouldn't she admit to what she had done? Hartmann had no real reason for suspicion. If she lied, a lingering doubt would surely remain.

"Yes, I did," she said, "for a brandy. I couldn't sleep. Seeing you again . . . well, I was wound up. Why?"

"Did you see anything on this table?" He looked down at the coffee table.

"No, should I?"

She looked perfectly innocent, half child and half woman, he thought, boldly inspecting her face and body. He couldn't help feeling desire. She was too beautiful to ignore in that way. But he still harbored doubts. The lists would mean nothing to her, of that he was certain. But merely seeing them would be enough to jeopardize the entire momentous operation. No matter her innocence or beauty, he could not allow that. He shook his head. "I only wondered," he said. "It doesn't matter."

She snuggled closer and kissed him on the cheek. "You businessmen," she said. "Always so suspicious."

He wished he could believe her. Then he had a thought. If she was indeed even a remote danger, what better means to circumvent her talking than keeping a close rein on her? Why not have her come with him to South Africa? That way he would take her off the path of any potential investigators—and her presence could benefit him in other ways as well. "Would you like to go out, or dine here?" he asked. "I'm getting hungry."

"Whatever you want, Ernst," she replied. She felt his suspicions were dampened.

"Here, then," he said, patting her hand. "Can the cook make us something light?"

"*I'll* make you something special." She got up, waving him toward the kitchen. "Keep me company?" she asked. "You can open a bottle of champagne."

They went into the kitchen. Hartmann sat at the wood peasant table as she produced eggs and slices of smoked salmon from the refrigerator. Then she handed him a bottle. She felt more confident as the tension slowly drained from her.

"You're really quite something, Ernst," she said. "Coming up here to talk with those businessmen, then off to Cape Town. My God, when do you find time to relax?"

"I don't," he replied. "Unfortunately there's been too

little of that, but then, there's been nobody to relax with."

"You said you weren't married, but you have girl friends."

"Some," he said. "But none who mean anything." His outlet for sex was whores, he preferred it that way. He looked again at Norah's body, sheathed in tight jeans and a loose blouse, and wondered what she would be like, submitting to him. He would have his chance, he decided. Norah was coming with him.

There was the other angle. Norah's presence in South Africa could help him. Steenkamp would not allow anybody in government to know the extent of Protégé's plans, at least until that moment when it became a fait accompli. So the work that Hartmann would do for Steenkamp demanded secrecy. Norah and her presence in South Africa would take suspicion off him. She would provide him with a cover, without her knowing, he thought. He was vaguely aroused by the idea of the game.

"Why did Peter go so suddenly?" she asked. "At least he might have said good-bye, I mean." She hoped for a clue.

"Why?" he asked. "I don't know. He went to Dar."

"Hunting, I suppose." She shrugged.

Hartmann shook his head. "I guess," he said.

Norah decided to ask. "I'd like to go again, to Africa, I mean, like I said at dinner last night." She waited, but there was no reply. She had to follow him, and she would follow him no matter what. Now that Hans Peter was out of range, she had to choose a secondary target that might lead back to Hans Peter and the poison he represented. Hartmann had those lists. They were important in themselves. But they also held out the prospect of finding the more demonic source, the group that gave *life* to the plotters. If Hartmann did not invite her, she would follow him to Cape Town.

There was something else as well, she confessed to herself: she was attracted to him. That much she knew, even though the thought was unsettling. He was much older and they had known each other for all those years.

But the feeling was there and she could not ignore it. Before she condemned him for being mixed up in this business she wanted absolute proof of his guilt.

Hartmann looked up from his plate. "Why don't you cancel your flight?"

Norah was bewildered. "Why?" she asked.

"And reserve a seat next to mine for Cape Town?"

She beamed at him. "Oh, Ernst, what a lovely, lovely idea."

He returned her smile. "Well? Can you come?"

Norah hesitated for longer than she needed. "I'd love to." She leaned over the table and kissed him lightly on the lips. "It'll be like the old days."

No, he thought. They would be together in the Mount Nelson, but it would certainly not be like the old days. "Now run up and pack for summer weather. Bikinis and sun hats and shorts."

"And I'll telephone for a reservation."

He gave her the flight and seat numbers, then went back to his meal.

Norah ran upstairs and quickly packed, then telephoned SwissAir. She got a seat next to his in first class. She hung up, then immediately lifted the receiver again and dialed the number in Tel Aviv.

Within seconds Eli Thre was on the line. He listened as she told him about Hans Peter leaving for Tanzania, which made him wonder, then about the lists she had seen. Last of all, she told him of the plan to leave for South Africa.

'With *whom?*" Eli Thre's voice threatened to crack.

"Ernst Hartmann," she repeated.

"Come home now! That's a direct order." The name sent off alarm bells in his head. The mission was too dangerous for her now.

"But, Eli," she whispered, "he can lead me to what you want, to the people Mengele told you about. I'm certain now that it's not just Hans Peter."

"I said drop it. I want you back here." He did not want to alarm her with an explanation.

"Is it Hartmann who bothers you? Eli, I know him. He's like a father to me."

He shouted at her: an order was an order. But she was stubborn and didn't want to understand.

"This is something I must do," she said, confused by the anger in his voice. "Good-bye, Eli." She paused. "Eli? It'll be all right. I promise it will. Don't be angry. Please?" Then she hung up.

In his office in Tel Aviv, Eli Thre covered his face with his hands.

"Yes, a suite is available," the desk clerk said. "We'd be delighted, Mr. Hartmann."

Norah stood to one side, nearly numb from the long flight, as Hartmann registered at the Mount Nelson. In all those years, nothing much had changed. The Nelly was still an oasis in the heart of Cape Town, surrounded by gardens and tropical palms. The same old matrons with white powdered faces played bridge and drank tea in the reception. Children, watched by parents from under latticed balconies, splashed noisily, as she had once done, in the swimming pool outside. She shifted her weight onto her hip, thinking how she only wanted a shower and to sleep. How wonderful this could be, she thought, if it did not have a purpose. She heard a bell ring and soon a porter led them to their suite.

"Everything to your satisfaction?" the porter asked, once inside a suite with a living room separating two bedrooms. Hartmann told the porter to turn on the air conditioning, then dug into his pocket for a Rand tip. Meanwhile Norah inspected the view of the gardens and the room itself.

"There's something here for you, Ernst," she said. On the desktop were a bouquet of flowers, a bottle of whiskey, and an envelope addressed in ink. It was an invitation, to a luncheon party in his honor.

Norah chose the smaller of the two bedrooms and unpacked. She jumped into the tub and let the hot water pull the tiredness from her body. The flight had been exhausting as always. Dinner, a movie, and then she had tried to sleep but had only catnapped.

She opened the shower door and grabbed a towel. Standing before a full-length mirror, she was indifferent to what she saw. Yet she was pleased by the certainty that Hartmann would not be. Her figure was evenly tanned and her hips slim and seductive. She crossed her arms beneath her breasts, then wrapped the towel turban-style on her head. She put on shorts and a T-shirt. Finally she returned to the sitting room as Hartmann was pouring himself a drink.

"Make me one?" she asked cheerfully, sitting on the sofa.

He turned to her, excited by what he saw, then smiled. "One thing is certain," he said. "You know how to test a man's friendship."

His words pleased her, but she teased him. "I don't know what you mean," she said.

"Oh yes you do."

"You mean Hans Peter?"

"The very same."

She frowned at the corners of her mouth. "He has no say at all in my personal life. He never has had."

"Be that as it may," Hartmann said. "He still wouldn't like this one bit." He handed her a glass and sat beside her.

"Who said we were doing anything? We have separate rooms, with locks, and I promise not to attack you. For Pete's sake." She crossed her legs Indian-style, revealing soft contours through the thin fabric of the shorts.

"Ah, but the temptation. You do enjoy making love."

"Of course."

"And so do I."

"But that doesn't mean——" She stopped herself. If this was going too far too fast, she still needed to have it happen. Sex was a vehicle that would lead her to a single, important truth that she had to discover.

Hartmann was aroused. He came closer and put his arm around her shoulder. It was thin and fragile. He wanted her now as he had wanted her the instant he had seen her with her hair shining in the light. It didn't make sense, he knew it didn't. He looked boldly at her breasts, then into her face. "Tell me what you want," he whispered, his voice thickening.

She sighed, responding to his touch. She led his hand to her breast. She relaxed as he caressed her body, his mouth closing on hers. They continued the embrace, each exploring the other, until he drew back and looked into her eyes.

"I want you," she said.

"Ummmm," he replied.

He led her by the hand into the bedroom. She wriggled out of her shorts and T-shirt, then rolled on her stomach as he undressed. The hair on his chest was flecked gray, his stomach flat and hard. The shoulders were broad and tightly muscled.

He lay down and caressed her, his hand moving gently along her back. She responded by turning over, lifting her hips to his touch. Neither of them for these moments had any world but this, the tremendous pleasure they shared, as though they had been lovers all their lives. Norah traveled through valleys and skies of ecstasy, disbelieving in herself the measure of her passion.

But he would not stop, unconsciously weaving the need to hurt with great tenderness, a thread he had not known for a lifetime of years. He could not have her enough, the meanness washed out of him by her body. Finally he spent himself and rolled beside her, breathing deeply, thinking of nothing but what just had been.

Completely relaxed, he raised his arms above his head and looked over, wondering at her sudden new expression.

"What's wrong?" he asked, gently.

"Nothing," she replied. But everything was wrong, everything, the instant she saw the dull green SS tattoo inside his upper arm. Everything was wrong, because that love she had felt only minutes ago was now swamped by hate.

"Nothing," she told him again, softly.

Two hours later nothing but love was what the guests suspected between them when Norah swept across the terrace of Kleene Schuur on Hartmann's arm. Radiant in a white summer dress, she seemed like a new bride, deferring to him, complimenting, affectionate. But behind her smile Norah was about to burst, knowing how very alone she was.

Eli Thre had never seemed so far away.

The party was hosted by Steenkamp, who doted on Hartmann, as though he, the Prime Minister of the country were in some way inferior to his guest in status. There was a bond between them that went beyond friendship, and it set Norah to wondering. What made the relationship confusing was the other guests. They were South Africa's establishment, the ranking politicians and cabinet ministers, the generals of the Army, businessmen, and diplomats. If there was something dark existing between her "lover" and Steenkamp, the others surely did not know what it was.

They were blunt in their language and to Norah's eye they all looked dowdy, as though they had only now discovered the fashions of the fifties. Except for one woman, whom Norah had spotted for her clothes. She was chic, with an intelligent face. Norah thought she looked vaguely familiar.

The smoothness with which Hartmann moved among these people, Norah surmised, suggested that he had met some of them before, probably through Steenkamp, when he had visited the country twelve years ago. In spite of the gap in time, they were outgoing and friendly toward him and inquisitive about his perceptions of African politics. They referred to him as a businessman. But none of them was specific about what his business actually was.

The Prime Minister was standing with a small group of people by the swimming pool. "Ernst," he yelled in their direction, "come say hello to my young Foreign Minister."

Hand in hand, they strolled over.

"You remember Connie Uys and his wife, Marie," the Prime Minister said by way of introduction. "Ernst Hartmann." Then, looking at Norah: "And Miss Hirsch." Then back at Hartmann: "And this is General MacIntyre. He heads up our Army." They shook hands all around.

"You've put our Prime Minister in good spirits," Connie Uys said to Hartmann.

"Old friends always do that to one another," Steenkamp interjected, grasping Hartmann affectionately by the arm. "Ernst and I go back before you were born, Connie."

"Indeed we do," Hartmann said. "Our reunions aren't often, but they are always special."

"Are you still doing business in Africa?" General MacIntyre asked.

"As much as ever," Hartmann replied.

Norah glanced at the Foreign Minister's wife, Marie, whom she had noticed before. She was certain they had met. She again searched her memory but came up with a blank.

"Ernst knows the independent kaffirs," Steenkamp said, referring to the people of black Africa. "What's it like to deal with them now? Have they become pigheaded now that they have political power?"

"You just don't want to get on their wrong side," Hartmann replied. "Play on their weaknesses. In many ways, they're still children."

"I feel the same," Steenkamp said. "Didn't they just come down from the trees?" He roared with laughter.

Norah thought her ears were deceiving her. No civilized person talked about other human beings as if they were animals. She didn't remember South Africans talking about any blacks, even their own, like this when she had last visited. What made it more astonishing, the blatant racism was coming from the lips of the Prime Minister.

She turned away to see the attractive woman, the wife of the Foreign Minister, staring at her. Recognition dawned on her face and she came over. "Is your name Norah?" she asked tentatively. "Are you *Norah* Hirsch?"

"Yes, but I . . ." Norah still could not place the woman.

"And you don't remember?"

Norah laughed. "I'm awfully sorry but I don't."

Connie Uys overheard the exchange and joined them, helping Norah in the guessing game. "My Lord, why should she remember, Marie? She was only a kid." He took Norah's hand, warmly this time. "You stayed with us for two days, remember, the summer you were here?"

Now Norah did remember. They were just married and he had a law practice in Cape Town. He was handsome and charming while she was a confidant, even to such a young girl. Uncle Ernst had arranged for the Uyses to watch after her while he went elsewhere on business. The Uyses were friends of friends, and very nice, Norah recalled. "Yes, of course I do," she said, embracing Marie. "Please excuse me. I should have known right off. It's wonderful to see you again." She meant it, too. Connie and Marie were special people.

Marie led her away in the direction of the buffet table. "You'll have to make do without us," she said to the men. "We have a lot of gossiping to do." Then when they were out of earshot she said, "Whew, what a relief. I couldn't take much more of that."

"Did it disturb you?" Norah asked.

"It always does, when they're so bigoted," she replied. They sat alone at a table, eating cold cuts, catching up, as old friends would. Norah told her that this visit was a sentimental journey, denying that there was anything between her and Hartmann. That she didn't know Hartmann well seemed to please Marie. Norah wondered why, and asked if she knew him.

"Only through friends," Marie replied evasively. "Connie, of course, met him while you were here."

"But you seem not to like him," she said.

"Between us," she said, "I don't like anybody who talks the way he does, which means almost everybody in South Africa."

Norah laughed, pleased that Marie was still the outspoken liberal she now remembered. Neither she nor Connie had ever run with the herd, believing differently about apartheid and the blacks. Even as a girl, they had told her what they felt, defensively back then. She wondered out loud how Connie had risen to the post of Foreign Minister.

"A fluke, I guess," Marie replied, smirking. "The Prime Minister at one point wanted to show how liberal we can be. He picked Connie for the UN first, then Foreign Minister. But now it doesn't matter."

"Why?" Norah asked.

"You heard what they said. To them our black people are subhuman, which they aren't. Blacks are bright as anybody else, just less experienced in *our* ways, as we are in *theirs*," she said frowning. "But that shouldn't make us superior, now should it? What I want to say is, Connie tried. I mean, we're not all like . . . well, like Steenkamp."

"But there's still time."

"No there is not," Marie said, a fierceness in her voice. "In a year or less, we'll be forced out, all of us. We waited too long. Connie's so certain, he bought us a house in England."

"I'm sorry for you, then," Norah said fleetingly.

"That's kind." She paused for an instant. "But I'm not sorry. We brought it on ourselves. Connie believes that some of the whites won't pack up and go peacefully."

"But they have no choice," Norah said, wondering at how little she knew of the situation. That it had become desperate surprised her.

"My dear," Marie said. "There is always a *choice*."

"Do you mean violence?"

"To a degree that will be horrible, believe me."

"But surely Connie can work to prevent it from happening."

"Not anymore," Marie said, with conviction. "God knows he wants to try, but he walks a tightrope in the Cabinet. If he were to speak out, Steenkamp would close ranks on him. Connie feels, for whatever it is worth, it's better to work on the inside. So he stays."

"But surely, Marie, this isn't a police state. There's a Parliament and a press and people like yourselves. That must count for something, even now."

"It was like that once," Marie said. "But in desperation everything changed. Believe me, now we have worse than a police state. The Cabinet doesn't do anything, and the press has been gagged. No, it's all Steenkamp. And that's what scares us. Because he's capable of *anything*." She waved her hand indifferently. "Anyway, I'll be glad to be gone."

Norah saw Hartmann look in their direction. She had been away from him too long. Marie winked at her and the two of them walked over and rejoined the men, who talked to Hartmann about his work in South Africa.

"You're just the man for the job, I'd say," MacIntyre remarked.

"How fast can we get it done?" Hartmann addressed his question to Steenkamp, studiously ignoring the general's flattery.

"I think we all agree, if need be, in a couple of days, Ernst." He chuckled hoarsely. "We're fairly practiced at it by now."

"But the element of risk—" MacIntyre started to say. He was cut off by the Prime Minister's pained expression.

Steenkamp had thought hard about the element of risk. It was important, damned important, that the blacks didn't act up. Steenkamp had the policy of apartheid working for him there. The blacks would be led to think that this was just another relocation from one homeland to another. So they more than likely would not riot. And after the killings at Soweto, they would be licking their wounds for weeks to come. No. He didn't expect trouble, but he could never be sure. There was one form of insurance that was infallible, and that was what they would use. "More than usual," he said, "they'll be guarded by armed police and soldiers. If they get out of line, we have a riot and they will give us no choice but to hit them hard."

Norah didn't understand what he was talking about, so she asked.

Steenkamp gave her a patronizing look. "It's nothing to worry yourself about, young lady."

"No," Hartmann interrupted. "Tell her."

Steenkamp thought for a minute. "All right, then. In South Africa we have a policy of apartheid. It is our way of keeping blacks separate from the whites. From time to time over the last fifteen or so years, we've moved the blacks where we needed them, from one of their townships, like Soweto, to another. We are moving them again in a day or so."

"I see," Norah said. She felt indifferent toward the politics of South Africa, although she thought them reprehensible. She didn't know enough to argue. What happened in South Africa was none of her affair. They deserved what they got, these bigoted whites.

They were soon joined by others wishing to hear the wise offerings of their Prime Minister. They stood there for another quarter hour until finally Connie Uys signaled Marie with a brush of his hand. "Let's go home," he whispered. Connie paid their compliments to the others and made an excuse for leaving early. "Another appointment," he explained simply. When he shook Hartmann's hand, Hartmann asked a favor.

"I want to stay for a little while," he said. "Will you drop Norah?" Connie readily agreed.

Relieved, wanting to be alone for even a brief time, Norah feigned reluctance, then agreed. She didn't know what to expect, but she guessed he would want to use her again soon for lovemaking, like a whore. The thought disgusted her. But she had no choice, knowing that he had enjoyed their sex, just as she had hoped he would. But now she wished it hadn't been *that* good.

The three went through the house to the portico, where they waited for an attendant to bring up the Uyses' car. They were joined by Dr. Robert Blum, Steenkamp's personal physician, an old bearish-looking man who shuffled through the door.

"Still not driving, Doc?" Uys asked, smiling genuinely at their oldest friend, who nodded. "We'll give you a lift, too. Come on."

A widower, Blum loved the Uyses. He had more or less adopted Connie as a young man, advising and guiding him across the terrain of a political career. And Uys thought of Blum as a surrogate father, while Marie loved the little man for his depth of character and the vulnerability he showed them alone. On the drive, made longer than usual by heavy traffic, they discussed the cocktail party and reminisced with Norah. Then Connie turned to what was really on his mind, the Prime Minister.

"You know the problem," Dr. Blum replied, aware

that Uys knew of Steenkamp's cancer. "It's literally killing him."

Connie didn't know if he should ask. After all, Blum was Steenkamp's personal physician, but the question was one that had to be asked. The Soweto riot and talk of crushing the blacks disturbed him. "Can something like that bend his mind, Doc," he asked. "Has it? I guess what I'm saying is that . . . well, he's not the same man. The Soweto thing can't be called normal."

Ethically it was wrong for Blum to answer, but what was said between them always had a special confidentiality, and Norah, sitting beside him in the backseat, seemed quite innocent and harmless. And she was the Uyses' friend, which was good enough for Blum. "Of course it wasn't normal," he said. "He *killed* a man. In a clinical way the cancer and the pressure of events right now have pushed him too far." Marie looked startled. "No, my dear, I don't think it's anything to worry about," he lied. "Most of the time his judgment is unimpaired, but he's still a horribly isolated man. Someone to be watched."

"But . . . he was in great spirits today, wasn't he? He seemed normal enough," Marie offered, expressing a hope she didn't feel.

"That he was," Blum said, turning to Norah. "Your friend Mr. Hartmann seems to have a restraining influence on him. He does him good."

"It surprised me that they are friends," Norah said. "From what you say, I hope Ernst *continues* to restrain him." She thought for a moment. "It's an awful accusation, though, about Steenkamp. Killing somebody?" She hadn't heard.

"It's a fact, Norah, not an accusation," Uys said. "Even he admits it."

"Then why can't you . . ."

"Impeach him?" Connie asked. "You tell her, Doc."

"The Boers support him, even if some of us don't. And they are the majority of whites. Connie and I are in a decided minority of two. What he did to that black?" He paused. "They loved him for it."

"I see," said Norah in a soft voice. It was insane. But

was it her problem? "Do you know how Ernst met Steen-kamp?" she asked, trying to sound offhand.

Each of them thought for a while. Connie answered, "No, I don't. But it's an interesting question."

Norah pursued it. There might be something in the relationship between Hartmann and Steenkamp to indicate why Hartmann was visiting, *with those lists*. "Can you tell me a little about the Prime Minister?"

"It's all well documented," Dr. Blum said.

"A farmer, local politician, up through the ranks, a Boer to his soul, right-wing—"

"Fascist, you mean," Blum interrupted.

Norah perked up her ears. "What do you mean, fascist?"

"He is," Connie replied. "During the Second World War, Steenkamp threw in with the Nazis."

"Threw in, hell," Dr. Blum said. He was not Steen-kamp's personal physician by choice. Because of Blum's skills, he had been commanded to the position.

"All right, cool down," Connie advised. It was a subject that still made tempers flare, at least among non-Boers.

But Blum didn't cool down. "Our *beloved* Prime Minister," he said sarcastically, "went to Germany during the war and worked with Abwehr I, the German external Intelligence service. Admiral Canaris headed it up. Abwehr sent Steenkamp back to South Africa. He tried to organize an overthrow of the government of Jan Smuts. It failed."

"And our *beloved* Prime Minister was thrown in jail, until the war ended," Connie said.

"And with that background, he became Prime Minister!" Norah was truly amazed.

"*Because* of that background, you should say," Dr. Blum remarked. "Apartheid is his policy and his alone. He created it."

Connie smiled. "You're wrong about that."

"All right, so he didn't. The policy of apartheid, my dear, is based on the Nazis' policies toward people who were non-Aryan."

"Like the Jews," Norah said.

"Now you're catching on."

"And the Boers, the dominant white group in South Africa, elected him Prime Minister because he knew how to take care of the blacks," Connie said.

"They *love* him for it," Dr. Blum said.

Abwehr, thought Norah. The SS *tattoo* on Hartmann's inner arm. That had to be the connection between the two men, and possibly the connection with the lists she had seen in Zurich. She didn't know how these facts fit with the deep group of her stepfather's that Eli had sent her to Zurich to discover, but she damned well was going to find out.

Just then they pulled into the drive of the Lord Nelson. As they said their good-byes, Marie insisted on Norah's joining them for dinner the following night. She would check with Hartmann, Norah said, but in principle she'd love to. They would plan on it.

South Africa was becoming her problem after all.

14

"I need concrete proof," Ralph Crawford told the American across the desk.

"Don't you guys ever work on circumstantial evidence?" James Profit wanted to know. After all, *his* agency had often gone out on a limb. As a CIA analyst, Profit's purview was black Africa—about forty nations whose economic indicators he monitored. On station now for ten years, he loved Africa, career backwater though it was, for the private delights of amateur archaeology, fishing, and, less often now, hunting. He watched Crawford shrug a reply, realizing his question had been unfair. No, IRS was definitely not into speculation.

Crawford was visiting him out of quiet desperation. He doubted if Profit, his only American contact in Tanzania, could help, but he would listen, and perhaps push him in the right direction. The way things were, he was playing blindman's buff, for any point of the compass now was as good as any other. IRS did not want his *theory*. He felt certain of MacKee, but that wouldn't wash with Washington. They wanted proof. On something like this, an "accident investigation," they'd laugh him back home if he didn't get it. He outlined for Profit what he knew, leaving nothing out, putting nothing special in, then waited for a response.

"I agree MacKee is probably alive," Profit said of the theory, shaking a shaggy head of black hair. "But I don't see how we can help." Then, after a pause: "Do I need to explain the situation?"

"I guess not," Crawford replied, embarrassed for him. They both knew how succeeding administrations in Washington had all but castrated the CIA. Nobody, including spy outfits in other countries, trusted the agency, or cooperated, except in the routine collection of routine data. Shameful but true, Crawford thought. He shifted uncomfortably in his chair, deciding to review the points again. Maybe they would send off sparks in Profit's mind. "Let's start with individuals," he said. "Do you know anything about MacKee or this banker?"

"What can I say?" Profit replied. "The stuff I know is the level of street gossip. Anybody will tell you the same. MacKee was a fixture in Dar, even though he kept pretty much to himself. But Dar just isn't that big a place."

"Did you ever see him, personally?"

"Every so often. I even talked with him now and again."

"Then what was he like? Was there anything unique about him?"

"Let me ask *you* a question," Profit said, turning serious. "Have you ever seen an elephant killed?"

"What's that got to do with any—"

"—Have you?"

"No."

"Well, I do a bit of hunting, ducks and antelope and the like. Nothing big. And I'll tell you, Ralph, anybody who'd hunt an elephant for *sport* is sick, really pathetic.

They're the most superb beasts on four legs. Jesus"—his eyes nearly misted over—"they have family structures that beat any that man has these days. Don't laugh," he said, sad and serious. "They're endangered, *tembo* are. Well, your MacKee and this banker you mention, Hirsch, got their kicks from just about decimating the herds around here. Cows, bulls, calves, the whole lot. It was illegal, but nobody paid them any mind, because they gave away the ivory. All they wanted was the kill. What I'm saying is MacKee was a bloodthirsty bastard with the emotions of a snake. The same goes for Hirsch."

It was a long way around, Crawford thought, but the point was made. He was no conservationist, but the recollection of the rhino he'd tracked with Farita helped him empathize, for the animal alive was majestic. Dead, it was as though that majesty had never existed. "Yeah, I guess you're right," he said slowly. "You say that Hirsch was MacKee's hunting budy? So they spent a lot of time together?"

"I don't know. Probably not, if you say Hirsch lives in Zurich."

"Then was there anything more than friendship? Like maybe business?"

"I can't say for sure, but somebody mentioned Hirsch's having a share in his coffee estates. You could check it out with the Finance Ministry."

That wouldn't be worth the hassle, Crawford thought. Right now what he wanted was a picture of MacKee, a psychological impression of the man. That's how his reading of mystery books told him it was done. And all those mysteries couldn't be wrong. "MacKee was a naturalized American, but the records don't show much of a past," he said. "Would you guess he was English or what?"

Profit smiled at how little Crawford knew. MacKee probably bought the American passport. Wealthy refugees did it all the time after the war. Profit's parents had no money, and look at the trouble they went through to become U.S. citizens. "German as Kaiser Wilhelm," he said. "Of the old school, too. He was always ramrod-straight and had this superior way about him, as if he'd just been ennobled or something. An Austrian accent, I'd guess. He had a sense of humor, but it wasn't one that'd get you and me laughing."

The more Crawford listened, the greater his confusion. A German with American citizenship—that is, before he renounced it—living in Tanzania, maybe dead, with an estate executor in Switzerland, and God only knew what else. Tracking MacKee backwards was going to be impossible. "What about haunts, his hangouts, maybe friends in Dar?" he asked.

"Again, Ralph, I really can't help."

"But you saw him occasionally. Where?"

"Oh, that," Profit said, passing it off. "He'd go to the Settlers' Club, where I drink now and then. Not a bad watering hole, but the members are a little bizarre." Crawford opened his mouth. "They're old German settlers, Ralph, with attitudes about Africa that are ancient. If you want to see what Tanzania was like when the Germans were around, go there."

Crawford thought he would do just that. He took down the name and address and asked Profit if the club was restricted to members.

"As long as you're white, you won't have a problem," Profit replied. The club did have a few selected black members who had been admitted after Independence, but they were made to feel so uncomfortable they rarely if ever went. "I'll take you after work," he said, feeling sorry for Crawford.

"That's all right," Crawford said, not wanting to waste the entire day. "I'll find it on my own."

Crawford walked along the sidewalk toward his hotel, looking in shop windows as he went. He wanted to find a souvenir store where he could buy gifts for the boys and Marcia, and something for Larry Calder. He finally found what he was looking for. The sign in the shop told him that African game trophies and ivory were sold there. He went inside and selected a Masai spear for Calder, wondering how he would get it home, two native shields for the boys, and a silver elephant-hair bracelet for Marcia. As he was paying at the counter he spotted a showcase with silver jewelry. He didn't hesitate to buy a bracelet. He owed Farita for her kindness.

Once back at the hotel, he saw that the same taxi driver as before, Kimau, was waiting for him. The fifty shillings he'd given him earlier in the morning had won over the African, who had declared himself Crawford's exclusive guide and protector.

He gave the souvenirs to the hotel porter to put in the safe and went outside to Kimau's Peugeot. The destination he gave was the German Settlers' Club.

The port city of Dar es Salaam was exotic as any could be; America had nothing to compare. It was a city out of Kipling or Joseph Conrad. The people who made Conrad's *Lord Jim* into a movie, he thought, must have visited Dar es Salaam. The colonial buildings were whitewashed and decaying in the humid climate. The streets were lined with a succession of small stores, each selling a different product. There was a broom store and one for pans and another for paper. He was enchanted by the singsong of Swahili, by the palms swaying over the entire scene. It struck him as the most beautiful city he had ever seen.

Kimau glanced in the rearview mirror. "Maybe, Mr. Crawford, you'd like a massage this afternoon," he suggested. "They make you feel better in the heat. And I know a place where the girls are—"

The touch, Crawford thought. "Clean?" he said, laughing. "I don't believe you said it. And your sister, Kimau? She's a masseuse, too?"

"And young." He also started laughing.

Crawford had decided about that. If he was going to fool around it would be with Farita, and not some local hooker.

They approached the outskirts of the Indian quarter, past the Aga Khan Hospital, and the Aga Khan High School beside the Aga Khan hockey field. A movie theater was showing a film with *Khan* in the title. On the sidewalks walked men in turbans and women in loose, flowing saris.

"I thought this was Dar es Salaam, not Bombay," he said to Kimau.

"The *muhindi* make a good business," Kimau replied. "We Africans go to them for credit."

"At what interest rate?"

"Nothing fixed," Kimau explained, tapping the Peugeot's steering wheel. "A car like this new is worth ten thousand shillings. An Asian sells it to you for maybe one hundred."

Either the Africans were downright smart, Crawford thought, or the Indians were philanthropists. "What's the hitch, then?" he asked.

"The hitch is you pay for one hundred and fifty months."

They were now in a residential suburb with large homes surrounded by high fences, on which signs were posted warning of police dogs. Guards stood watch along the gates and Crawford asked why.

"The *muzungus*," Kimau answered, as if that were adequate. "Many Tanzanians are very poor. In order to live, they steal from the whites. So the *munzungus* hide behind fences."

God, Crawford thought, the sad Africans. Those who had money were exploited by the Asians, and those who didn't lived outside electric fences. No wonder they were sometimes bitter.

He watched Kimau turn the steering wheel and felt him apply pressure to the brakes, as they drove through gates and cautiously over speed bumps in a driveway. Ahead of them was a low stucco building painted the color of cherries. A zebra-striped awning at the door was marked "GSC," the German Settlers' Club. Crawford told Kimau to wait and soon was in the cool of the club's entrance hall.

The furnishings struck him first. Overstuffed chairs with flowered slip covers, leather sofas that long ago had conformed to the demands of a hundred white bottoms, a glass case in the corner with a lion's head—"Killed in 1905" read the corroded brass plaque—a scarred reception desk on which a half-dozing cat licked itself. An antique wooden telephone switchboard buzzed like a bluebottle fly. He heard a clicking noise and peered into a side room where elderly men were racking up for a game of snooker. Through the window he saw matrons lounging by a swimming pool. They were served by liveried blacks voicelessly carrying trays of lemonade and orange squash. The place smelled of age and boredom and twice-told tales.

At the other side of an empty reception room with a skylight he saw a bar with animal heads mounted on the walls. Dark and scented with stale cigar smoke, it had backgammon boards with the ivory pieces neatly in their places, a card table, and plaques, he saw, which were the gifts of visiting European regiments. While he was looking at the rows of bottles behind the bar, he suddenly came face to face with an African barman who had been sitting hidden on a low stool behind the barrier.

"Jambo, bwana," he said cheerfully.

"Yes," was all that Crawford could think to say. The African pushed forward an order book. Crawford guessed that at GSC gentlemen ordered drinks in writing and not with spoken words. He put down "Vodka and tonic" and was immediately served with the drink and a wooden bowl of dried plantain chips. The bartender stood almost at attention, looking into space. Jesus, thought Crawford, this place was lost in time.

"Do you speak English?" he asked.

The bartender now gave Crawford his full attention. "Yes, I do, *bwana,"* he said smartly. "And German."

"You're one up on me, then," he said, wondering why he worked as a barman. "It's not very busy."

"The gentlemen arrive just before noon."

"Do you know many of the members?"

"Know them?" he looked bewildered. "No, *bwana,* not *know* them. I serve them."

"It's the same thing, I guess," Crawford said lamely. "I wondered if you knew Mr. MacKee, or maybe you know other members who did?"

"I served him for many years." The bartender's eyes clouded over. He mistrusted whites who were inquisitive. He wasn't used to them speaking so openly. *"Bwana* MacKee was a gentleman, like the other members," he said simply.

Crawford saw that he wasn't getting anywhere and

doubted he ever would. "And Mr. Hirsch?" he asked on a long shot. "Is he a gentleman, too?"

"Yes, sir. He should be coming in soon."

Crawford wasn't sure the barman understood, so he repeated the question. The barman told him that Hirsch was presently a guest in the club and would soon arrive in the bar for his noontime drink.

"Which room is he in?" Crawford asked. "Can you tell me that?"

"In the Military Wing," the barman replied. "I believe Room Four."

"Thanks," Crawford said, drinking the last of the vodka tonic and paying with a five-shilling note. "Keep the change," he said.

Crawford couldn't believe his good fortune. Luck had returned: he felt his spine tingle. If MacKee was alive, Hirsch would know. If he was indeed dead, Crawford would be within touch of his estate. But what if, considering their friendship, they had contrived together to fake the death? Then Crawford would have tipped his hand, and MacKee *and* the estate would be gone, probably forever.

He opted against direct confrontation, at least for the time being, choosing instead to watch what Hirsch did and where he went. His heart started to pump strongly. At the very least, thought Hirsch, he might find *proof* that his man was alive. That would be a solid beginning. Crawford looked at his wristwatch. By what the barman said, there was plenty of time before the members arrived. He could snoop around more, maybe even . . .

As he considered the question, he was walking outside near the swimming pool, searching for the Military Wing. There were no signs for the names of different residential blocks. But the doors to the rooms, he saw, faced outward. Finally he had no choice but to ask a pool steward, who pointed a finger.

Room 4 was locked. Crawford backed off and stood in the shade of a tree, wondering how to get in. He saw swallows darting to nests in the eaves. The windows were closed and presumably latched. He couldn't ask a steward to open up, thinking of the fences and guards on the houses they had passed. Everybody was probably suspicious of everybody else, whites of blacks and blacks of whites. He wouldn't take the chance, he decided, shifting his weight from one foot to another, the thought of a cold drink coming to mind. Then for the first time he noticed the pail beside the doorframe of Room 5.

Minutes later a stooped cleaning man shuffled out of the room, picked up the pail, then with a house key on a ring around his neck opened the door to Hirsch's room. Crawford waited, checking his wristwatch, slightly worried now about the element of time. Hirsch would probably stop in the room before going to the bar. Crawford had another twenty minutes.

Sooner than he expected, the cleaning man came from Room 4. Crawford moved.

"*Bwana* Hirsch," he said, wondering if the old man spoke English. He kept his hand on the edge of the open door. "He asked me to fetch something. Thanks." And he slid into the room, smiling at the cleaning man, who seemed to think nothing of the intrusion.

Crawford's eyes adjusted to the darkness. Several items caught his attention at once. A Halliburton suitcase was on the luggage stand at the foot of the bed, opened and empty. He went to the wardrobe. It contained two identical gray safari suits, a three-piece striped business suit, dress shoes, and chukka boots. The pockets were empty. Nothing was hidden in the shoes. He checked his watch again. Now he was shaving it thin.

The bed was covered with a mosquito net attached to the ceiling. Through the opening, he saw a shortwave radio on the nightstand and a black attaché case. His hands were sweaty as he picked it up. Sitting on the bed, he placed it on his knees.

He was unfastening the locks when he heard a key in the door.

The case fell on the floor with shattering noise. Now trapped, Crawford couldn't hide. He looked at the door through the white gauze of the netting, trying to will it not to open. He put the case back on the bed and got up. As the door cracked open, he muttered loudly that they had shown him into the wrong room.

As though he didn't see Crawford, the cleaning man came through the door, went into the bathroom, then seconds later left with a can of Omo cleaning powder.

Crawford was faint with relief, breathing in shallow gulps. He really was an amateur, he thought. The lock on the door had an inside catch, which prevented anyone from getting in, even with a key. He turned it up, then went back to the bed and the case.

Items in the case were arranged in order. He looked at the checkbook from the Commercial Credit Union, wondering what line of credit a bank gave its owner. Next he found a yellowed document of several hundred pages written in German. He would have given it a miss, if he hadn't recognized the swastika and the salutation "Heil, Hitler." at the bottom of the covering letter. He took out his pen and notebook, copying from the front page and paragraphs in the body of the letter. He didn't know what it meant, though perhaps it tied in with MacKee. Once he had finished writing, he flipped through the document. Near the back tucked into the spine he found a photograph, again old, of three men in German uniforms with a backdrop of snow-covered mountains, taken from a distance that made the men's faces indistinct. He put the photo in his coat pocket.

Now he had to work fast, he thought. It was after noon. He turned to a red-leather desk diary below the document. On a day column, the next day, there were several notations, which he also copied in his notebook. They also made no sense.

"OLDUVAI H 1300, 250 DAR intl. 1500."

He lined up the items as he had found them, closed the case, then quickly inspected the room. Carefully now, he unlocked the door, opening it slowly, listening for the sound of a footfall. He slipped out of the room, looking right and left. There was nobody. Outside, the heat felt almost cool to him as he stood by the tree. For the first time in his life, Crawford wished he smoked.

Moments later, a man with slick gray-flecked black hair wearing a safari suit walked down the sidewalk from the main club building. Crawford took a good look. The man opened Room 4 and went in.

His appearance fit the impression Crawford had formed in his mind. He was thin, of medium height, and severe-looking. He conformed to the image Crawford had of all bankers. For that matter, he could have been a senior administrator at IRS. The slicked-down hair struck him as old-fashioned. It was oiled, perhaps with pomade, a smooth, tarry dome of hair.

"Okay, Kimau," he said a few minutes later. "Let's move out." He got in the taxi.

Halfway back into Dar, they stopped at a telephone booth. Crawford borrowed a shilling from Kimau and called James Profit.

"I need your help," he said.

"What did you find out?"

"I don't know, it's in German, that's why I'm asking." They agreed to meet for lunch, but before that, Crawford had one important stop to make. He hung up, returned to the taxi and told Kimau what he wanted.

Kimau, maneuvering the Peugeot more with courage than with technique, set a course through noontime traffic into the city center. People were disappearing from the streets: the heat was becoming unbearable, even to the natives. Crawford removed his jacket. His shirt was soaked.

The waters of the Dar estuary shimmered in the heat. On the other side of the road from the seawall, *dukkas* advertising cloth, hardware, silver and gold jewelry, were boarded with metal grates, while their proprietors went home for siesta. Kimau pulled to a stop. They got out, Crawford following down a narrow alley. The smell of rotting fruit, urine, and spices assaulted him. He put a handkerchief to his nose, watching bony dogs with hungry eyes cower in doorways as he passed. Finally they found themselves in front of Ram Singh Chemist's.

They saw the owner through the window. His back to them, he turned at the sound of tapping on the pane and looked at them through chipped eyeglasses. He had enormous girth, tiny, ringed hands, and a rust-red turban that was a work of origami. The flesh of his face moved easily into a smile, but his eyes were suspicious. Kimau had told Crawford that Singh was a provider of services, from black market shillings to illegal medicine, drugs, pornography, and, on demand, even abortions. Singh was always willing to do what others wouldn't, or couldn't.

"My driver says you'll do this right away," Crawford said, handing Singh the photograph. "Can you enlarge it enough to see the faces?"

"No problems," he replied.

They went with Singh behind an apothecary shelf into a room bathed in red light. There was an enlarger, racks of chemicals, and trays containing strong-smelling liquids. Photos were tacked to the wall, Crawford saw, looking at one of a young Indian girl no more than ten years old having intercourse with a man with grandfatherly gray hair and wrinkled skin. She sat astride him, her back to his face. She wore a child's expression of glee, as though the sex act was a perfectly normal endeavor for girls her age.

"They start them young here," he said to Singh, who glanced at the photo.

"Oh, her," he said with a note of pride. "A good little girl that. My niece. If you can pay the price, she is upstairs."

"Thanks," Crawford said. "I'll pass."

"This won't take long now," Singh said, sliding a negative of the print into the enlarger's frame. Crawford leaned over. A beam of light on paper, then paper in the developing bath. Shades started to appear on the paper. At first like ghosts, three figures appeared, then more clearly, dressed in tailored uniforms, smiling, their arms fraternally around each other's shoulders. Now their faces were distinct. Crawford didn't recognize the other two. But Hans Peter Hirsch was the one on the right.

The restaurant on Numiery Street, where Kimau took Crawford, had a sign above the door, " urried   bster." Africans at the bar slaked their thirst with Tusker. Farther inside, the ubiquitous ceiling fans circulated a spicy curried aroma. Indian families at the tables ate masala and tandoori with peppers and chilis rolled into chapatis with greasy fingers. In the far corner, Crawford saw an arm shoot up and wave at him. It was James Profit.

"How did you find this place?" Crawford asked, amazed.

"I followed the dogs," Profit replied, smiling and getting up for Crawford to take a seat. He saw the dampness of Crawford's shirt. "You're getting to look like an old hand," he said, meaning it. "But we've got to get you out of long sleeves and wool jackets."

Crawford had decided earlier that morning to buy a safari suit. He wondered where he'd find the time or how to go about it. At home, Marcia bought most of his clothes.

"What'll it be, gents?" a voice asked. The owner of the Curried Lobster was an Indian without a turban. He handed them plastic menus.

"Give us a cold beer. Cold, I said," Profit told him. He wrote down the order.

"Have you got fish curry?" Crawford asked.

"Always, and it's fresh, right out of the Indian Ocean."

Profit looked at the owner, then back at Crawford with a sympathetic smile. "The fish is *frozen*, Ralph," he said. "It was probably caught months ago in Jap nets."

Unperturbed, the owner neither apologized nor made excuses. "Then I recommend the tilapia," he advised.

"Sounds good," Profit said. "Give me the mutton and a tilapia for my friend, two papadam, saffron rice, chapatis. Okay, Ralph?" Crawford nodded. The owner vanished behind a bead curtain.

"I went to the Settlers' Club," he said, telling Profit about what he had discovered. "But I'll be damned if I know what it means."

"Let's have a look," Profit said.

Crawford took the notebook from his pocket, its pages rimmed with the wet of perspiration. Profit read, while the owner put down two bottles of beer with ice chips melting down the sides.

"Do you understand German?"

"I'm a bit rusty, but I was born there," Profit replied, pointing to the notebook. "It must be a working paper, on a project they called 'Tanganyika.' That's this country. Hey," he said. "This is amazing." Crawford leaned on his elbows. "From what you have here," Profit said, "this is some wild Nazi scheme to bring all the Jews into East Africa. *This* was in his briefcase?"

"Along with this." Crawford produced the enlargement. "Do you recognize any of these three men?"

Profit looked at the enlargement. "This one looks like Hirsch." He looked much younger, but the features were the same.

"That was my guess, too."

"And this one on the left . . . damn if he doesn't look like our man James Langway MacKee."

"But that can't be." Crawford's voice was pained.

"Jesus, an SS officer, too, by the looks of the uniform."

"It just *can't* be. MacKee was an American."

"Naturalized, remember, with a German accent. Didn't you do a background check on MacKee?"

"Not before 1973 we didn't."

Profit looked at him with a serious expression. "If you had checked, I'd bet you would have found nothing."

"And what about Hirsch? The Swiss were neutral, weren't they? Why the Nazi gear?"

"Finance doesn't recognize borders or ideologies," Profit remarked, looking again at the print. "The one in the middle has the rank. Look at the bars. He was an admiral. The face doesn't mean anything, though."

"Leaving that aside for a moment," Crawford said. "What does this mean to you?" He showed Profit the diary notation, "OLDUVAI H 1300, 250 DAR intl. 1500."

Profit stared at the cipher for several minutes, testing different approaches. Olduvai he knew, and Dar International Airport. "Have you ever heard of Olduvai?" he asked. Crawford shook his head. "Well, it's a place near Arusha in the Serengeti. I know a bit about it because I'm an archaeology buff."

"What is it, a ruin?"

"It's a gorge, a twenty-five-mile-long gash in volcanic rock, three hundred feet deep. But it's famous because of what a couple of ethnologists found there. Louis S. B. Leakey and his wife, Mary, discovered the bones of man's oldest ancestors in that gorge. Some people even call it the birthplace of mankind."

"And 'DAR intl.' is probably the airport. But the other stuff is gibberish."

" 'Thirteen hundred is one o'clock; '1500' is three o'clock. What about '250'?"

"I don't know."

" 'H'?"

"Christ, I repeat, I don't know. It could be a person or a place or a thing."

"We have to go on assumptions," Profit said to him. "Because we just aren't going to get facts."

"All right, let's assume," Crawford said. "For the sake of argument, let's assume that 'H' stands for Hirsch himself. Let's go further and say that Hirsch is going to kill someone at the Dar airport at 1300."

"Then what about Olduvai?"

"I don't know. That doesn't fit."

Crawford put Olduvai aside for a moment. "Or should we assume that Hirsch is going to kill somebody and escape through the Dar airport on flight 250 leaving at 1300?"

"How about this scenario," Profit said. "What about the killing taking place at Olduvai at 1300—Hirsch is either the killer or the victim—"

"The victim? It was found in his room!"

"The killer, then. Hirsch kills someone at Olduvai at 1300, then he escapes through Dar airport on flight 250 at 1500?"

"Well, that way we include Olduvai, all right."

"But that doesn't make sense, if you knew Olduvai. It's an inhospitable place that ethnologists mainly visit. Christ, if you were going to kill somebody, you could certainly find a better place, unless your target was an ethnologist."

Then Profit remembered. The thought was frightening, but somehow it made as much sense as any of what they were discussing. "Ralph," he whispered so faintly that Crawford didn't hear. "Ralph?" he said again, louder. "It's Nyerere. Hirsch is going to kill Nyerere."

Crawford wondered if he had heard right. "Nyerere?"

"He's going to Olduvai tomorrow. It's been in all the newspapers. He's going to commemorate a plaque in the gorge to Louis and Mary Leakey. Hirsch's target is the President of Tanzania."

15

Perhaps it was the wine, or the two dozen oysters, or the tension, Crawford didn't know, but he felt quite giddy some six hours later when he, Farita, and James Profit left the Bistro Restaurant and headed down Nyerere Avenue to the most popular dance hall in Dar es Salaam. They had promised themselves one drink and a dance or two while they waited for the old man they were to meet.

As with any good African discothèque, the "New St. Tropez" could be heard well before it was seen. A mushroom-shaped structure resting on a concrete pedestal over an Agip petrol station, the place was a crush of white and black bodies swaying to an electric rock band.

They edged toward the bar, with Profit in the lead, Crawford holding Farita's hand. She looked stunning in cream slacks and a rose blouse. Crawford liked the quickness of her mind and her readiness to laugh. She flattered him by her presence and made him feel good. Profit handed them drinks, then leaned against the cushioned bar, looking toward the dance floor. A black girl in tight pants and a revealing bolero walked past and without a word, placed Profit's hand on her breast, rubbing her thigh against his leg.

Crawford was shocked, less for himself than for Farita, who seemed not to notice. "Either you're Robert Redford," he said to Profit, "or this place is a bordello. Maybe we should leave."

Profit ignored the suggestion, leaning over to kiss the

girl, asking if she wanted a drink. Farita smiled at Crawford, knowing an explanation was in order.

"Does that shock you?" she asked.

"No," he lied, wondering why it didn't seem to bother her. He had never been in a place like this, and he guessed that she hadn't either. "I thought it might upset you, though."

"This is Africa, Ralph," she said lightly. "It's very easygoing. You might call these girls by some name, but you'd be surprised—if you wanted they'd sleep with you for nothing; sex isn't complicated, but because they have no money or a job, they might expect you to help them out if you could. And only then. They don't push anybody."

If sex wasn't complicated, what was it, he wondered, watching the men and women in tight embraces. That was how it had always been with him and Marcia, fraught with guilt, ego, and a half-dozen other hang-ups that neither could seem to conquer. "But they're still prostitutes," he heard himself saying.

"No, they are girls having fun," she said, more forcefully now. "Please don't make it something it isn't, with names and definitions and prejudices. Nobody here sees it like that. So relax and be the *bwana* in Africa." She squeezed his hand.

Just then Crawford saw a black dwarf threading a path toward them through a forest of bodies. He had large hands and a friendly face, Crawford noticed, and he was now tugging at Profit's pant leg. "Buy me a beer, James?" he asked.

Profit looked down and patted the dwarf on the shoulder. "Sure, Herc. Tusker for Herc!" He waved to the barman, then introduced Hercules to Crawford. The little man swaggered even while standing still, as though he had long ago come to grips with his size.

"You're with the finest lady in Dar," he said to Crawford. "I call her *Bibi iko chakula.* You're lucky, Mr. Crawford. She doesn't go out with just anybody."

Farita smiled, then touched his cheek. "What a rogue, always making a girl feel wonderful," she said.

"Where's the action?" Profit asked.

"That one over there." Hercules pointed to a girl on the edge of the dance floor. Profit liked what he saw. She had plaited hair with colored beads. Her childlike eyes sparkled. He left them and went over to her.

Farita led Crawford by the hand to the dance floor. Crawford pressed her lightly to him. She moved in his arms like a column of air.

"I agree with Hercules," he said. "You are very beautiful."

She moved closer, so that now he could feel her body against his, supple and strong. They danced without talking, then Crawford looked at her. "Was that true about you being choosy?" he asked.

"I guess so, because I don't often go out." She tried to explain. "What with the work . . . and, well, most men aren't very interesting. I'd rather be by myself."

Emboldened now, Crawford kissed her lightly. She held him even tighter, until the music stopped. They walked slowly back to the bar, where Profit was standing alone.

"I guess he isn't coming," said Crawford, checking his watch.

Profit didn't indicate one way or another. "We'll give him a while longer." He put down the glass of beer. "Do you mind if I have a dance with your girl?"

The expression "your girl" embarrassed Crawford slightly. "Why, of course, if she wants."

The band was playing a disco number, and Crawford saw that they danced well together. Profit seemed to have combined all dance styles from the jitterbug to disco into one. Farita smiled over at him from the dance floor.

While he stood sipping his beer, Crawford reviewed some of the later events of the day. It had been exhilarating and altogether productive, though in the end they still had nothing more than conjecture to go on.

After lunch he and Profit had decided to confront Hirsch. Together they went to the German Settlers' Club. When they got there, Hirsch had checked out, but they'd managed to wangle their way in to his vacated room. All they found was a piece of note paper with an address on it. That had led them to the rifle shop and a man named Gabby.

Mounted heads, zebra and lion skins, umbrella stands made from elephant feet, lay in a clutter around the shop. Racks of guns and rifles lined the walls. Inside a display cabinet Crawford had seen cartridges the length of a man's large finger, and he had wondered what beast—or man—the cartridges were intended to kill. The man named Gabby had come out from the back workshop. He was polite and soft-spoken and wore a black eyeshade, similar to what a jeweler might wear. He had delicate hands and polished nails. Profit had handed him the piece of notepaper and demanded an explanation. There was some haggling, and the exchange of dollars.

Finally Gabby had motioned them to follow him into the workshop. "Those are specifications for mounting a telescopic sight on a rifle," he told them, sitting down at his workbench.

"For Mr. Hirsch?"

"Yes, he was the customer."

"On what kind of a rifle?"

Gabby did not hesitate. "A .457 magnum, double-barrel Holland and Holland."

"An elephant gun." Profit had paused. "Was it a new Holland and Holland?"

"It did not appear to have been test-fired." Then he had added, "It's a beautiful instrument, very costly."

"Yeah, right," Profit had said. "What kind of range does it have?"

"With the telescopic sight, I would guess complete accuracy at two thousand yards. It is the most powerful precision rifle made."

They had left the gun shop and gone to Profit's office. During the drive, Profit had explained that Nyerere had banned the hunting of elephant a year ago. The Holland and Holland was impractical for smaller game. But it was perfect for taking out a man over a great distance. They had enough proof, he had said, to contact the office of the President, warning Nyerere that an assassin was loose.

Profit had placed the call, but he got no closer to

speaking directly with Nyerere than a cop on the beat would get to the President of the United States in similar circumstances. Instead he had been passed from one security adviser to another. Each one had demanded to know what proof he had of an assassination plot. When Profit explained, Crawford visualized their raised eyebrows.

Profit had thought of one last idea and telephoned the man they were waiting to meet at the St. Tropez. "Proof," he had said to Crawford. "Nobody will listen until we get hard evidence. Until then, we're on our own."

Crawford had by now emptied the glass of beer and placed it on the bar. The disco tune was drawing to an end. From what he could tell, Profit had danced himself out, but Farita was as fresh as she had been at the start of the song.

"Whew," Profit said, wiping the sweat from his brow with his shirt sleeve. "I should stick to the fox-trot."

"That's crazy," Farita said. "You dance like Travolta. Doesn't he, Ralph?"

"Almost, or as they say at the carnival, close but no cigar." They all laughed.

Profit looked around the room. "He still hasn't shown?"

"I guess not."

Hercules appeared again beside Profit.

"What is it now?" Profit asked. "Do you want another beer?"

Hercules motioned for Profit to bend down to his level. He whispered in his ear.

"Jesus," Profit said to Crawford. "He's been here all along. Hercules says he was too shy to look for us in this mob, so he took a table in the corner over there. Let's go."

They left Farita with Hercules and went to a table beside the bandstand. Sitting there was a little, furry-looking man with bright, childlike eyes, tufts of white hair sticking out from behind his ears, a high forehead, and a small, sensitive mouth. He was dressed in a suit, necktie, and white shirt. He had placed his hat on the table. All in all, Crawford thought, he looked like a gentle bear that had been startled out of hibernation.

Profit greeted the man in a tone of deep affection, then introduced him to Crawford. His name was Egon Bloch.

"How long have you been here?" Profit asked, a bemused look on his face.

Egon Bloch spoke so softly that neither man could hear his answer above the music. They moved their chairs closer and leaned toward him.

"For one hour," he repeated.

Profit smiled affectionately. Bloch rarely ventured from the comfort of his bungalow in a northern Dar es Salaam suburb. He could not leave for long because of his menagerie: two or three bush babies, a Labrador retriever, several cats, and a Congo gray parrot with a salty vocabulary.

Egon Bloch had been one of the first MOSSAD operatives, from the founding days back in 1949, and had worked for the Intelligence Service during the Nazi hunts. Block had been assigned to Africa in the late fifties, and, finding Dar es Salaam a perfect place to which to retire, he had bought a house. Several years later he had moved in permanently. But Bloch still commanded deep loyalties, even in retirement, with the men who now ran MOSSAD. If anybody could help them, it was Egon Bloch; he had often helped out with Profit's CIA work.

"We've come for a history lesson," Profit started off.

Bloch looked around the room. "I would have thought of a library or a park bench. This place might be appropriate for the history of sex." He chuckled. "But I don't mind."

"Ralph," Profit said. "Show Mr. Bloch the photograph."

Bloch took the enlargement in his hand, then reached into his coat pocket for a pair of spectacles. He brought the photograph up to his nose and stared at it for several long moments.

"*Ich kenne ihnen,*" he said so softly the others didn't hear. The photograph spun Bloch into a time warp. He loosened his necktie. The images on the photo evoked in him a chorus of German voices from a horrible era of history. Voices commanding him to separate from his family: men to the right, women left. Can you work? *Jawohl,* you're fit enough. The tortured voices in freight cars, muffled sounds of people moving, moving toward oblivion.

"What's the matter, Mr. Bloch?" Crawford asked, seeing his distress. "You're very pale."

"A glass of cold water," he said weakly.

Profit trotted to the bar and got a bottle of Perrier, then returned to the table, anxious to know what had happened to the old man. Bloch gulped the water and with a conscious effort composed himself.

"Are you all right?" Profit asked.

Bloch ignored the question. "Why have you shown me this?" he asked.

"We want to know if you recognize them."

"Yes, I do, all but one. But you don't want the information for history. Two of these three are still alive. Is that correct?"

"We only *know* that one is. The one on the right is a man named Hans Peter Hirsch, a banker from Zurich. He is in Tanzania right now."

"The man in the middle," Bloch said, now in total control of himself, "is Admiral Wilhelm Canaris, the leader of Abwehr I."

Profit nodded at Crawford, then turned to Bloch. "And the man on the left of Canaris?"

"Lieutenant Ernst Hartmann, Abwehr. He was a protégé of Admiral Canaris."

Crawford remembered what Profit had said about MacKee's being naturalized and how people purchased passports after the war. "But I know the man as James MacKee."

Bloch held up his hand. "I can't say anything about your MacKee. A false identity, I would guess. This man was known during the war as Ernst Hartmann." He dug his fingernail into the photographic paper at a point beneath Hartmann's chin.

Crawford spoke. "What did you mean, the protégé of Admiral Canaris?"

"Canaris recruited the young geniuses in the Reich. They were to be the genius of the second generation of Nazis. He brought them along, formed their minds, and gave them inordinate responsibility for men of their age. His chief, or first, protégé was Ernst Hartmann. And I might add, after the war MOSSAD always feared the protégés and what they might do. But none was ever caught."

"Why were you so upset by this picture?" asked Profit.

In some way these men had stumbled onto something critical, Bloch was sure of it. After a few instants of silence, he decided to relate what he had learned from Tel Aviv in only the last day. MOSSAD had nothing to lose by his telling; they would share the information. It was the only way now to proceed.

"Ernst Hartmann is *alive,* gentlemen. I must know how and where you got this photograph?"

Crawford felt the hair on the back of his neck tingle. Bloch had just said that *Hartmann was alive,* which meant that *MacKee was alive.* Which meant that his guess about MacKee was correct. The image of the cadaver in the morgue, the lump of stripped flesh, came to mind. His assumption was correct. He felt exhilarated and confused at once: because if MacKee had faked his death and returned to his former identity as Ernst Hartmann, what they were in pursuit of now was much, much bigger than the simple matter of a few million in owed taxes.

Crawford felt as though he had fallen into a very dark pit of confusion. He was already on uncertain footing with a tax investigation of this magnitude, but now that it had grown larger, he was in the dark *and* on uncertain footing. This was an affair for national Intelligence organizations, not him, not IRS. What was he doing here? An overwhelming sense of bewilderment, of unreality, swept over him.

"How do you know?" he asked Bloch. "How can you be so certain that Ernst Hartmann is alive?"

"You are right to ask," Bloch replied. "If Mr. Profit did not tell you, I will. I am recently retired from the

Israeli Intelligence group called MOSSAD. But I still keep my hand in. I pass along things that I hear. One *never* retires. Am I right, Mr. Profit?"

"Unfortunately yes," he said.

"Yesterday I received a coded message through our consulate here—we do not have an embassy in Tanzania —that Tel Aviv had learned about Hartmann. Specifically they had learned that he is alive. Furthermore, one of our agents in Zurich has learned that Hartmann may be part of some sort of pseudorevolutionary, neo-fascist 'deep group' that has strong anti-Semitic and anti-Israeli convictions. At least some members of his group served under Admiral Canaris before he was killed near the end of the war. They had enormous wealth, which they deposited with the bank owned by Hans Peter Hirsch. The wealth increased two hundred, three hundred times through prudent investment. That money was used to finance various organizations in Europe and the Middle East—anyway, *that* is why MOSSAD originally wanted the deep group destroyed. It is highly lethal, because of its anonymity and the resources at its command."

"Excuse me if I ask," Crawford said. "It's a rude question. But how does this tie in with James Langway MacKee?"

"That is the question we are trying to answer at present." Bloch took off his spectacles. "All I know is that MOSSAD got information from Zurich that something might be happening in Africa. Since we don't have many agents—active or retired—in this continent, it was only natural for them to contact me and ask if I had heard anything. Until this evening, I had not."

Profit had listened to enough explanation. "I suggest you tell Mr. Bloch what else you found."

Crawford told him the whole story in as much detail as he could recall: about his IRS assignment, the morgue, the Nazi document on transporting Jews, the cipher in Hirsch's diary, and the rifle. Bloch listened closely, and when Crawford finally finished he put his hands on the table.

"First of all," said Bloch, "none of us is in a position to make complete sense of what Mr. Crawford has just said. We must leave that to our respective headquarters. I suggest when we finish our meeting here, we relay the facts to Tel Aviv and to Langley."

"Right," Profit said.

"And then we address ourselves to a matter we *can* do something about."

"Nyerere?" Crawford said.

"May I speculate out loud?" Bloch asked.

"Please do," Profit said.

"James MacKee was being expelled from Tanzania and sent to stand trial in America. He faked his death to avoid detection. Then he went to Zurich under his real name, Ernst Hartmann. There he met with Hans Peter Hirsch, who is now in Tanzania. We suspect that he is about to kill the President."

"Yes, just as I said," Crawford remarked.

"Their common ground, then, is Tanzania. They were disgruntled, or at least Hartmann was for being thrown out. There are hundreds of others in Tanzania who also are angry with Nyerere for expropriating their land and taking away their jobs in the civil service. What does that suggest to you, Mr. Profit?"

Profit pulled his chair closer to the table. "That it is not just Nyerere. That he will be assassinated as part of a coup d'etat. Killing Nyerere alone wouldn't do anybody any good. What they probably have in mind . . . these white settlers and Hirsch and Hartmann . . . is a takeover in Tanzania."

"Precisely what I think," Bloch said. His eyes glistened.

"The classic operating procedure for a coup," said Profit, "is *first* to take out the leader, then sow confusion, take control of the army and communications—"

"But *first* of all, kill the leader," Bloch said.

"Then we *must* get to Hirsch," Crawford said. "Hirsch is the key to it all."

"And we have to warn Nyerere," Bloch said.

Profit shook his head. "We tried, this afternoon. His security people wanted to know what proof we had. They laughed at us."

"Then we'll leave the warning up to our governments.

They can get to Nyerere directly. It's the only certain way."

"And in the meantime?" Crawford asked. "What about Hirsch?"

"Until we get help, it's our responsibility to track Hirsch," Profit said. "We know where he's going, and we know what he plans to do. That makes it a bit easier."

"But not a whole lot," said Crawford.

Bloch turned to Profit. "The two of us should remain in Dar and stand by to coordinate intelligence. Which leaves you, Mr. Crawford, as the odd man out."

"But I'm not equipped to . . ."

"None of us ever is," Bloch said. "Find Hirsch and follow him. Don't try to stop him. Once you have found him, tell us and we will send help."

The dark pit was swallowing him again, only this time it was darker and much, much deeper. The elements of time and coordination had thrust this responsibility on him: the responsibility for the safety of a President. He felt uncertain, he wanted to run. This was not in the IRS's bailiwick. He swallowed hard. "If there isn't a choice, I guess that's it," he said. The other men nodded, preparing to leave the discothèque. Crawford motioned for them to sit down again. "Please," he said. "I need *some* direction."

"Like what?" Profit said.

Suddenly Crawford got very angry. "Like what, my ass! Like how do I get to Olduvai, where in hell is the fucking place, how do I move when I get there, like—"

Profit sat down next to him. "Okay, cool it, Ralph. I didn't mean to be so cavalier. I guess we're all a little edgy."

"Edgy? I can't even think where to begin."

"Well, it sounds like Olduvai—that *is* where he's got to end up. Let me see, the nearest airport is Arusha . . . ."

"So it's back to Arusha?"

"Yeah, maybe Farita will help you out again."

When they rejoined Farita a half hour later, she was sitting alone sipping a Coca-Cola. Crawford apologized for detaining her.

"That was some summit conference," she said impishly. "Will you tell me about it?"

"Will you take me to Arusha?"

"Anywhere. Right now, though, I want to go home. Will *you* take me?"

"Gladly," Crawford said.

Outside on the sidewalk, Profit pulled Crawford aside. "Call me from Arusha," he said. "I should have some news by then. And Ralph, if you get in a spot, run. Don't be a hero."

"Not my calling," Crawford said with a grin. "I'll be in touch."

Crawford and Farita took a taxi to her apartment near the harbor, a short walk from his hotel. At the door he kissed her again and was about to say good night when she invited him inside, for a grasshopper.

"Thanks, but I'll have coffee," he said. "I've had enough booze for one night."

She giggled and put a record on the player, then told him to relax. She disappeared into the kitchen. Crawford took off his jacket and necktie and leaned into the cushions on the floor. He could hear the crackling sound of something being fried in the kitchen—probably bacon. She soon reappeared with a plate of food, offering what Crawford thought were french fries. He bit into one.

"What is this?"

Laughter sparkled in her eyes. "Like I said, grasshopper."

When they started kissing, Crawford was slow to respond. Making love really couldn't be this simple, or could it? Then he remembered what she had told him in the discothèque. As he leaned forward on the cushions, he was struck by guilt. He had never been unfaithful to Marcia. But wasn't it about time he was, just once? And what about the boys? They wouldn't even know, and if they did, what would they care? Then he thought about Farita, who was bending down to take his hand. Was it fair to her?

She answered for herself. "I know what you're thinking, or at least I think I do. Can I tell you something?"

He was now on his feet. "Yes."

"We think of love as play, like children play. It needn't be complicated. But it must be fun." She laughed and led him to the bedroom, where she slipped out of her pants and pressed him back, taking off his shirt, then helping him with his trousers. She sat on top of him naked, her face a mask of pleasure. As she moved over him, so concerned for his enjoyment, he started to shed the layers of inhibition and guilt, the demons that usually attended love, and he heard himself laughing. Farita continued to take the initiative, showing him things he thought he would never know. He never wanted it to end, but it was too new and his excitement went too fast out of control. And soon it was over.

"That felt good," she said, finally, raising herself up on an elbow.

"It did?" He caught himself. "Yes, I mean, it *did*."

16

David Monshoe delicately weighed the pouch of death's-eye powder in his hand. Now that he had done its bidding, the powerful juju was no less malignant. But the King was in Lesotho, and for the man seated across the breakfast table, that was everything. King David had become his last resort.

Earlier in London, David had sought an explanation for Loba's desperate gambit. With no concrete thoughts of his own, he had visited the British Foreign Office in Whitehall, where he spoke to Hamilton Touhy, a political officer in charge of southern African affairs. Touhy had then conferred with another official, Robert Apple of the British Intelligence Service, but neither man knew anything. South Africa was desperate, of course, they had told him, but they saw no tie-in with Lesotho. David had expressed his anxiety, then had gone to Heathrow.

His arrival in Maseru had been unannounced, even a surprise to Chief Loba. He had gone directly to his room in the palace, telling Loba's secretary that he expected to see the Prime Minister at breakfast.

"Yes, I used the death's-eye," Loba said, looking at the pouch in Monshoe's hand. "Otherwise you wouldn't be here now. So you must know how important it is."

David looked at his uncle with loathing. His mother's brother, Loba was a caricature of the worst African leaders. Fat and with an open, expressionless face, he symbolized the venality of the Idi Amins who pillaged and plundered, until finally their people rose up to destroy them. Tribal leaders, David knew, had always sold their people into one form of slavery or another. But Black Africa was maturing. The lunatics of the continent were fast dying out. Soon each country would be ruled by men of stature like Nyerere and, David thought, perhaps even himself. He placed the pouch on the table.

"You invoked a power, Loba, that should never be used," he said quietly. "I hope the end justifies the means, because if not . . ." His voice trailed off.

Loba wanted to approach the young King gently at first. "When were you last in Lesotho?" he asked.

"Four years ago."

"Then you'll see many changes. More than ever, the politics of pragmatism . . ."

David listened with half an ear. The word *pragmatism* went off in his head like an alarm bell. Pragmatism excused any illegality. Pragmatism had become a rationale for dictatorships. But what about the politics of idealism, like those of Nyerere? It was time that somebody in Lesotho tried, but it wouldn't be Loba. Never.

" . . . Mind, David, I don't defend apartheid," Loba was saying. "But we must live with South Africa. If we antagonize them, moralizing will be our destruction. So why not agree, and even take a small profit from the situation?"

"As a leader, you have morality or you don't. Unfortunately, it's part of your character that never existed."

"Be practical, David," Loba said, unperturbed by the insult. "Moral weight sinks the ship of state. You wouldn't know. But believe me, it does. We must try to strike a balance, an equilibrium if you will."

David shook his head, realizing that Loba's mind still obeyed jungle laws, where survival alone counted.

"While you are here, you should visit the villages," Loba said. "The theory you learn doesn't always work in practice. Go out and see some of the problems I face. Practical problems with practical solutions."

How could Loba know, David wondered. He had no education, so how could he understand theory?

"In your absence I have forged an alliance with South Africa," Loba said. "Prime Minister Steenkamp and I, we see eye to eye. Lesotho has not criticized apartheid, nor joined in the condemnation of South Africa. But we must grow closer together, if Lesotho is to survive. We must extend the limits of our cooperation."

Now it was coming, David thought, the reason for the death's-eye powder. The palaver was finally nearing its purpose. "What do you have in mind?" he asked.

"As a poor country, Lesotho doesn't have much to offer. But we do have labor. My conclusion was to agree."

"To what?" David asked. Loba had jumped an entire gulf of explanation.

"To put Lesothan contract labor in South Africa's mines," Loba said, watching David tense. "We are speaking of twenty-five million dollars in transfers. Hard currency." He wanted to test David's idealism. Perhaps a share of the commissions would turn his head. "Of course a percentage of the transfers is earmarked for you."

David smiled. The people would never work in the mines. Contract labor, he thought. If they were to go down into the mile-deep shafts, it would be *forced* labor. "What would *I* have to do?" he asked.

"I'd help you to tape it beforehand," Loba replied, as he had rehearsed. "A speech to the Lesothans broadcast on Independence Day. Just talk to the people."

David rubbed his leg, remembering the burning pain, the delirium and the boyhood fear of dying. Loba had told him to be a man. Well, that he was, and that he would be. "I'll do it," he said.

"Now you're starting to sound like a *king*," Loba said. But he wondered at how easily he had convinced his nephew. No arguments, no tantrums? That wasn't like David Monshoe, of that much he was certain. He knew how stubborn he was and he envied the extent of his physical courage, even when he had been a boy. He knew how the youngster had suffered after he had cut his leg. Loba had watched him fight delirium. And he had never once yelled out in pain. It had been a remarkable thing, and Loba hated the King for it.

"I'll go on the radio, just as you ask. I'll speak to my people. In fact, if you want, I'll be heard in South Africa. And for anybody else who wants to listen, I'll be heard by the world."

"Good, good," Loba said. He was frightened of David. He sensed that this student King hadn't meant a word of what he had said. Loba imagined him sitting there, across from him, savoring the moment, playing him like a mindless fish, waiting to lower the net and trap him. He became wary. Unless the death's-eye powder really had scared Monshoe to the bottom of his soul.

"And when I go on the radio, Loba, I'll tell the people this: *Don't* go in the mines!" The tortured expression on Loba's face made David feel wonderful. He wanted to laugh. "*Don't* listen to Loba! *Don't* do *anything* against your nature." He was shouting now. "You are free. Remember what that means, *free*. That's what I'll tell them. Did you hear me, Loba?"

Loba angrily threw his napkin on the table. There was really no other choice now. "I hear, you young fool. But believe me, nobody else will. Ever!" He got up from the table, rattling the dishes and tipping over a glass of water, and went to a sideboard. He looked back at Monshoe as he raised the receiver of the telephone. Then he dialed a three-number extension in the palace. "Get down here!" he yelled.

David took his napkin and wiped his mouth, then folded and placed it neatly beside his plate. He shoved the chair back and got to his feet. He knew exactly what Loba was doing, whom he had called, but he would never give him the satisfaction of knowing he was frightened.

He thought quickly. He would go down the hallway off the breakfast room toward the kitchen, then out the door onto the back terrace. He would climb over the rocks of the promontory, where he had gashed his leg those many years ago. He knew the rocks and could hide there until dark. His people would shelter him. And he would tell them what Loba was trying to do.

He started to walk down the hall.

Loba yelled, "Don't try to escape. They have orders to kill you if you try."

He pretended not to hear and continued toward the door to the kitchen.

"Catch him!" he heard Loba scream.

The kitchen door opened. Blocking it were two heavy-built white men. They wore suits and had the fleshy faces of thugs. David did not hesitate a step. He went up to them and, inches away from the face of the one on the right, he bent with lightning speed on his good leg, then snapped upward, his shoulder in the man's chest. In the same movement he butted his head against the man's heavy chin, catching it on the point. The man reeled back into the kitchen and fell across the larder table. The second man had his pistol drawn. David reached for his gun arm, but too much space separated them, and he could not swivel fast enough on his false leg. He stumbled and fell toward the man, who brought the pistol butt down on the back of his head. David crashed to the floor, but he was not unconscious. The second man bore his knee into the small of his back and pinned his arms. David heard the first man moan and stagger over to help.

He turned his head toward the open door. He saw a woman in a white dress. It was starched, like a maid's. And a white cap, like a nurse's. She had something in her hand. She leaned down and punctured the flesh of his shoulder with the needle.

17

A modest and religious man, Dr. Henry Bloosens never seriously thought that his creation would be used. But the inconceivable order was now as real as Valindaba, the name of the nuclear enrichment plant Bloosens supervised.

In the Zulu language, *vala indaba* means "The talking is over."

Prime Minister Steenkamp had chosen it for South Africa's secret nuclear complex in the Magaliesberg range near Pretoria. "Secret" because the nuclear installation was meant to be peaceful. But as the third-largest supplier of uranium, South Africa had traded six thousand tons of "yellow cake" oxide every year in return for bomb technology. The United States had sold South Africa its maiden reactor, then fueled it with enriched uranium. When the Americans unilaterally canceled the treaty, West Germany was perfecting a jet nozzle centrifuge for the separation of isotope 235, the uranium used in atomic and hydrogen bombs. And the first buyer was South Africa. Local mines fed U_3O_8 yellow cake into Valindaba, then refined it into bomb-quality U_{235}.

"I'll need to check the codes," Dr. Bloosens told his visitors. "If you'll have a seat?" He left the office.

General MacIntyre was dressed in full military rig, with braid, ribbons, and medals. The uniform gave him a confidence he didn't feel. "It shouldn't be long," he told Hartmann, whom he had met at the helicopter base in Pretoria.

MacIntyre followed orders, especially when they were issued by the Supreme Commander of South Africa's military, Johannes Steenkamp, who had summoned him last night. He was given the bomb authorization, a magnetic key, and Steenkamp's rationale. "Separating the bombs from their delivery bases makes no strategic sense, Mac," the Prime Minister had said. "I want them assembled now." When MacIntyre had tried to argue, he was challenged with an irrefutable logic. "I need the political leverage, because I expect even more pressure," Steenkamp had said.

In a way it made sense to the General. The bombs made sense, and he was not one to question.

Hartmann took out a pack of cigarettes and lit one with a gold Dupont, watching General MacIntyre pace the office. This neat touch had been Steenkamp's idea, and he liked it. If the blacks caused trouble, they would be told about the bomb. It also would keep the Americans or whoever at a respectable distance. They would not dare to intervene. "Simple and foolproof," Steenkamp had called it.

A man in a white coat entered the office, introducing himself as Dr. William Grisco, second in charge of Valindaba. "Dr. Bloosens is checking, sirs," he said, trying to sound offhand. "Please understand, this isn't a procedure we go through every day."

"While we're waiting," Hartmann asked, "can you show us the bombs?"

"I don't see why not," Dr. Grisco replied, knowing they were authorized. "We can get the okay from there by telephone."

They took an electric cart from Administration past a solid mass of reactor housing to a gentle grass mound in the hillside, where two army sentries guarded a steel door. Grisco inserted a flat-nosed magnetic key in a double lock, then asked MacIntyre to do the same with his. The door opened automatically with a whooshing sound into a vestibule that contained one elevator.

"Here we are, gentlemen," Grisco said as the elevator door opened and they stepped in. He pressed the button for G-20; the doors closed. They felt weightless in the rapid descent.

"How far down?" Hartmann asked.

"Five thousand feet," Grisco replied. "We converted an abandoned gold mine shaft."

Several minutes later, the car braked and the doors

opened onto a long narrow tunnel, again guarded by soldiers. Hartmann felt the heat from the shaft's extreme depth and heard the sound of automatic vents and coolers. Grisco and MacIntyre repeated the procedure with the keys at a door in the tunnel wall.

"Here is what you want," Grisco said proudly. The room was bare except for a canister a man's height in diameter. Gleaming, it lay on a wooden ark. Hartmann pressed his hand against the shiny surface, leaving a print that Grisco wiped clean with his handkerchief. For several seconds nobody spoke.

"Beautiful; don't you think?" Grisco finally said.

Hartmann had never seen an atomic device. This looked benign. "I'd like a rundown," he said.

"Allow me," General MacIntyre said, rattling off specifications. "Thirty kilotons, basic design, like the one used against Japan. Tactical and not very complicated. Is that right, Dr. Grisco?"

"Essentially, yes," he said. "But this is only the casing. There is nothing inside."

Hartmann thought he was being duped and said as much.

"I thought you knew," Grisco said.

"The Prime Minister told me there was a bomb here," he said, his anger rising. "A bomb, Dr. Grisco, is not a stainless-steel tube."

"Please let me explain, Mr. Hartmann," the general placated. "This is a screwdriver bomb. The basic assembly exists at Valindaba, but it is not joined into a bomb—"

"For political reasons," Dr. Grisco interrupted.

"Yes, because until now we preferred to keep a balance of power," MacIntyre said. "That's also why we haven't tested them."

"Then how do you know it'll work?" Hartmann asked.

"Because our computers say so," Grisco explained. Actual tests were not required for simple casings of contaminants. "This is the detonator," he said to Hartmann, who looked over his shoulder at the inset of the casing. There was a small digital readout above three red programming buttons. "It works by pressure, like conventional bombs when they're dropped from altitude, or by time delay. Whichever, a nitrostarch explosive bombards the uranium at twenty-thousand feet per second. There is critical mass, and chain reaction follows."

"And when that happens?"

"A blast hole that's a quarter mile wide," MacIntyre said with near-awe.

A telephone rang outside the tunnel. Dr. Grisco went to answer, then seconds later returned. "That's the authorization, gentlemen," he said, tapping the casing. "We'll have this assembled and delivered inside ten hours."

Norah was pretending to be asleep when she heard the hotel room door slam shut. From the other bedroom came the sound of a coat hanger dropping on the floor, then a muttered curse. That morning Hartmann had told her that he was dining with the P.M. *Alone.*

Norah moved her head sideways on the pillow. The day had been a waste. She had accomplished nothing positive. She had searched the hotel room, rifling through Hartmann's suitcases and clothes, but she had found nothing, neither the lists nor anything else that she could pass along to Eli Thre. If things continued this way she would be forced to confront Hartmann directly.

Norah had the feeling Hartmann was tiring of her. His conversation with her when he had returned from the luncheon party was distant and cool. Thankfully, he had slept in his own room. She tried to think if she had given him reason for suspicion. She hadn't: everything was just as it had been the evening they flew from Zurich. Except the Uyses. Her friendship with the Foreign Minister and his wife had surprised Hartmann. He had asked her about it last night. It was as though he wanted to keep a distance from everyone but Steenkamp. By association, she should do the same.

But why? What threat was Connie Uys? Steenkamp had all the power in South Africa, Marie had told her so. Steenkamp was omnipotent, now that the country was in a state of emergency. Was it perhaps that Hartmann feared questions about him, that Connie might find out something that only he and Steenkamp knew?

That must be the answer. But then, what did she know that could compromise Hartmann? In her guise as the innocent, she would know nothing about his identity. She could not tell Connie; that is, unless she became desperate and needed an ally within the country.

Now she heard Hartmann cross the carpet, then open the door and leave without saying a word to her. She swung her legs off the bed and dialed the hotel operator, asking to be connected with the Uyses' home number. Connie answered.

"Is it *tonight* we're having dinner?" he asked, confused.

"No, Marie said tomorrow, but that's not why I'm calling." She paused. He didn't help by asking what. "Can you possibly do me a favor?"

"Of course."

"Connie, the Prime Minister and Ernst are dining together tonight. Call it jealousy"—she tried to giggle but it came out wrong—"but I'd like to know where."

"Is anything the matter?" He sounded concerned.

"Not a thing, except I'd like to know that he's not gallivanting with strange women." She hoped it sounded like a joke.

"You said he's with the P.M.? I'll be back to you in a few minutes. 'Bye."

Norah got dressed, then sat with legs crossed by the telephone table. It bothered her that she didn't know where Hartmann had been during the day, and that there had been nobody to ask. The telephone rang, interrupting her thought. She picked it up immediately.

"You've no need to worry," Connie said cheerfully. "He's gone to a stag party, all right, but there won't be any women. The P.M.'s secretary told me they went to the German Club."

"Do you know where it is?"

"They don't allow women," Connie said. "And you'd have the devil of a time passing for a man."

"Do you know the address?"

"To the north of the city, in the seven hundred block of Stuttaford Street. But I don't want you going there."

"No, of course not."

"You promise?" Even if she did go, they would not let her through the door. As far as he knew, it was a club for men who enjoyed German food and music, a sort of rathskeller.

"I give you my word. I'm just about to go down to the restaurant for an early dinner, then right into bed."

"We're looking forward to tomorrow, Marie and I."

"Me too," she said, then rang off.

It took Norah five minutes to dress and leave the room. She found a taxi in front of the hotel and gave the driver the address. As they drove, the streets were so empty that even the driver wondered why out loud. Usually there were pedestrians and late evening shoppers, he explained, and the blacks by this time were en route to their townships. But now there was nobody. "I can understand about the blacks," he said. "The police have them penned in after the riot. But the whites? Maybe they know something I don't." He smiled at her, turning around.

"Will you wait for me, to bring me back to the hotel?"

"Certainly, miss, so long as I keep the meter running."

Norah agreed, looking out of the window. They had entered a district of plain-fronted shops. A water truck had sprayed the streets, so that pools of yellow lamplight reflected in windows. The taxi tires hissed past stores with signs advertising produce, wholesale meats, and electrical appliances. Norah strained to see the street numbers on the doors.

"Stop just up there," she finally said. Beyond the corner cars were parked even on the sidewalks. The taxi pulled up and the driver turned off the lights. Norah got out—she would be back soon, she said.

"Take your time, lady," he yelled after her.

Now that she was here, she needed a plan. She wouldn't go inside. The spectacle of a woman would draw the attention of Hartmann or Steenkamp. As she approached the brick building, she heard the sound of a brass band. The music made her wonder. Perhaps this was nothing more than an evening of drinking beer and camaraderie? She stood by the wall for several minutes. Not a person in sight.

By listening against the wall, she could imagine the layout inside. The band was close to the back, the members nearer the entrance. The band got louder as she walked down the side of the building to the rear. When she turned the corner into an alleyway the music got louder still, and she stopped at the point of the greatest volume. It was a plywood stage door, recessed into the brick wall. She stepped up onto the concrete lip and concealed herself in the recession. From this vantage the sounds were clear. She stood there for nearly a half hour.

Just as she was deciding to leave, the band stopped playing. She pressed her ear against the door. There were shuffling sounds, which she guessed to be the band moving off the stage, then the whine of feedback from a microphone and the voice of somebody testing the sound levels. Applause. An oath, spoken first in a language she did not understand, but repeated in English.

"As ek storm, volk my."

"If I advance, follow me."

"As ik omdraai, skiet my."

"If I retreat, shoot me."

"As ek sterwe, wreek my."

"If I die, avenge me."

Norah felt completely vulnerable. If she was caught, there would be no mercy. She wanted to run for the safety of the Uyses' house, then get the first airplane to Tel Aviv. But she stood her ground.

A man was speaking. She didn't recognize the voice, but she guessed he was Steenkamp. Parts of what he said registered as the same bigoted filth from the cocktail party. "This makes us more determined to pursue our own destiny. . . . It wants to lower us to its level. . . . Not ever. . . . This condemnation has forged us into one committed people. . . . You in this room are the soul of South Africa."

Minutes passed and Steenkamp led another oath of allegiance. It wasn't ritualized like the other had been. "All my strength is for the freedom and independence of the Afrikaaner, for the building of a New Nationalist State. In this spirit, I declare myself prepared to suffer and, if called upon, to die. I will serve with my whole heart, body, and soul."

Then she heard another voice. It was Hartmann's.

"Your Gruppenführer Steenkamp," he was saying, "has asked me to address the troopers among you in particular." He paused. "Tomorrow many of you will be at my side. You were chosen for this mission personally by Gruppenführer Steenkamp because you can be trusted and would die to ensure its success. Remember, all of us on the tanker will be following in the footsteps of Admiral Canaris. The Tanganyika Projekt was his vision, as it is now our responsibility. You are sailing to a new land, which soon will unite to form a new state with South Africa. You must all remember: be diligent and show no mercy. You have your orders."

The applause drowned out the sound of Norah's running feet. She sprinted blindly back to the taxi, her mind frozen by the realization of what she had just heard. These madmen had a plan that nobody suspected: a plan to destroy an entire continent. She replayed Hartmann's words in her head as the driver took her back to the city and the hotel. He had addressed the "troopers." Did he and Steenkamp have a private army, troopers who were not in the South African military? They must. And these men were going to guard blacks on a tanker? They were sailing to a new land that would be the beginning of a new state with South Africa. What new land, where?

She had to tell someone.

The drive seemed to take a lifetime. She had to hurry: Hartmann would return soon, and by the time he did, she had to be finished and gone. She could not hide. He would kill her for knowing what she did.

When she got to the hotel, on an instinct she went to Hartmann's bedroom. She picked up the trousers he had thrown on the chair. Nothing in them but a page of instructions and a diagram, with three digital buttons. She kicked the trousers across the bedroom and reached for the jacket. There was a sheet of paper in the pocket.

The sight of the lists took her breath away. What she

had waited for so long, what had caused her such anguish, was now in her hand. She could barely believe they were here. At the bedside light, she scanned them to make certain.

"No," she said, nearly screaming. "No." These were not the same lists she had seen in Zurich. "No, no." Tears of frustration welled in her eyes. Hartmann had outwitted her again. He had planted these sheets, wanting her to find them. Or had he? Frightened, she looked toward the door.

She went to the telephone extension in her bedroom. Now not caring who knew, who interrupted, she dialed the memorized number in Tel Aviv. There wasn't time to go through the charade of Lime Tree Catering. Eli Thre answered instantly.

"Norah, Norah, slow down," he said as she babbled into the phone. "You're making no sense."

"Nothing makes sense anymore, Eli." She was crying. "The whole world has gone mad. They are madmen. I don't have what you want, nothing of it. I've failed."

Eli Thre let her talk herself out, neither interrupting nor questioning, until finally, when she did nothing but sob, he started talking.

"You're doing fine, baby," he said. "Now listen to me, please. I'm putting you on tape. Answer my questions, like you were taught. Fact only. Put away your anger. You're doing fine, just fine. Are you listening?"

"Yes," she said, defeated.

"Okay, first, you have the lists. But they are not complete, is that right?"

"Yes," she said.

"Don't worry. It's a miracle you got what you did. Now, what I want you to do, clearly and slowly, is read all the information from the lists. How long are they?"

"Two pages, that is all." Her voice was flat. There had been at least twenty pages on the table in Zurich.

"Go ahead, you're on tape."

"Henrik Müller, tel. Munich 7490-201, LH 766. Claudio Arenas, telex 35-83455, ansback Riospan, VA 79. Robert Follet, tel. N.Y. 212-472-1669, TW 012." ·

Norah read them off more rapidly now. They were

useful, or Eli Thre would tell her to stop. She was regaining control, as she heard her voice recite numbers and codes from different countries. Most were in Europe, she noted, trying to find a thread of meaning.

"Jean Fouquet, tel. ODÉON 5538, AF 629. James Goodwin, tel. London 01-385-6498, BA 720."

She had gone through two thirds of the list when Eli stopped her.

"Hold on, Norah. This is important." She heard his muffled voice. Then less than a minute later, he uncupped the phone. "Yeah, Norah, here we go."

"What is it?"

"The last numbers on the list. They're flights." He stopped for a second. "And they all go into Zurich."

"But I don't understand."

"Give me the rest, I'll explain later." His tension now came down the phone line.

Norah read off the last of the names as fast as she could. "That's it, except for a notation at the bottom," she said.

"What is it?"

"Aeroteck (Zur) 0800 ETA 1500."

"Beautiful!" Eli exclaimed. "This is beautiful stuff."

Confident now, she told him about the German Club and the conversation with the Uyses and Dr. Blum. "Now will you explain?" she pleaded.

He did, rapidly. "Now get out of that hotel," he said. "Hartmann is dangerous. Tell Uys about all this. Now go!"

Norah dropped the receiver, thinking that she heard a noise. She ran into the sitting room and stood there, waiting for it again. But nothing came. She was jumping at shadows. Back in Hartmann's bedroom, she slipped the lists in the jacket pocket, then ran from the room. She didn't think to close the door.

18

It was nearly one in the morning by the time Norah got to the Uyses'. The house was dark, and the only sound in the quiet suburb was the far-off barking of a dog. She paid the driver and ran up the front walk. At first nobody stirred. She pushed the bell again and again. Finally she saw a light go on at the far end of the house. Connie Uys, in nightclothes, opened the door.

"My God, Norah, what's wrong?" He was shocked by the wild look on her face. Something terrible had happened. "Come in, come in," he said, tying the sash on his bathrobe.

"Norah, dear," Marie cried from the hallway. She rushed up to embrace her, then: "Are you all right?" She looked aside at her husband. "Let's calm her down. You stay with her, Connie. I'll make tea."

"What did he do to you?" he asked Norah once they were in the living room. "You went there, didn't you? I told you not to, damnit, I told you to stay away."

He was scolding her as though she were a child. It was ridiculous, because for the first time since she had left the security of Tel Aviv, she was fully a woman in control. There would be no more tears, no more mistakes. She was Norah Hirsch, and she had to stop madmen.

"Forget all that, Connie," she said in a clear and purposeful voice. "Listen to me. I want to know who in the government you can trust. Dr. Blum?"

"Yes, of course, but why?" The sudden change in Norah took him by surprise. Marie came into the living room with a tray of tea, but neither Norah nor Uys paid her any attention. She took a seat nearby and was quietly attentive.

"And who else?"

"Why . . . I guess Mac. General MacIntyre. At least he

169

listens to reason. He is neutral. The others are all Steen-kamp's men."

"Then call the General and Dr. Blum please, right now. Ask them to come here immediately—"

"You're acting crazy, Norah. Of course I won't—"

"Tell them that an agent of MOSSAD has information critical to the survival of South Africa. Unless something is done in the next few hours, your country won't exist."

"What?"

"I'll explain when they get here."

Dr. Blum took longer because he didn't drive. Or at least, he hadn't driven in fifteen years. But the old Ford was still in the garage and, for some quirk, he maintained it in good repair.

He had not gone more than five miles when he saw that the road ahead was blocked. A traffic jam at this time of the morning? he wondered to himself. Probably a wreck, he guessed. Somebody had nodded off at the wheel. And it must be bad, by the looks of the backup of traffic.

Up ahead he saw road flares and police lights. Then he recognized that this was not an accident. Police were searching each of the cars, first the drivers, then the trunks. He couldn't see why, but he was curious to find out.

He folded his hands while he waited. He couldn't believe what Connie had told him on the telephone. What nonsense, the destruction of the country and all that other business. Pure fantasy. It wasn't like Connie. But they were all under strain. The girl was probably hysterical. He had brought a sedative just in case.

"Can I see some identification?" the uniformed police-man asked when Blum reached the head of the line. He dug into his pocket for his wallet.

"What's the trouble?" Blum asked. The officer read his official ID.

"Sir, excuse the bother, sir," he replied politely to Dr. Blum, who noticed a machine pistol slung on his shoul-der. "It's only the blacks. Some of them are trying to escape the transport. Not many, but we're rounding up the ones who think they're better than the rest."

"Ah, the relocation camps. Yes, I know. But why check here?"

"The rail convoys are going through Cape Town. A bunch of trucks with blacks traveled down this road today, too. It's pretty quiet now, though."

That seemed odd to Dr. Blum. The resettlement camps were well to the *west* of Cape Town.

"What's going on?" The officer's voice was filled with surprise and anger. He dropped Blum's identity paper on the ground and turned toward the lines of cars and trucks behind them. He crouched beside the door of Blum's car and unslung his machine pistol.

Blum turned to see what was happening. Blacks were spilling out of the truck two back in the line. They hit the ground running for the safety of a field off the road and a line of protective trees. The first who had jumped out were near the treeline, but others, the slower of them, were in the middle of the field.

"Freeze!" the officer shouted. "Freeze or I'll shoot." Then there was the staccato of pistol and rifle fire. Car horns blared. Some drivers reversed their cars and pointed their headlights into the field.

One black man darted right and left, like a broken field runner. Phosphorescent orange tracers arched over his head. The arc flattened, like a beam of light locating a target. The orange stream of death touched the man, who was thrown to the ground by the bullets' impact.

"Dear God, dear God, dear God," Blum yelled at the officer sucking air into his lungs. *"What are we doing? These are our people!"*

General MacIntyre also saw something that disturbed him. But unlike Dr. Blum, he couldn't identify why. He, too, had been roused from a comfortable sleep. The Foreign Minister would not have called unless it was very important, he knew that for certain. He didn't question the order to appear. The thought wouldn't have occurred to him.

He drove from his apartment building in downtown Cape Town. The streets were deserted, which was normal for this hour. He made good time up the steep road from the flatlands into the foothills of Table Mountain, directly in back of the harbor. From here only a few lights twinkled in the city center. But as the road curved, facing back toward the harbor and the docks, he saw something strange.

MacIntyre stopped the car and looked far away at what had caught his eye. The dock lights never burned this late at night. And they extended into the harbor, like a string of Christmas beads, along the old pipeline catwalk that was once used for the offloading of oil. And there, nearly in the middle of the bay, at the end of the lights was a ship! But what a ship, he thought. It was enormous, like nothing he had ever seen. A supertanker with spotlights on its superstructure that beamed into the water. But why? South Africa had no oil to unload, had it? And imports were embargoed. Or were they? He put the car in gear and drove with greater urgency now toward Rondebosch.

They had their doubts that this slim, lovely girl was indeed an agent of MOSSAD. But MacIntyre had the corroborative evidence of the bomb and the ship. As for Dr. Blum, he had watched the Prime Minister's deterioration and knew him capable of anything, even this. And then there had been the black man in the field.

"What can *we* do?" Dr. Blum asked when Norah had finished a long and detailed monologue. "Steenkamp has the country by the throat." His hands were trembling, and he folded them so the others would not see.

"You can stop it!" Norah said, angered by the question. "Do I need to remind you? You three are Chief of Staff of the Army, Steenkamp's private physician, and the Minister of Foreign Affairs. What can *you* do?" She shook her head.

"Easy, Norah," Uys cautioned. "Accusations won't help."

"But the doctor is right," MacIntyre said. "Steenkamp has us checkmated."

"We can't be certain about the tanker, for instance," said Blum.

"Then find out," Norah said, even more angered by their equivocation.

"It's not that easy," Uys remarked. "We can't call Hartmann, or ask Steenkamp. And I'll bet the port is sealed off tight. They will be guarding the gates——"

"Can't you see?" Norah said. "Why else would the transport of so many blacks have struck Dr. Blum as odd? They're not moving them into relocation camps near Port Elizabeth. The blacks are being herded aboard that ship."

"Would your people know?" Uys asked MacIntyre.

"*I* don't even know."

"What kind of time are we talking about?" Blum asked.

Norah tapped her foot impatiently. "Gentlemen, it's now three in the morning," she said. "The ship might leave at sunrise. Should we work on that assumption, do you think?" They all nodded. "Then the first line of defense, obviously, is you, General. I suggest that the Army take over the port. And have the Navy blockade the entrance to the harbor. But act—now!"

All three heads turned to MacIntyre, who was silent. He wasn't going to be pushed by a hot-headed young woman. There was a question of loyalty. The Army was sworn to support its commander in chief. The judgment of the highest elected official was not for him to question. He had always obeyed. Her suggestion was anathema.

"I won't do it," he said. "Not that way."

"Then you're as much a criminal as Steenkamp," Norah said bitterly.

"I can't, don't you see?" MacIntyre appealed to Blum and Uys. "What she's asking for is anarchy. There are laws——"

"What about the law of conscience?" Norah asked. "You, General, hold fate in your hands. And you say there are *laws?* What about Steenkamp's laws? He makes them up as he goes. I have no doubt that he thinks this is for the best. Best for the *white* South Africans. Didn't

Hitler have similar ideas about what was best for his Aryans?"

MacIntyre felt cornered. South Africa could not be compared with Hitler's Germany. That was wrong. "I can't," he said finally.

"All right, Mac, we can't force you," Uys said. "Will you do this, though? Will you order all army units back to their barracks? In other words, will you *neutralize* the Army? Neither help Steenkamp nor hinder him? Will you do that? Ignore his orders?"

"Yes," he said, this time without hesitation.

"So where does that get us?" Norah asked.

"To Steenkamp," Dr. Blum said fiercely.

"If we stop him, we stop the ship," Uys said.

"I don't see how," Norah said.

"I do," Blum said, turning to Uys. "I know how." And Uys knew, too.

19

"See, where we were?" Farita turned the control column and banked the Cessna. "There's Loukie's camp." She banked the airplane sharper. "And the *manyatta,* over there."

"Do you think the rhino is still around?" Crawford asked.

"Long gone by now. You liked doing that?"

"The biggest thrill I've had," he said, then, seeing the little pout on her face, he quickly added, "In the category of stalking rhinoceroses, anyway." She laughed and touched his hand.

"Where is Kilimanjaro?" He wanted a look at the fabled mountain, which he knew was somewhere nearby.

"She's a cranky old witch," Farita said. "And this time of year she's shy, only comes out for a few minutes in the morning. The cloud bank up ahead is all she's showing of herself. Sorry."

"And Olduvai?" A look might be helpful.

"Way off to the west, unless you want to detour."

"No, let's get down." He opened a book on his lap. "Can I read to you?"

"Go ahead."

Crawford turned to page 97, on which were inset photographs of Mary Leakey on her knees sifting through the sands of the gorge, and her husband, Louis, proudly holding in his hand the tooth of a million-year-old elephant.

" 'If we travel north again,' " Crawford recited from the book, " 'as far as the south-east edge of the vast Serengeti plain in Tanzania, we find a complex of extinct volcanoes surrounded by land which is today quite dry for most of the year.' "

"Over there," Farita said, pointing to her left. Crawford saw the ridges of the old volcanoes.

" 'But about two million years ago, under the shadow of this great volcano complex was a lake fed by innumerable streams draining from the highlands. Animals came to drink at the lake edge. And it is certain too that these animals shared the lake shore with bands of hominids.' "

"What's a hominid again?" Farita asked.

" 'Early representatives of the human family,' it says here. The first representative of the human family."

"Read on."

" 'From about two million years ago, lake sediment and wind blown sand steadily built up and up, until now that distant past is buried beneath some three hundred feet of deposits. Earth movement associated with the geological stirrings in the Great Rift Valley drained the lake.' "

"You can see the rift, up ahead and to the left."

"I sure can," Ralph replied. A geological fault ran north and south as far as the eye could see. One side formed cliffs of dizzying heights. "It's a fantastic sight."

"And scary sometimes. It's still settling. There aren't many adults around here who don't know what an earthquake is."

Crawford read on. " 'Ultimately, a quirk of nature—' "

"Ultimately?" Farita mimicked. "God, what a word. Ten letters to mean a million years."

"Yes. 'Ultimately, a quirk of nature, in the form of a seasonal river, has carved out a gorge, slicing through the deposits of sediment so that now you can stand on the bedrock and gaze at millennium after millennium stacked neatly as a layer cake of time. . . . This is Olduvai Gorge, a 25-mile-long gash in the arid plains containing a rich array of human prehistory.' "

"That's where we're going," Farita said, excited.

"Do you think we were *all* really descended from that hominid? He was a black man, wasn't he?"

"Tell that to the bigots of the world and they'll tar and feather you. But the proof is there, all right, in black and white." She took a chart from the door pocket. "Excuse me, Ralph, I've got work to do."

Farita expertly guided the Cessna on its final leg into the Arusha airport, touching down perfectly. They taxied to a parking space, and Crawford helped her tie down the wings and chalk the wheels. Soon they were in the office of Simba Rentals, where they picked up a Ford escort. Crawford drove.

"The first thing we do," he said, "is reconnoiter."

"Why not go to the Gorge?"

"That comes later," he said. "We're going to need communications—"

"Okay, let's do the tour."

Tanzanians drove on the left, which caused Crawford several miles of disorientation behind the wheel. It seemed to him that every oncoming car or truck was heading straight at them, and when he had to make turns it reminded him of Dodg'em cars in those chilling seconds before a collision. But he picked up the technique quickly, and even found it a challenge. The last couple of days had given him a new, almost inexplicable feeling of euphoria. Maybe that was it, he thought, why people climbed mountains or took balloons across the Atlantic, because the feelings that came with success more than compensated for the dangers.

They were now approaching Arusha's outskirts. It was cooler than in Dar es Salaam. Lush fields of tea and coffee edged between the whitewashed colonial buildings on the outskirts. Practically every shop and hotel was named Kilimanjaro after the bashful mountain that rose up behind the city. The air was astringent and dry.

They pulled into a parking space around the corner from the PTT, which Farita had pointed out.

"Should I go with you?" she asked.

"I'll only be a minute. Why not get some picnic food, so we can have lunch in the gorge?" He gave her money, then set off, alone.

The PTT building was a jumble of post, telephone, and telegraph facilities all crammed together into one large room. He had to ask how to make a call.

"Go to Inquiries for the number," the attendant at the Information Counter said. "Then to Receipts for a chit. The booths are against that wall. Wave the chit to the man at Connections. When he sees you, he'll connect you with Dar."

Crawford had memorized the instructions and was able to complete steps one and two without a hitch. But once in the empty booth he could not seem to get the attention of the man in Connections.

He lowered the piece of paper, frustrated and about ready to return to the desk, when suddenly the man turned to look Crawford's way. Crawford fanned the chit back and forth, but Connections lowered his eyes again. This was insane, he thought; then he discovered the reason he was being ignored. Four other men in booths along the wall were also waving their chits. One of them had graying black hair and was dressed in a charcoal-gray safari suit. It was Hirsch, no doubt about it.

Crawford turned his back to the room. Then he peered cautiously over his shoulder. He had to keep him in sight. Hirsch stepped forward, gave the man money, then turned and went through the side door.

Crawford went outside by the same door. Up the street, Hirsch was standing near a car, reaching in his pocket for keys. He unlocked the door and got in. Crawford stepped inside an alley. He made note of the car and tried to memorize the license. He summoned his courage and stepped from the alley, trying to walk casually past the Fiat. As he glanced into the car, Hirsch looked up.

"Can I help you?" he asked. But the question was more: What are you doing?

"Ah, no. Thanks, anyway," Crawford said nervously. He kept walking. Hirsch couldn't have his description, could he? Crawford went to the middle of the block and turned. The Fiat was pulling out, rapidly, he thought. He ran down the sidewalk in the same direction, then around the corner. He could see Hirsch's car heading straight along the main road west of town. He started running again and seconds later was in his car, fumbling with his keys, trying to tell Farita, who looked confused.

"It's a red Fiat," he explained. The tires screeched when he pulled into traffic and turned right onto the main road. "Does this lead to the gorge?"

"Yes, straight," she said.

"Put your belt on," he told her. "This could get rough."

"I don't see him," she said.

"Keep looking. He may have turned off."

"There are hundreds of roads in the coffee fields," she said.

"Let's hope he hasn't time to play cat and mouse."

"What's he going to do?"

"What?" Then Crawford remembered that he hadn't told her. "Kill Nyerere, that's what."

"Oh, dear God!" she said, now straining against the belt for a sight of the Fiat, without saying another word.

Crawford looked at the speedometer and gasped. It read 120 kilometers per hour. The traffic thinned out. But they slowed, stuck behind a truck. He steered into the right lane to see if he could pass. The road was straight and slanted down. He swerved back into the left lane seconds before a bus swept past with horn blaring.

"Could he be so far ahead?" he asked.

"It doesn't seem so," Farita replied.

Crawford took his foot off the accelerator and pulled the car off the road.

"No sense in that," he said, sounding defeated. "He's hiding up there in the fields."

"Then what should we do?" They'd need a helicopter or her Cessna. "What about the airplane?" she asked. "We can go back—"

"No good. What happens when we spot him?"

"You're not armed?" She sounded incredulous. "After an assassin, and you have no gun?"

"I'm afraid so." He gave her a quick smile. "Nobody offered."

"But you could have—"

"I know, but frankly, I didn't expect this to happen—ever. And anyway, I don't know how to use a pistol."

"But you do know what you're doing?"

"Oh, sure Farita. I go after presidential assassins ... well, four or five times a day. Of course I don't know what I'm doing. This is known in the trade as ad hoc pursuit."

"Then let's ad hoc, as you say, together."

"Thatta girl," he said.

"We have one real choice." Crawford raised an eyebrow. "Keep heading to the gorge. He's going there eventually, unless he scrubs his plan."

"You're right."

He started the engine and pulled onto the asphalt surface. He kept the speedometer at a comfortable sixty kilometers. As they went, he told Farita what he knew and how they had come to be where they were. When he finished, she giggled.

"It's not a laughing matter, you know," he said. He couldn't understand the response.

"A laugh doesn't need to mean something is funny." She sounded defensive.

"Then what is it?"

"You make judgments about other people based on your own experience, as if everybody in the world was an American, or should be. And it isn't fair or accurate."

"Farita, I'm trying to understand, so please don't be angry."

She saw that he was sincere. "Laughter, or a giggle, as

you say, is a way of showing tension and, if you like, fear. That's one way *we* express it."

"I'm sorry. I didn't know." Then he smiled at her. "Any other weird responses you'd like me to learn? Laughter is sadness and sadness is joy, that kind of thing?"

She didn't think he was being witty at all. "Stop making fun of us," she said.

"I'll bet comedies out here are genuine tearjerkers."

"Ralph, leave it alone, all right?"

"I won't say another word."

The road started to bend from the highlands to the flats of the Serengeti. Some of the turns were sharp and banked on one side by cliffs, but Crawford kept his speed, even though the comfortable sixty now was a tense sixty.

They passed a sign for the Ngorongoro Crater.

Twenty miles in diameter, the crater of the extinct volcano formed a grassy basin. Once trapped within the steep walls, herds of animals rarely got out, but the Ngorongoro was more an Eden than a prison, for the balance of nature inside was perfect and harmonious.

Hans Peter Hirsch thought of the American as he sped along the southern rim. He had looked at him suspiciously, and the voice was definitely American, not that there had been any difficulty identifying him. He had seen the short trousers, the rumpled blazer, the button-down collar. America was painted on him like a flag.

Of course he still could not be certain, but he would be cautious. He had worried when Michael, the barman at the Settlers' Club, had told him that a gentleman had been asking for him and MacKee. The man at the club's front desk had said something about it, too. But he had seen no one, nor was there any reason to believe that anybody, especially an American, had the slightest idea of what they were doing. That was why he had not mentioned it to Hovagny. The Baron had enough worries of his own.

Hirsch had seen the American go into the telephone booth at the PTT, and he had tried to make himself obvious. He had to know whether he had fallen prey to paranoia or to a real hunter. The best way to do that was to draw him out.

He took his foot off the accelerator. Nobody had followed, and he had gone far enough for a hunter to catch up, even an American hunter. He wondered now if he should turn around and head back.

He came out of a sharp corner and glanced in the rearview mirror. A blue Ford Escort had come up on his tail. He leaned forward into the mirror for a closer look at the driver. Then he saw. It *was* the American.

He stepped on the accelerator and reached down on the seat. He felt the comforting weight of the 7.65 mm PPK. If it came to that, he would force the American off the road and kill him. But first he wanted to try something different. He wanted to see if the American would do his work for him. He would force the American to kill himself. He would lead him into a game of hare and hounds.

The Ngorongoro road followed the rim, then branched off to the left in the direction of Olduvai. Hirsch went right, the volcanic precipice just beyond the far lane. In places the road dipped sharply where the rim had been eroded to a level with the crater floor. Now, as he gained speed, the rapid descent into these depressions made Hirsch's stomach rise to his throat, as if he were riding a roller coaster. Again he checked the rearview. The American was struggling to keep up.

Hirsch decided to see how good the American was. He braked viciously hard. The Fiat slewed toward the embankment, then fishtailed straight. Expertly he stood on the accelerator and watched the American struggle with the wheel, almost out of control. The Escort slapped the Fiat's rear and nosed into the far lane. Hans Peter thought the American was going over the rim, but one wheel gripped the asphalt, spinning the car back into the middle of the road. He slowed to a crawl, as the American regained control and continued the pursuit, hanging back a cautious twenty-five yards. His reactions were sluggish, Hirsch thought, now certain that the Walther PPK would not be necessary.

Having exploited the braking maneuver, Hirsch now

opted for speed. His confidence soaring he touched the accelerator to the floor. A truck in the far lane blurred when it passed in the opposite direction. The speedometer read 180 kilometers, flat out for the Fiat. It couldn't give more. Five hundred yards ahead in the gradual right curve, he saw the top of another recession. A blind spot, the dip was steep. Hans Peter gripped the wheel hard and pushed back against the seat, ready for a short flight over the lip, hard through the basin, and up the far side. Only a few seconds now, and the American would be dead.

A small herd of kudu was crossing the road at the bottom of the basin, heading toward the crater floor. Their gray faces and large, bull-like bodies loomed in Hirsch's windscreen. He had to go around them; he spun the wheel right, and felt the car lurch as the tires separated from the ground, then slammed down hard. Almost in slow motion he saw the kudu scatter as the Fiat went up on its side. Now completely out of control, the Fiat spun violently end over end.

Crawford saw the ball of flame and tapped the brakes in time to negotiate the lip. Engulfed in fire, Hirsch's car had not yet even come to a stop. Crawford stopped on the shoulder of the road just as the Fiat exploded. For several minutes he watched the Fiat flame up. Even behind the windshield, the blast of heat burned his skin. He looked at Farita, but could think of no words. His mouth was dry and his eyes stung from the black smoke. The kudu were gone.

They waited for several more minutes. Slowly a feeling of triumph came over Crawford. And limitless relief. He had faced Hirsch and beaten him. Still without words, he reached over to Farita and drew her close. Together they watched until the flames died out.

"I'll have to look," he said finally.

"He can't be alive," she said.

"I have to make certain."

The car body was like a griddle. Crawford touched the door handle and brought his fingers away quickly, then wet them with saliva. Kneeling down, he saw inside the front seat and turned to Farita, telling her not to look. Hirsch was charred beyond recognition.

20

Eli Thre bit a fingernail so it bled.

"So the assassin is dead," he said to himself. And now the jigsaw was complete. He was not just going to defuse this thing. He would turn it to MOSSAD's advantage.

An assistant put a cup of coffee on his desk. He hadn't slept for thirty-six hours. And it was going to be another few hours yet before they knew. In real terms the gamble was not worth the consequences of failure. But what choice did they have?

Throughout the long night, since Norah and Egon Bloch had called, he had coordinated with the Americans. They had been slow because, of necessity, the President and the National Security Council were brought in. Winfield Cowles and Andrews at the CIA, whom he had contacted first, had understood immediately. They had had much of the same information sent by their man in Dar. But Thre had offered an offensive, and that required decisions from the full American security establishment and the President.

Earlier he had put together the strategy during the meeting with the Prime Minister. He had driven to his home and laid out the facts. Thank God the P.M. was a military man, understanding better than most the need for immediate decisions.

"To hell with them," the Prime Minister had said of his Cabinet. "We go now!" Seconds later he had ordered the Minister of Defense to put a StarLifter in the air, loaded with two companies of commandos, many of whom were veterans of the Entebbe Raid. "Get them within range of Dar, then circle them," the Prime Minister had told his defense chief. "I'll get back to you if we get immediate permission to land." He had sat there pensively for several more minutes. Then he said, "I want to speak with Nyerere. Let's get him now!"

The two heads of state had spoken for the better part of thirty minutes. From an extension in the Prime Minister's house Eli Thre had listened and offered his advice, then outlined what must be done. Nyerere was a great man, he thought. For who else would take the risk? He gained by having the Israeli commandos, but he didn't have to agree to the full Israeli position. Yet he had. Even while he listened, Nyerere had ordered the GSU to find Hirsch.

"I will go only if they find this assassin Hirsch," Nyerere had told them. "That's a risk I will not take. If we get him, I will go to Olduvai, as planned, and we'll see what vermin come from under the rocks."

"And you understand fully about this group?" the Prime Minister had asked. The plan, as it had been worked about by Eli Thre, had been hastily explained, and the Prime Minister wanted to be perfectly certain that Nyerere knew what he was doing.

"As I understand it, this is a fanatical group of South Africans and neo-Nazis."

"Among others. The members coming into Dar seem to be from all countries."

"International scum reborn, is that it?"

"That seems to be the shape of it from the information we have. There doesn't seem to be much clear ideology. But they are a menace to us all."

"I appreciate your help in this. It is deeply embarrassing."

"According to our sources, the members are to come together in Zurich. They will leave in a chartered Boeing 707, and should land at Dar International just after you are supposed to be dead."

"And these people are responsible for helping carry out the coup?"

"From the information we have, yes."

"Then your commandos, Mr. Prime Minister, can do what they want with them. Kill them for all I care."

"We want them alive," the Prime Minister had replied.

"When they land at Dar International, we will be waiting. They will be trapped, I guarantee it."

"And what of the others?"

"Are your troops loyal?" A question for a question.

Nyerere paused for a moment. "The GSU are," he had answered finally.

"Then our commandos will work with GSU. Together they should have no trouble from the others, the vermin, as you say, Mr. President," the Prime Minister had said. At the end he had raised an important point with the Tanzanian leader. "You don't have to go," he had said with great understanding. "You needn't go to Olduvai."

"Thank you, sir," Nyerere had replied, equally sincerely. "If I don't go I will never know. I will never be certain who is loyal. This is a great tragedy for Tanzania."

"All right," the Prime Minister had replied reluctantly. "The charter flight is from an outfit called Aeroteck (Zur). Our understanding is that the aircraft's transponder is American military, code 0473. It's IFF, Mr. President, so have your people ask them to squawk. When that number comes up on the radar screens, ferry them in, like everything is normal. Our unit commander will be on the ground by then. He'll take it from there." Disconnecting, the Prime Minister had turned to Eli Thre. "It's set," he said in a soft voice.

The Prime Minister had lifted the telephone one last time, to the Defense Minister.

"When the StarLifter approaches Tanzanian air space, tell them to land. Do *not* circle."

"I want an emergency Security Council meeting this morning," he said. It was now 6:30 A.M. and the President was standing in the Situation Room of the White House surrounded by electronic screens, computers, and communications equipment. "The UN must know about this." The aides who listened were impressed. They had not seen him so determined, as though the bottled-up years of ineffectiveness for the President were now being released. He replied to an objection from his Secretary of State. "I don't give a damn," he said, angrily. "Believe me, this thing will not happen. It can't!"

Winfield Cowles and Andrews from the CIA had briefed him hours earlier on the crisis, then coordinated with Uys in South Africa and, later, with the Israelis. The United States was to handle the South African connection, leaving Tanzania to the Israelis.

"And the fleets?" the President asked his Chief of Naval Operations, who frowned.

"Four days from South African waters."

"I want them moved, anyway. What's the status on the tanker?"

"It's in the harbor," Cowles replied.

"What the hell are they doing, then?"

"Uys won't tell us, sir," Cowles replied. "But he doubts if the ship will leave."

"And what do you think he means? I want certainty, not doubts."

"Uys reasons that he can stop this thing once Steenkamp is out of the way."

"How does he plan to do that?"

"He won't tell us."

"Wonderful, sweet and wonderful. He won't tell us. We've got a crisis like never before, and he won't tell us?"

"No, sir," Cowles said.

"Then forget him. What did you figure out about troops?"

"The risk obviates them. Uys still doesn't know for certain about the bomb. Those blacks are hostages, sir. Steenkamp will blow them up."

"And Steenkamp refuses to talk?"

Cowles nodded. "You heard what he said. 'Stay out of it.' "

The President balled his fists. "The tanker must not leave South Africa's territorial waters. You talked again to Tikkoo?"

"Yes, sir. Our specialists should be there in an hour. They went in F-4s."

"London?"

"Yes, sir."

"Will it work?"

"If the ship leaves, yes, sir, I believe so. It has to work. We have nothing else."

"All right, then get me the Israeli Prime Minister."

Within seconds he was put through to the Prime Minister of Israel, with whom the President had enjoyed a productive, if sometimes strained, working relationship.

"You can't talk to Steenkamp?" the Prime Minister asked. There was a note of amazement in his voice. "He must know that he can't succeed. Can you persuade him?"

"Of what?" The question answered itself. The Prime Minister of South Africa was a madman.

"I understand." The Prime Minister paused for an instant. "Rest assured, Mr. President, we have Tanzania under control . . . or will in a few hours' time. But that's nothing if you don't stop the tanker."

The President knew all too well. If that many black South Africans were harmed in any way, let alone killed, the Cubans and Russians would wreak a terrible vengeance on white South Africa, and morally, America would be helpless to prevent it from happening. Privately he admitted to having pushed South Africa too far. Part of Steenkamp's madness was his fault.

"Have you told the Russians?" the Prime Minister asked.

"I will, before we take this to the UN."

"My only thought is that relatively few people know. If we can do what we hope, there is no need to alarm the Russians. And if we fail, they'll know anyway."

"Thank you, Mr. Prime Minister, let's keep one another advised." They rang off.

Now that a counteroffensive was in place, there was nothing left to do but worry, and Eli Thre's thoughts automatically turned to Norah. She had done the impossible. Without her, Egon Bloch's input would have told them only half, if that much. And with half they would have had nothing. Now that her part was finished, he wanted her home.

She had no way of knowing about Hans Peter

Hirsch's death. But he doubted if she would care. No, he reconsidered. There would be something in her that would mourn, if only a little. For despite what Hirsch was, he had sheltered her. He had been her stepfather. Eli wondered what that would mean as the red light flashed on the emergency telephone. "Yes?" he said, picking it up.

It was Norah.

"Eli, Dr. Blum and Uys are certain. They can do it," she said, breathlessly.

"What, Norah? What can they do?"

"I think they're going to hold Steenkamp. It's the only way, Eli. The ship can't leave without his instructions."

"How do they mean to do it?"

"They won't say."

"All right. Now, what about you?"

"Like you, I can't do anything but wait."

"Has Steenkamp closed the airports?"

"I don't think so."

"Then I'm giving you another direct order. This time you are to obey it. Get the first plane out to anywhere, now! I want you in Tel Aviv by tomorrow noon. Do you understand?"

"I have one more thing to do," she said, and disconnected the phone.

21

Midmorning, the room was dark and smelled of damask and dried leaves.

The man on the bed opened his eyes and stared at the ceiling, remembering that distant morning on the ridge. He breathed deeply, for the memory gave him pleasure. Even now he could smell the grass, the soft tufts he had lain on as he watched them moving down the escarpment. They were Mau Mau *bibis* taking supplies to their men, who hid by day in the volcanic rocks, storing energy for their forays in the night. He had spread his legs and raised his rifle. The power in his finger had been transformed into that of a god as he touched the trigger. He had absently wondered as he inspected them through the telescopic sight. Who this time would live and who would die? Finally he had chosen three targets; then the bullets, all perfectly timed, had exploded from the barrel.

He gave a little sigh as he now swung his legs off the bed and went to the dressing room. He had selected the clothes last night, still folded neatly on the chair. Slowly he stepped into the forest-green trousers and cinched the belt. The shirt felt cool on his skin as he did up the buttons. Next came socks and black riding boots. Then he went to a box inlaid with ivory. He lifted the lid and looked inside. Reverently he took out the neck chain, fastening it behind his neck.

The Abwehr amulet that Canaris had given to him gleamed at his throat.

He went downstairs to the Trophy Room and opened a glass-fronted cabinet. The clean smell of oil delighted his senses as he reached in and stroked the smooth wood of the stock. He took the .457 by the breech and looked down the twin barrels, tooled with precision rifling. Balancing the rifle in the crook of his arm, he brought out a leather shell case and slung the strap over his shoulder.

Outside, the sky was clear and the air perfectly still. Chakka, his bearer, waited for him.

"Is the target ready?" he asked finally in Swahili.

"Ndio," Chakka replied.

Together they walked away from the house. Resting against a tall thorn tree was a jute bag filled with sand. The head of a Thompson's gazelle lay on top.

"Mazuri," he said. "Okay."

They paced off a thousand yards.

"Lay it down here," he said, as Chakka spread a cloth on the ground.

He lay flat on his stomach and tucked the butt into his shoulder. He then slid two blunt-nosed cartridges into the barrel. As he focused the telescopic sight, the gazelle head seemed not more than an arm's length distant. He sucked in a breath of air, then let it out slowly, applying steady pressure to the trigger. The Holland and Holland exploded, recoiling into his body.

Instantly he got to his feet. The bullet had entered the gazelle head to the right of where he had aimed. With his thumbnail he compensated for the error by turning the grub screw on the mount. Again he got into position, aimed, and squeezed. The rifle bucked against his shoulder. Without looking, he knew this shot was true. Chakka melted a small drop of sealing wax onto the scope's screw to hold it in place, then wrapped the rifle in soft leather.

He went through the plan in his mind. He would be concealed above the target. When Nyerere came into view, he would shoot twice. Then confusion or hysteria. He could stay on the rock or ride off. It didn't matter, because no one would guess. He had planned too well for anyone to interfere.

They walked to the stables, where a gray mare was being led into a trailer hitched to his Range Rover. The horse was his favorite. Sure-footed and solid, she balked at nothing. He slapped her rump and told the groom to close the gate.

"You've put everything inside?" he asked Chakka and the groom. "The saddle, the bridle, the gun sheath?"

"Not the sheath," Chakka said, apprehensively. *"Bwana,* the strap broke."

"All right," he said. He would carry the rifle across the pommel of the saddle.

He put the rifle next to him on the seat and drove down the dirt road from Tembo, raising a dust cloud in his wake that could be seen for miles.

The Baron was precise in everything he did. It was how he had stayed alive, through the war and during his escape from the Allies. Baron Hovagny planned ahead in minute detail. He never had to scramble because he thought of every contingency. When the unexpected arose, it was expected.

The Baron had planned. He had known the inevitable outcome of the war. One after another, the battles had turned against the German war machine. Then came the invasion. Normandy was a wound, he had known, that would bleed all life from the Third Reich. But before the Allies could trap and imprison him, he was in Switzerland, then from Genoa by steamship to Dar es Salaam. Those who didn't plan deserved their fate.

Yesterday, with Chakka by his side, he had covered this same route. He had chosen a site above the road, which curved into the Olduvai Gorge like a coiled black mamba. He had lain on the smooth rock and judged the angle of fire. He had imagined what it was going to be like. Nyerere's limousine would slow to negotiate the sharp hairpin. The President would show himself, as he always did. From the waist to the top of his head, a perfect and easy target.

Now the odometer showed another three miles before he would reach the turnoff. He was beginning to pick up signs of the presidential visit: an occasional flag tied to a telephone pole, groups of natives walking in the direction of the gorge, and police guards stationed at half-mile intervals along the President's route. Nyerere went everywhere by car. He had not flown since before Independence and helicopters were as alien to him as anything on earth. Nobody seemed to know why, but he feared flight —a superstition that would be his undoing.

The Baron slowed the Range Rover and turned off the asphalt highway onto a dirt track. He stopped and engaged the lever for four-wheel-drive, then started again through the dense bush. Two miles farther along he stopped and cut the engine. The silence of the terrain was unearthly, as he unhinged the gate and backed the mare from the trailer. First he put on the bridle and tied the reins to the door handle. Next came the saddle blanket and saddle. Smooth to his touch, it was English and made of fine leather. He cinched the girth, then took the rifle from the seat, mounted the horse, and cantered in the direction of the gorge.

Crawford was struggling with a can of peaches.

"I can't do this," he said, handing the opener to Farita, who laughed happily. They were sitting on the seat that

Crawford had taken from the car and put in a clear spot she had chosen for their picnic above the gorge. Secluded, they could see into Olduvai without being seen themselves. Watching Farita, Crawford leaned back against a rock, then tilted his head into the bright sun. His nostrils filled with the scents of wild flowers, sage, and African mesquite.

"Do you feel better?" she asked, threading the opener around the rim of the can.

"Much," he said.

After the accident he had felt heady and wanted to return to Dar to follow events. But the Arusha airport had been closed. The adrenaline in his blood took time to dissipate. But the high he had experienced in the chase now left him lethargic and spent. He had done enough; he had killed the assassin.

"Stop that," Farita scolded, brushing his hand off her breast. "One thing at a time, sir."

"But I only want one thing."

"Eat or make love, I mean. It's your choice, silly."

"Let's have lunch, then drive into the gorge. We have to find a good parking place."

Larger and larger groups of Tanzanians were walking into the gorge. They were coming to see their beloved "Mwalimu." There would be thousands by the time he arrived.

"It really is a layer cake," Crawford said, looking into the gorge. To his eye it resembled pictures he had seen once of the Grand Canyon, without a river flowing at its bottom. The layers of rock were an ocher color, like the American Painted Desert. He wondered what each of the striated levels would mean to an archaeologist.

Farita handed him a cheese sandwich and a paper cup of wine. He ate quickly, thinking hungrily of the dessert that was to come. He sipped at the wine.

"If I ask you a question, you won't get angry?" Crawford said.

"That depends."

"The wine and all. Aren't you rather . . . well, urbane, for a young woman from around here?"

It was a fair question, she thought, and one she didn't mind answering.

"I was lucky, I guess," she said. "A teacher I had thought I was attractive. He encouraged me to become a stewardess. The job literally opened up the world, and I learned fast."

"What about lovers?"

"Oh, I had those. They were sort of teachers, too, in London and New York, and later in Germany. Through them I learned about how Westerners do things. Wine, for instance. Clothes, makeup, grammar, conversation, for others. Like a finishing school, but it was better."

"Why did you come back here?"

"It's my home," she answered simply.

"I wouldn't have," he said.

"But then you're not African." She wanted to explain but didn't know if she could.

"How does it draw you back?"

"If you can't see why, I can't help you."

"Try," he said, taking her hand. "I want to know."

She shook her head. There were ways people felt that went beyond explanation. If Ralph gave himself the time, he might feel the same.

He hoisted the car seat on his shoulder, while Farita collected the picnic debris. They climbed down the ledge, put everything in the trunk, then drove the Olduvai Road into the basin of the gorge.

Crawford watched the people who lined the road. They wore native costumes with feathers and beads and carried drums and whistles. For old and young alike, a glimpse of their President was worth a morning's wait.

"Look at that one," he said, changing gears into second around a hairpin. A young man had climbed a telephone pole and was comfortably perched on top.

"Don't you turn out for your President?" she asked.

"Oh, some people do, but most of us see him enough on television. Anyway, the Secret Service won't let you near him."

"Normally Mwalimu could walk across the country without anyone harming him. And millions would come. You don't hurt what you love."

"He stays cooped up in the car, I hope."

"Today he will. Usually he waves to the people from an opening in the roof."

"Is it bulletproof?" Like all Americans, he remembered the assassination in Dallas twenty years before.

"It's just a hole, like a sun roof."

Crawford had been so keyed up about finding Hirsch, he had not stopped to consider just how he had planned to kill Nyerere. But now he did. The gunsmith, Gabby, had said that the Holland and Holland had a range of two thousand yards. That meant Hirsch would have fired the rifle from a great distance. He would have concealed himself carefully in the brush or the rocks—but where? He had never been a student of assassination, but he had read parts of the Warren Commission Report. Oswald had been concealed, well concealed. And he had chosen his place of hiding for the vantage it commanded over the plaza and, most important, for height. If you were going to assassinate somebody with a long-range rifle, you would go for height. And if height was the key to success, Hirsch had chosen well. The gorge was tailor made for an assassin.

"Look!" Farita exclaimed. "The monument."

They had come out of the last turn. Off the road in the distance was a tall obelisk of stone quarried in Tanzania. The base was covered by a shroud, which would be removed as part of the ceremony. A policeman stood in the middle of the road, waving them to stop.

"Hello, Officer," Crawford said, smiling. "Can we go for a look?"

"You'll have to turn around," he replied. "We're clearing the road of cars soon. If you want to see the President, you'd better find a place fast."

"Thanks," Crawford said, reversing the Escort and driving up again to where they had just been. He turned to Farita. "I'd almost forgotten. Is the camera still there?" He had brought his Pentax for tourist pictures, but in the chase and the excitement after, he had forgotten about it.

Farita leaned over the seat. The camera had fallen on

the floor. She took off the lens cap and snapped a picture of Crawford.

"You're nearly out of film," she reported.

"There's more back there somewhere," he said, then, "What spot looks good to you?"

"Right up there." She pointed to the soft shoulder on the edge of the asphalt. It was on the outer edge of the sharpest hairpin. "He'll slow to a crawl past here."

Crawford stopped and reversed, the front wheels of the Escort just resting on the asphalt. They wouldn't be more than a few feet away from the limousine when it passed. He wanted a good look at the man he had saved. "This is perfect," he said. "A ringside seat."

"Take my picture, okay?" Farita offered a model's profile.

"Not like that," he said. "Go out and stand in the road." Crawford opened the door and snapped her picture. "Now come on back. It's getting too crowded around here."

The Africans were everywhere now, and the sound of their anticipation was getting louder by the minute. They sang and danced and cheered, making President-watching into a party. Crawford felt comfortable among them. They peered into the car at him and smiled. He loved being where he was, and he told Farita so.

"The enthusiasm is infectious, isn't it?" she asked.

"Lord, yes. It makes me want to get up and dance with them."

"Then why don't you?"

He looked at her. "Give me a little time and I just might." He checked his wristwatch again. "It shouldn't be long now, if he's on schedule. Another eight or ten minutes."

Farita sat up, like a schoolgirl.

President Nyerere felt the sun and wind on his face. "Is everything set? he asked the man on the seat next to him in the limousine.

"Yes, sir," the GSU colonel replied. "But is there no other way?"

"Not if I'm to be sure," Nyerere replied. "The vermin must be found."

After they had gone into the gorge, the GSU colonel was to report an accident. It would be broadcast on national radio: Nyerere has been shot. Nothing more than that. One simple message that would trigger the coup. Those who responded to the broadcast message were traitors. They would be arrested by GSU troopers assigned to every battalion and police brigade in Tanzania. No matter who they were, black or white, they would be brought swiftly to justice. The penalty for their crimes would be death. Then Nyerere would return to Dar. His country would be clean.

"This must be right," he said to the colonel. "They mustn't suspect."

"And you're certain about the assassin?"

"That he is dead? Yes, as certain as anyone can be."

"No other backup?"

"Not that we can tell. The Swiss was working alone: it was easier for security reasons."

"The others," the colonel said. "They are horribly desperate."

"The fascists?" Nyerere said. "Yes, very desperate or crazy."

"Maybe both," the colonel said.

"How soon?" Nyerere asked, now growing apprehensive.

"Another few miles yet, sir." He felt the tension.

"You're certain of GSU, Colonel?"

"Positively, sir."

"And the Israelis?"

"At Dar International and waiting."

As though it were a final decision, Nyerere turned to the colonel and said, "All right, let's get it over with."

The Baron kneeled on the rock, then found a comfortable shooting position.

The cartridges felt heavy, as he slid them into the twin chambers of the Holland and Holland. He rested the barrel on the rock and aimed through the scope. The line of sight fell directly on the hairpin turn, just as he knew it would. He scanned the field of vision, taking practice aim on the heads of African bystanders. The angle of fire was five or ten degrees off target. Though Nyerere would be moving, he would appear fixed until the limousine went into the curve. He would wait for the last second, when the car crawled into the turn.

He had looked for signs of danger, but there was nothing but normal security. A thought crossed his mind that this kill wasn't much of a challenge. Hunting leopard required more cunning than shooting a President. Smiling, he wondered how he might have made it an even contest. Maybe if he stood in the middle of the road?

He rolled over on his side. Two Egyptian condors were specks high above in the sky. The ridge was clear, as was the terrain to either side. The mare pulled at some brush, but the reins stayed tied.

He slid into position when he heard the wail of sirens. The lead car of the motorcade passed swiftly below.

"For Protégé," he whispered, putting the scope to his eye.

The Africans around Crawford went wild. Now that Nyerere was close they were in a frenzy, dancing, beating on drums, blowing whistles, singing, and chanting. The din was overwhelming.

"He's coming," Farita said needlessly.

Crawford put the camera to his eye and caught a Masai warrior with a long spear. His body was covered with red dirt. Crawford took one photo after another.

They heard the siren. The crowds on the side of the road pressed forward. Farita told Crawford to put the camera down and look. He tried to advance the film for another shot, but the lever didn't move.

"Aw, Jesus," he said so that Farita heard.

"What's the matter?" she asked.

"The damn film." He held out the camera.

"There's a roll in the back. Hurry, Ralph. He'll be here any second."

Crawford strained over the seat. As he was reaching

for a box of film on the back deck, a reflection caught his eye. It came from several hundred yards away, on the ridge, near where they had picnicked. He wondered what it was, a shimmer of sunlight off metal, as though somebody were signaling with a heliograph. He turned and changed the film. Now he was ready for the President.

He raised the camera again to his eye, advancing the film as he shot without moving it from his face. Click! a dancer suspended in midair. Click! a drummer with ecstasy in his eyes. Click! an old toothless woman.

"I see him, Ralph! He's standing up!"

Crawford didn't hear her for the noise. He framed a mounted policeman. Click! He wore jodhpurs, polished black boots, a maroon beret. Across the saddle, an Enfield carbine. Through the lens, Crawford followed him.

Sunlight glinted off the shiny breech.

Like the tumblers in a lock, everything fell in place.

"An assassin on the hill!" he screamed. "He has a rifle! They're killing him! They're going to kill him!" He looked up the road. The black limousine, Nyerere standing in the sun roof. The killer wasn't Hirsch. "Oh, my God," he shouted.

He reached down to the ignition and turned the key. The motor failed to catch. He held the key in the start position. The Escort bucked forward, propelled by the starter motor. It was now almost blocking the road. Farita brought her arms up and braced against the door. She started to scream when the limousine slammed into them.

Crawford crawled over Farita and threw open the door. He fell to the ground, then quickly picked himself up and stumbled in the direction of the limousine. He caught a brief glance of Nyerere as he threw himself between the gunman on the ridge and the President. He heard an explosion. A bullet whined past his shoulder and, he saw, pierced the thin metal of the limousine, directly in line with the President. Through the window he saw Nyerere fall onto the seat, then roll on the floor of the car.

The second explosion went off in Crawford's head.

What happened? he thought dreamily, feeling the hole where his stomach had been. Part of him was falling out. He had been whole, and now they had torn at his flesh.

He slid down the side of the car and rolled on his back. He looked up at the sky, a lovely blue, and he wondered what he and Farita would do when all this was over. Where was she? And where was Marcia, was she off with the boys, playing?

The sticky wetness on his legs, was that part of him, too? He wanted to raise his arm and touch the spot. It wasn't that bad, was it? He would make it, the President would . . . Oh, the President, was part of him falling out, too? He opened his eyes as wide as he could, to see the President, but nothing was there but sky. He felt calm now, peaceful and silent, and nothing could touch him again. He welcomed the dusk. The sky closed to a pinpoint of blue, then it darkened, gray, then black, then nothing.

Farita ran from the car and bent over him.

"Anatoka damu vibaya," she repeated again and again. But nobody touched him. *"Iko wapi daktari."* She saw the light disappear from his eyes and bent down closer, tears falling from her eyes.

"Leave him!" the GSU colonel said. Crawford had already left them all. "Get out of the way," he said, shoving Farita aside. "Move out," he ordered the driver. "Get the President to safety."

As the limousine backed around and with tires screeching burst up the hill from the gorge, the GSU colonel wondered where the shots had come from. He scanned the ridge. Near the top he saw a slight movement, a touch of gray disappearing behind a boulder. He ran and spoke rapidly in Swahili to a group of Masai warriors, then he sprinted up the road and into the bush on the incline. His legs pounded at the dirt. Now he saw: a horse and rider. Walking! So cocksure, he was walking!

The colonel increased the pace, so that his lungs burned. He checked his stride and glanced back. The Masai were right behind. Then he pressed on.

Seconds later he was throwing distance from the man.

Hovagny heard his footsteps and turned in the saddle. He jabbed the horse's flanks, but the mare bucked and slipped in the loose gravel.

"What—" Hovagny started to say.

"Mwuaji kwa hila!" the colonel yelled at him. *"Mwali-mu ni hai!"*

Hovagny's eyes opened wide.

The colonel turned to the Masai who were standing behind him. *"Kuchoma ni mkuki muzungu,"* he said. He started to repeat the order, but there was no need. Spears whistled past his ear. Thrown with an accuracy that killed lions, all four hit Hovagny in the chest. Such was the impact, the colonel did not bother to look. *Mwuaji kwa hila.* The assassin was dead.

22

Sir Derek Erskine stood in the antechamber of the South African Parliament, reading a private diplomatic dispatch. He was in Parliament this morning to hear the Prime Minister's speech. All the diplomats were.

"Well, well, old fellow," said Brigadier M.M.O. Cunningkim, a member of Parliament. "What news?"

He handed him the dispatch. Sir Derek had no reason to keep the Whitehall message secret. Soon it would be public knowledge. "They shot Nyerere. Dreadful . . . just dreadful," Sir Derek said.

"Who did?" There was surprise mixed with pleasure. Cunningkim disliked all blacks.

"It's not clear, either mercenaries or a junta."

"A coup?"

"Looks that way." Sir Derek shook his head sadly. "And I thought Tanzania was stable."

"So the coup succeeded?"

"We don't know. The Foreign Office is reporting only that Nyerere was shot."

"And killed?"

"It's too early to tell."

"Ummmmm," Cunningkim replied, secretly wishing.

"He was a decent bugger, really," Sir Derek said. "I had great respect for him."

"Come off it. He was a white baiter."

"You're wrong about him," Sir Derek said, purposeful. "Nyerere was a humanitarian." He looked to the chamber door. "Shall we go in?"

In its design, Parliament was a smaller version of the British House of Commons. Government benches faced the opposition. The sergeant-at-arms, in a black tailcoat, greeted the members and guests as they went down the center aisle to their seats. There was a festive and excited air, as every member, for once, was in attendance, anticipating the words of the Prime Minister. Now, ten minutes before Steenkamp was scheduled to begin, Cunningkim decided to forego taking his seat and joined Sir Derek in the gallery.

"What's Steenkamp got up his sleeve?" Cunningkim asked.

"More gibberish, probably. Let's hope he doesn't speak in that dreadful Afrikaans."

Cunningkim leaned over the balcony. From where he was, opposition benches were on the right, government on the left. Front benches were occupied by government ministers, the Cabinet, and their deputies. Cunningkim noticed one seat, the first on the front bench. It was empty.

"He's not even here," Cunningkim said, slightly offended by Steenkamp's breach of etiquette. "It would be uncommon of him to keep Parliament and the diplomatic community waiting." He checked his wristwatch.

"Quite," Sir Derek said. "And it's after the hour." He felt a hand tap him on the shoulder. It was his American counterpart, who whispered in his ear. Sir Derek and the American got up and left the gallery.

Twenty minutes later, the atmosphere changed. The press at the far end of the house grew restless. Polite chatter was now a loud murmuring. Members left their seats and gathered near the back benches. Decorum was gone.

Then a hush fell over the room, as the sergeant-at-arms walked the length of the aisle to the Speaker's box. He banged a gavel, then waited while guests put on earphones for a simultaneous translation from Afrikaans.

"Honorable members, ladies and gentlemen," he began in a monotone. "Prime Minister Steenkamp, as you know, was to address this morning's session. However, I was just informed. His plans have been changed. He withdraws the privilege of speaking to you today. He offers sincerest apologies for the inconvenience."

He banged the gavel again, as the house erupted in noise. Eyes followed as he went to the gallery reserved for relatives of members. He spoke to the Prime Minister's wife, who followed him out at an unsteady pace.

Lena Steenkamp was driven from Parliament to the Groote Schuur Hospital. At the door she was met by a nurse, who led her toward the operating rooms. Lena was an elderly woman; her face registered shock, for the sergeant-at-arms had told her some of what she was about to see.

He looked almost normal, she thought, after she had entered the intensive-care unit—except for the horrible tubes attached at his throat and arm. Above his head, she saw monitoring screens. Thank God for that. His heart was strong and beating regularly. So then what was wrong?

"I'm so very sorry, Lena dear." It was Dr. Blum, dressed in green surgical robes and a cap. A surgeon's mask hung from his neck. Behind him stood Connie Uys.

"How is he?" she insisted, a trembling in her voice. She clasped a handkerchief.

"This is not easy to say," Dr. Blum replied, then added more softly, "He has suffered a massive stroke, dear Lena. Your husband, our Prime Minister, is completely paralyzed."

"Noooo," Lena wailed, stumbling toward his bed, refusing to believe. She then fainted on the floor.

"Sedate her," Blum ordered a nurse.

It had been so simple, Blum thought. Carrying the black bag into the house, sounding cheerful and so very matter-of-fact about the checkup, then feigning surprise at the high blood pressure. Steenkamp had been so helpless, so trusting, as Blum had prepared the light sedative. The needle had found the artery above the collar bone. Then Blum had winced and squeezed the embolus from the syringe. He had waited for the seizure to strike. It had been that simple to turn Steenkamp's body into a terrifying prison.

Lena Steenkamp now was on her feet, woozily going to her husband. "Can you hear me, dear?" Lena asked.

Yes, he heard. But his mind was locked forever in a frozen body.

General MacIntyre rushed, out of breath, into the intensive-care unit. He saw the Prime Minister and turned to Blum with a questioning look. "I got your message," he said. "How is he?"

"A vegetable, General. A medical vegetable."

"But how?"

Blum thought for a moment. "Only his mind could tell us the answer to that, General."

Uys stood beside MacIntyre. "Your commander in chief is no more, Mac. As a member of his Cabinet, I'm going to give you an order. Get your troops to stop that tanker."

The general nodded. He took one last look at Steenkamp. Then he went to find a telephone.

Norah had gone to the port. Uys had told her to wait there until MacIntyre arrived with his troops. She was the only person who could talk sense to Hartmann.

A guard, one of Steenkamp's private army, the men she had heard being briefed at the German Club, prevented her from entering the gates. But she had to try to reason with Hartmann! The guard repeated his orders: no one was to be admitted to the facility until the ship had sailed.

"Is Mr. Hartmann there?" she asked, pointing toward the far end of the docks. She saw cargo nets lifting mounds of clothing and depositing them in large containers, a line of black men and women moving in single file toward a covered pipeline bridge. Steenkamp's private soldiers, armed to the teeth, formed a cordon on either side of the line.

"He arrived a short while ago," the guard said.

The lines of blacks had nearly ended, so the loading was almost complete. When that was done, the ship would sail.

Norah had never felt so helpless. They were so close to stopping the madness. . . . They had only to restrain—or kill—Hartmann for the transport to fail, and he was only a few hundred yards away from where she was standing.

She thought about Hartmann, her "Uncle" Ernst. He had been the one behind all of this. He had manipulated her stepfather, the South African Prime Minister, and so many others. But how had he done it? The instant she asked the question she knew the answer. She had always known. She had felt it herself the night they had dinner in Zurich, and later when they made love. She couldn't explain it logically to herself, but there was some power in Hartmann that nobody could deny.

Hartmann possessed power over others. An evil power, but the force of persuasion was the same. She wondered seriously what she would do if she was faced with the prospect of refusing him, denying him, of killing him. Of course she could do it, she thought. But she shuddered at the thought of ever being tested.

She heard a Jeep behind her. General MacIntyre jumped out and ran over to her.

"Where have you been?" she asked, the tension making her voice shrill.

"It took time to get men organized and down here. We're in place, and we're ready to spring our trap."

"How many are you?"

"We have two thousand men ringing the facility, and that number again in reserve. I don't think they'll put up a fight. They're not stupid."

MacIntyre's personal contingent of troops had disarmed the guard at the gate. The general thought for an instant, then ordered his men to stay where they were.

"There is no sense alarming them inside there. It will only cause civilian casualties. They can't go anywhere, so we'll wait."

Norah was amazed. "Wait for what? My God, General, the ship can leave any minute."

"Wait to talk with Hartmann." He told a communications aide to use the telephone in the guardhouse. Somehow he had to reach Hartmann; Uys had told him what to say. "We don't know what he has in there. And we don't want him and his goons going berserk with machine guns on those people. We'll talk to him, then we'll make our decision."

"General," the communications aide yelled from the guard shack. "I have someone on the line, sir, who says that he is Mr. Hartmann."

MacIntyre and Norah ran over to the shack. MacIntyre grabbed the telephone and put it to his ear.

"Listen, Hartmann," he said. "This is General MacIntyre of the South African Army. You have no chance to escape. Steenkamp has had an accident. He is paralyzed and cannot speak. Control of the government has passed to Conrad Uys, who has commanded me to stop you. My troops are ready on my order to close in on you. We are offering you this chance to give yourself up. We will hold our fire."

"I don't think you understand, General." It was Hartmann.

"I understand all I need to," the general replied angrily. "You are trapped."

Hartmann laughed. "Maybe I've made a mistake then, General. I thought it was you who went with me to Valindaba."

"Oh, my God," MacIntyre said, drawing in his breath.

"That's right, General. 'Oh, my God.' And you and all of Cape Town will be visiting that God sooner than you thought, if you interfere in any way. Do you hear me?"

"Give me a few minutes. I'll talk with Uys."

"You have no time, because there is nothing to negotiate. I want out; I go out. Like a cruise ship. Or Cape Town becomes a desert."

MacIntyre hung up. Ashen-faced, he turned to Norah. "He has a thirty-kiloton bomb on board the ship which will detonate if we interfere."

Norah's shoulders slumped. She felt as though she had taken a physical blow. The snake, she thought. Unless you crushed its head, it would continue to bite and bite again. Hartmann was never further from defeat than right now. "Then what do we do?"

"I'll see what Uys has to say."

She started to cry, then, remembering, stopped herself. "There isn't time, General," she said.

She watched MacIntyre go into the guard shack. She turned and went to his Jeep, got aboard, started the engine, engaged the gear, and drove through the facility gate. It was what she had to do; there was no question of choice. She had to talk with Hartmann to convince him.

She braked the Jeep inches from Hartmann's back. He was standing at the edge of the pier and was preparing to take the launch out to the tanker.

"Ernst," Norah yelled. She stayed in the seat. Hartmann turned around, confusion on his face. He couldn't know why she was here, what she was doing. He thought of nothing to say, so he said, "What in hell?"

"I've come to ask you to stop this insanity."

"You know nothing about it. It is none of your business. Now go away, Norah. Get out of here."

"Ernst, you didn't hear the general."

"I heard him clearly."

"It's over." He started to walk toward the ladder leading down to the launch. "It's over, Ernst," she yelled. "Steenkamp is paralyzed. The ship can't leave."

He found the first step of the ladder, and then he took one last look in her direction.

Norah was desperate. "I *know*, Ernst. I am MOSSAD."

The word seemed to lash at him. The muscles in his jaw tensed. He stared at her with contempt in his eyes, then slowly climbed back up the ladder onto the pier.

"MOSSAD," she said again. "Your enemy. You are defeated. You, Hans Peter, the Baron, all the others. Defeated."

The color was gone from his face. "We'll see who is defeated," he said, clamping a fist on her arm. "We'll see," he said again. Then, to a guard: "Put this woman on the ship."

23

The giant turbine sent shudders through *Bronze Maru*'s miles of plating. The signal had been given to sail after the heavy lines were cast free from the pipeline bridge, and the helmsman began to negotiate the huge ship through the narrow channel. In the holds below, thousands of ears strained to interpret the sounds of motors and creaking metal. Their world was cold and bathed in eerie blue light; it was a universe of cramped cages, catwalks, noises, and silent fear. In the stern on the bridge, the sun shone through the expanse of windows that looked down on the flat length of deck. Level 9 of the bridge was the command post, from which the ship's captain and Ernst Hartmann controlled within the reach of their arms all navigational gear and most communications equipment.

"Once we clear the harbor entrance," Hartmann told Captain Koch, "set this course." He handed Koch a piece of paper with the coordinates.

"Robben Island off to port," Koch reported mechanically. The passage around the small island was the narrowest in the bay. Koch watched the depth sounder, which registered the fathoms from the hull bottom to the floor of the bay. "We have twenty feet," he said, nervously. If they were carrying crude, even half tanks, they would never clear. "Down to eighteen." He referred to a chart. "And now steady, at seventeen," he said, relieved. The twin beacons towered ahead on either side of the port's mouth.

"Do you see anything?" Hartmann asked, scanning the horizon. Would they blockade?

"Nothing, er, sir," Koch replied. He was resigned to follow orders. No matter what, he vowed to get them to their destination alive. Anything else was beyond his comprehension. "No obstructions," he said finally. "We have a free passage."

Hartmann relaxed for a moment, looking to the sea. The Cape of Good Hope, it was called, where rollers the height of buildings could whip in a frenzy of violence. He now had only the elements to face; nothing human dared touch him.

With Steenkamp paralyzed, South Africa was lost. But the loss changed nothing. Protégé was alone in Tanzania, which made their survival more tentative. Building their state was going to be slower and harder, but it would be done. Yes, Steenkamp was removed, but so was Nyerere. One for one. He looked at his wristwatch. By now Protégé and the German settlers were preparing for *Maru*'s arrival. *Bronze Maru* had a safe harbor. The thought gave him pleasure.

"These guards aren't necessary," Koch said to him. Hartmann had assigned three soldiers to watch the captain and his first mate. They were armed and vigilant, and they made Koch nervous.

"They are here to work, not to guard you," Hartmann said, and he was not altogether lying. The guards would take the bomb from its crate, if the need arose to threaten the South Africans or anybody else, but for the moment he wanted the bomb to remain as it was. He looked at the crate. A loading crane on the top of the superstructure had lifted it from the launch and swung it onto the control deck. It was surprisingly small, Hartmann thought, much smaller than it had looked in the deep shaft at Valindaba.

"What's in that?" Koch asked, looking at the crate. He recognized the international symbol for radioactive material, but the thought had not crossed his mind that it was an atomic bomb. Hartmann ignored his question—not that Koch cared. He had wanted to know the contents for safety's sake. If the crate was heavy it could smash against the control consoles in a turbulent sea. "Make certain it is secure," he ordered the guards.

Koch had been angered when the *Bronze Maru* was first commandeered in Swakopmund by Admiral Voerwerk. But he had thought that Ravi Tikkoo, the owner, would soon straighten out what must have been a horrible mistake. They had sailed down the coast of Southwest Africa to Cape Town, and then his anger turned to fear. He had thought that they were to carry crude oil. When he saw the cargo, at first he was uncomprehending. People! Hundreds of thousands of them. He had watched, and he had nearly become nauseous. Under heavy guard, they had been prodded and threatened along the pipeline bridge from the pier, then through the gaping cargo door and into the holds. From there they had been locked in the sheep cages.

Koch thought he had gone mad.

Nobody, least of all Hartmann, would answer his questions. He had asked their destination; he had wanted to know how the people below were being fed and sheltered, for they would all surely die of exposure in the holds in two or three days. He could not have that on his conscience. But from the very start he had no choice.

They had been at sea now for three hours.

"Sir, permission to change course," he said to Hartmann. "We are off Cape Agulhas."

Hartmann looked through the windows to the port side. The Cape was barely within eyesight. "All right, Captain, make the change," he said. Then he went to the charts. They were to sail due east past Port Elizabeth, then north toward Durban and Lourenço Marques with the island republic of Madagascar to their starboard. They would follow one of the most heavily traveled shipping lanes in the world. "What about weather?" he asked.

Koch read a teleprinter with meteorological data. "Clear for a few hours, like it is now."

"And then what?"

Koch shook his head. Hartmann knew nothing about the sea. "Around the Cape, sir, expect anything from glassy seas to gales. They'll come up without warning." He paused, trying to be more precise. "Simonstown is reporting storms." Koch knew what that meant for the people in the holds. In a storm, it would be hell. "We should think about those people," he said, nodding downward.

"What?" Hartmann was genuinely surprised. "They're safe, aren't they?"

"They are *humans,* sir. You treat them like a slave cargo."

Hartmann gave a little laugh. "You've been at sea too long. Wake up!"

Bronze Maru rode the seas lightly, dangerously lightly with the curve of her shovel hull bucking into the Cape rollers, which were coming at them with increasing frequency. In the south the sky was dark. A storm was moving rapidly north from its point of origin in the region a couple of hundred miles off the Cape. It was there that the warm winds and waters of the Indian Ocean collided with the cold of the Atlantic, forming a continuous storm. By the looks of the dark clouds off their starboard, they were in for a serious blow.

Hartmann was seated in the captain's chair, looking dreamily out to sea. In a few minutes he would go below to Deck 7 to the sophisticated communications room. He was worried about Dar es Salaam, and he needed to know how they were doing. He had told Hirsch that he would call. They had established a prearranged frequency, and presumably by now Hirsch would be in the Voice of Tanzania transmitter station coordinating the work of the 250, the advance group, and the white settlers.

The coup in Tanzania would be over by now. They would be mopping up and reestablishing order in the city of Dar, preparing for *Bronze Maru*'s arrival in port. Hartmann felt his hands perspire in nervous anticipation. Soon he would be returning home.

"Watch him closely," he said to the guards, pointing to Koch. "I'm going below."

He took the elevator to two decks below and found the communications room without difficulty. It was amazing, he thought as he looked at the banks of relay equipment, how much money Tikkoo had spent to outfit the tanker. Of course it carried no weapons under normal conditions, but it was nevertheless as sophisticated in most respects as many of the most advanced of the world's warships.

He handed the prearranged frequency to the guard in the room, who went about contacting the number in silent efficiency. He read out call signals, then handed the microphone to Hartmann.

"Hans Peter?" he asked, his voice filled with expectation. "This is Hartmann, over."

"Go ahead, go ahead," came the reply, crackling with static.

"Dar es Salaam, I want Hans Peter Hirsch."

"Go ahead, go ahead," the reply was repeated.

Hartmann was angry. "Who is this?" he demanded.

"One of the settlers, sir."

"Then where is Hirsch?"

"I don't know."

Hartmann thought for a moment. Hirsch should have been in Dar es Salaam all along. He was the main coordinator. If he was not there, something could have gone wrong.

"Dar, has the coup succeeded?"

"The President is shot, and we are proceeding as planned. But there is much confusion here right now," the settler replied.

"Has the flight from Zurich landed?"

"I am getting various reports, but they are all positive. I repeat, there is much confusion."

Only to be expected, Hartmann thought. "Do you know what happened to Hans Peter Hirsch?" he asked.

"I repeat, no. I do not know."

"Then who is coordinating? Who is in charge?"

"You must understand. We are isolated here. I can't answer you, because I do not know."

Hartmann persisted. "What about resistance? Are there any reports?" he asked.

"Only the GSU are resisting, sir."

This, too, had been expected. "What specific information do you have on Nyerere?"

"He was shot in Olduvai. He is dead. We received confirmation here at the transmitter of his death, and we broadcast the news for the start of the coup, sir. I assure you, it is going as planned. Repeat, as planned."

"All right, Dar. Tell Hirsch to call *Maru*. Out." Still, by now he had expected the coup to be over. He wondered darkly what he would do if they failed. He turned to the guard. "In two hours call Dar again. Can you relay communications to the bridge?" The radioman nodded positively. "Then do it. And relay anything else that comes up to the bridge."

"Sir, Cape Town called," the radioman said, almost as an afterthought.

"With threats?"

"More an invitation," he said, smiling, "to return."

"Don't talk to them again."

He had not given much thought to what he should do about Norah. He had blanked her out of his mind on purpose—thinking about her was too painful. He had trusted her; he had reached out to her; he had loved her. She was the daughter of his only real friend. She was the single person in his life whom he had allowed to get close. And she had worked all along to destroy him.

He wanted to hurt her in the most painful way. He knew how to use pain, but nothing in his memory was sufficient for what he wanted her to feel. He wanted to scar her mind as well as her body.

24

Tall and dignified, Ravi Tikkoo stood in the control center of his shipping empire. In the London district of St. John's Wood, the center monitored the minute-by-minute progress of his fleet, which at any given time was spread across four oceans. He was a man of deep philanthropic feelings, and his thoughts now bordered on disbelief as he watched the two CIA specialists, who had been flown to London that morning in F-4 supersonic fighters, coordinating with his technicians. They worked to set up lines of communication between London, the White House Situation Room, and *Bronze Maru*. Soon they would try their single chance to save his ship.

"Will your President listen in?" he asked Roland Gandre.

"They all will, Mr. Tikkoo. If need be, final decisions must come from them."

Gandre, a stocky man of middle age with an open, cheerful face, was the CIA's expert on terror psychology. In the last decade he had faced down a score of terrorists, from Munich to Kampala and Tripoli, but he had never conceived of confronting a thing like this. He opened a folder and shook his head at the dearth of pages.

"If only we knew more about him," he said.

"Would it help?" Tikkoo asked.

"To find his weaknesses, the soft spots that I could probe? Everybody has them, including this nutter."

"But you don't expect him to surrender."

"It's happened before." He looked over at the CIA's communications technician. "Are you nearly ready?"

"In a few minutes," he replied, holding up five fingers.

"What about the Nazi background?"

"I don't think so," Gandre replied. "The trick is to walk a tightrope. You can't push these people into a corner."

"There's nothing else to do, is there?"

"I'll try to prove that he can't win. If I can do that, we will succeed. Unless, of course, he is insane." He threw up his hands. "Then we can kiss the ship good-bye."

Tikkoo couldn't believe that there wasn't a better solution. "Yes, but if he gets to Dar es Salaam?"

"Don't even think it, Mr. Tikkoo."

But he did. They both did. A city leveled and all those people atomized, with the simple coding of three buttons on the bomb.

"What can you tell me about"—Gandre referred to his clipboard—"Captain Koch?"

Tikkoo didn't hesitate. "Perfectly solid judgment and cool. Count on him."

The communications man waved from across the room. "We're ready," he said in a hushed voice.

"Right," Gandre said, still wishing he knew more. "First put me through to Washington." He took a seat at a horseshoe-shaped desk. "Start taping, and connect through the speakers. Mr. President?"

"Gandre, this is Winfield Cowles. We hear you loud and clear," the CIA chief said. "I am with the President, his advisers, and Mr. Chapin from Defense."

"Thank you, sir," Gandre said. "Is there any more news from Tanzania before I begin?"

"You have it all."

"Keep your fingers crossed, then."

The connection with *Bronze Maru* crackled and hissed. Somebody to Gandre's left calibrated the frequency. The ship's radio operator came through clearly. He was told to connect them with the bridge and Captain Koch. Finally the connection was made.

"Captain, I'm speaking from your owner's headquarters," Gandre said. "Is Mr. Hartmann there?"

There was a pause. "You have to stop him," Koch said, excited. "He's a fanatic, sir."

"Where is he?" Gandre asked in an even tone.

"Belowdecks. In the radio room."

"Thank you, Captain," Gandre said. "Please call him to the bridge." He turned and asked Ravi Tikkoo, "Where is the radio room?"

"On Deck Seven."

"Washington? Has there been any communication in the last few minutes between the ship and Dar?"

"Yes." It was Cowles. "They made him think that the coup was a success. He doesn't suspect that it failed."

"Right, thanks." Then he flipped a line toggle back to the *Maru*. "What is Hartmann's status, Captain?"

"He was in my stateroom. Are you tracking us?"

"Yes. You are fifty miles southeast of Port Elizabeth."

Then Hartmann came on the line. "From here on in, you speak only to me," he said. "Who is this?"

Gandre told him that he was CIA, and that the President of the United States was listening to their conversation. "Will you tell me, Mr. Hartmann, what it is you want?" he asked, as though he were speaking with a friend.

"Nothing, so long as you don't interfere."

"What you're doing is senseless, Mr. Hartmann. Do you hear me, sir?"

The game was beginning to get interesting, Hartmann thought, wondering what ploy they would use. How would they try to convince him? What could they say? He grinned, deciding to play out the line. "No," he said. "What *you're* saying is senseless. I hold the cards."

Gandre didn't think so. "Prime Minister Steenkamp is ill, Mr. Hartmann," he said. "The government of South Africa is now in the hands of Conrad Uys. Do you know him?"

Was this really their trump? Of course, they guessed he didn't know about Steenkamp. He didn't respond.

"Mr. Hartmann, we have talked with Conrad Uys. You no longer have allies. You are alone, sir."

Hartmann said nothing. If they didn't know about Tanzania, he wasn't going to tell them. They would learn soon enough.

"Will you wait one minute, Mr. Hartmann?" Gandre shifted the key, blocking out *Bronze Maru* and opening the voice channel to the Situation Room. "Mr. President, it's your decision whether we tell him." There was a second's pause.

"It's the next card. Play it," the President said.

Gandre again switched the radio channels. "Mr. Hartmann," he said, "the coup did not succeed."

Then they did know, Hartmann thought. "Nice try," he said. "But I know different."

"President Nyerere is alive, sir. The assassin killed an American. Nyerere was only shaken up."

But the coup started with Nyerere's death, Hartmann thought. They were trying to trick him, but it wouldn't work. "What else do you have to say?" he asked, impatient.

"You don't believe me, Mr. Hartmann. How can I convince you?"

"Don't waste your breath."

"Is there any way we can convince you, Mr. Hartmann?"

Hartmann paused. There was only one way he could be certain. He would call Dar himself. But first he had to know what this American had learned about Tanzania. "Tell me what failed in Tanzania?" he asked.

"The coup. As I said, Nyerere is alive and in good health. Second, sir, the two hundred and fifty members you sent to Dar aboard an Aeroteck charter, which had a stolen transponder, have been arrested at Dar airport by Israeli commandos. Third, the white settlers you had convinced to join you in the coup have also been arrested, by the Tanzanian GSU." Gandre hesitated for a moment. "Would you like to hear more?"

Hartmann could not believe that the Americans knew. "Call me back in fifteen minutes," he said.

Hartmann told the radio operator on Deck 7 to connect him on the same frequency they had used before. He wanted Voice of Tanzania in Dar es Salaam. He waited several minutes while the connection was being made.

"Hello, Dar es Salaam, this is Ernst Hartmann."

"And this," came the reply, "is Major David Eskol, Forced Reconnaissance, First Israeli Infantry Brigade. Can I help you, Mr. Hartmann?"

Hartmann did not answer. So the coup had failed! Now he was isolated. The shock of failure numbed him and left him speechless. First South Africa, now Tanzania. How could it be? They had waited so long, planned so well. They had nearly limitless resources, they had his confidence, his brilliance. They could not fail; but they had failed. He slowly put down the microphone and waited for the call from London. Now he must entertain their offer.

Gandre came back on the line to *Bronze Maru*. "Do you believe us now, Mr. Hartmann?"

"What are you offering?" Hartmann asked.

"We want you to turn the ship around. We want you to go back to Cape Town. We want you to unload those people and put them safely on land. And we want you to give yourself up."

Hartmann laughed. "That's not much of an offer."

"We are in a position to make demands. You are not in the same position, Mr. Hartmann."

"Oh no? Then let me tell you *my* offer." Hartmann's voice was cold. "Listen well. If my people in Dar es Salaam are not set free by the time this ship arrives in the Dar harbor, I will not hesitate to detonate the bomb. Shall I repeat that, Mr. Gandre?"

"What bomb?" Gandre's voice was heavy with concern. Conrad Uys had informed the Americans, through General MacIntyre, that Hartmann had loaded a thirty-kiloton atomic device aboard the ship. But the threat of its being used was of a magnitude that Gandre had not fully considered. It was inconceivable to him and the others in Washington that anyone would detonate a bomb which would incinerate those thousands of people in the holds. And now Hartmann was threatening to blow up the capital city of Tanzania.

"Don't play games with me," Hartmann said. "You know I got a bomb from Valindaba."

"You wouldn't," Gandre said.

"There is one way to find out." Hartmann paused. "I'm not going anywhere except onward to Dar. Let me know when your superiors make their decision."

Gandre sat there in silence, listening to the hiss of the broken connection. Slowly he reached up with his hand to disengage the line. For several minutes nobody said anything; then he heard the President's voice.

"Gandre, put Mr. Tikkoo on the line, please."

Ravi Tikkoo stepped forward and took Gandre's seat. "Yes, Mr. President?" he said, his voice flat.

"Are you dead certain, sir, of the satellite capability?"

"Of course. Yes."

"Then we have no option, I'm afraid."

"He said not to interfere! You were listening, Mr. President."

There was a lengthy pause. They heard the sound of the President's breathing, muffled voices in the background.

"I will not take responsibility for the devastation of a city as well. Use the satellite, Mr. Tikkoo."

"Uncrate the bomb," Hartmann commanded. Soon the metal presence, snub-nosed and ugly, lay exposed on its cradle. Captain Koch stared at it, uncomprehending, as an animal would at sculpture.

"They said we can go back," he told Hartmann. "They will protect you." Then, seeing he was getting nowhere, "Why are you doing this?"

Hartmann felt in his coat pocket for the diagram and the bomb arming code. "My colleagues have failed; all of them, failed," he said. "But with this bomb in this ship, I will force a victory. The Americans can't refuse, Mr. Koch. They will do what I ask."

"But you were bluffing." It was a question and statement.

Hartmann shook his head. "Bluffing? No, Captain, I wasn't."

"Isn't there something you'd accept? What you're suggesting is insane."

"You heard my demand," then, thinking for an instant, finally, "Insane? What is that, Captain? Insane is what they called Steenkamp."

Koch's first mate caught his eye, then glanced furtively at the navigational console. Koch could feel it, too.

"May I make a suggestion, Mr. Hartmann?" he asked.

"Yes, by all means."

He had to distract Hartmann. "We might anchor until the Americans decide."

"We have supplies of food . . ." Hartmann said, thinking, " . . . supplies for four days at sea. Then the cargo begins to starve." His face cracked in a smile. "Don't think I care about their welfare, Mr. Koch. But when we finally do land, I want them alive."

Yes, Koch definitely felt *Bronze Maru*'s gradual course change. The ship was being turned by an unseen hand east, then eventually, he was certain, south, back toward Cape Town.

"If we choose a lay-by port, we could reprovision," Koch said.

"It probably will not be necessary," Hartmann said. "They will make their decision soon and then we head straight for Dar. But show me what you have in mind, anyway."

"We'll have to look at the charts," said Koch, and led the way into the room in which the navigational electronics were stored.

Hartmann hesitated for an instant. He thought he felt something different, something wrong. He looked out the window but there was nothing on the horizon but sea and dark clouds. Then he followed Koch into the navigational room.

"We are approximately one and a half days' steaming time from here," Koch said, pointing a finger at the four islands on the chart in the group, Territoire des Comores. "We will have to stand off Moroni, here, on Grande-Comore. But from here we can sail to Dar within one day." He ran his finger across the strait. The Comores were almost due east of Tanzania.

Hartmann was interested. A contingency now made sense. He looked up, trying to discern what was different, then back again at the chart. "Do these Comores present any danger?"

"It's a dozy place, sir," Koch said, tensing. Now they were almost on a southerly heading, back toward the Cape. "A Guard Nationale, but nothing to concern us."

"And food?" He paused. "Koch, are we going into a storm?"

"Yes," he stuttered. "Yes, sir, like I told you. But the food? There isn't much."

"Let's wait and see, then," Hartmann said, walking into the bridge area. He looked through the large windows toward the bow light. The sky was darkening fast. To one of the guards he said, "Watch things up here. I'll be in the radio room."

On Deck 7 he talked with the radio operator. "Anything from Tikkoo?" he asked.

"They test the line every thirty seconds, sir. But no communication or I'd have looped it to the bridge."

Hartmann started to go. "Sir?" the radio operator asked. He didn't know if he should ask the question.

Hartmann looked back over his shoulder. "What is it?" he asked.

"Maybe nothing at all. I learned radio communication in the Merchant Marine and I—"

"I don't want your life story," Hartmann said.

"What I wanted to say, the ship is turning, sir. I'm positive of it."

Hartmann stood for an instant, trying to feel through his feet. He had sensed it. They were turning.

He ran down the corridor and took the elevator to the bridge deck.

"Koch, turn us back," he yelled.

The captain looked uncertain. "What do you mean?" he said.

Hartmann went to the navigational console, where the digital compass read out degree headings. He slammed his fist on the Plexiglas plate. "One seventy-seven, southeast!" he screamed. "Put us back on course, I said."

Koch raised his hands in a helpless gesture. "I can't," he said. It was brilliant, what Tikkoo had done. "This was not my doing. That's the truth." Now every second counted.

"I don't believe you," Hartmann said. "Nobody else swung us around. I'm warning you, Koch."

"You're wrong. Ask the guards."

"Did either of them, him or the first mate, touch these controls?" he asked the guards.

"No, they did not, sir."

"What about the rudder, Koch? Can it be turned from underwater?"

Koch didn't know what he meant. "Like how?" he asked, bewildered.

"Divers, off a submarine, or a submarine itself. Could they freeze the rudder?"

The question, of course, was idiotic. The huge rudder was positioned behind the screw. At their present speed, the wash would prevent a person in scuba gear or a sub from even getting close. And if they managed somehow, the rudder was just too large. The steering engine was of a thousand horsepower!

"Perhaps so, sir," Koch said. "I can't say."

"All right." Hartmann had arrived at a decision. "Shut down the turbine. Stop the engine, Koch."

"In this sea? Impossible!"

Hartmann found the engine controls with the universal designation "All Stop." He pulled the lever like a throttle and the vibration ceased.

"Don't you realize," Koch said. "We can't drift a ship this size."

Hartmann needed Koch's help. "Is there a way to check? Can we get to the rudder?"

"In weather like this, no." He pretended to go through the standard procedures. "I can't figure it out," he said finally. He knew exactly what had happened, but he could not let Hartmann know.

Hartmann spoke through the intercom to the radio room. "When the Americans make their next line test, tell them we want to talk," he said to the radioman.

They waited as the minutes passed. Hartmann had to steady himself by the brass handrail in the heavy sea. Koch sensed now that they had beaten the madman. They had him on the run.

"We have London on the line, sir," the radioman announced through the intercom.

"Whatever you're doing, stop!" Hartmann yelled into the microphone. "Stop this immediately! Do you hear?"

Gandre's voice was calm and reasoned. "Mr. Hartmann, maybe you'll explain what you think we've done. Because we don't know."

"I'm ordering you to release control of the rudder."

"We are in London, remember, Mr. Hartmann."

"Contact the submarine or whatever it is. Tell them to back off."

"I can assure you, there is no submarine." Gandre had to keep Hartmann talking. "You can't see for yourself, of course, so you must take our word."

"Start the engines, Koch," he said. "Enough speed to stabilize the ship," then, into the microphone to London,

"Whatever you did, it must end now. The bomb," he continued breathlessly, "has a five-minute delay, as you probably know."

"Yes, we are aware of that," Gandre said.

"Koch will confirm what I am doing," Hartmann went on. "I will set the code. You have five minutes to desist— or I will blow all of us to hell."

Koch knew that Hartmann was serious.

"We don't care, Mr. Hartmann," Gandre said. "I repeat, we don't care. Blow yourself up, and those people too. A decision has been made. The President of the United States himself made it, sir. Obliterate yourself. We have no means to stop you."

"Tell them what I'm doing, Koch," Hartmann said. He got the code from his coat pocket, then went to the bomb inset. He pressed three buttons. The small readout registered the first number, then "Enter."

"He's doing it," Koch said. He felt convulsed, dizzy, his breathing shallow. "Mother in heaven, you can't let him, do you hear? You can't," he yelled at Gandre in London.

The second number; "Enter."

"We just don't care," Gandre said twice. "Kill yourself."

"The others, all the others," Koch gasped. "In the holds, what of them. Of me?" He started to cry, gulping air. "You can't let him. Please, dear God, please."

The third number; "Enter."

Now there were five minutes to oblivion.

"No, no. . . ." Koch whimpered.

"We *want* you to blow yourselves up," Gandre said. "At sea. The decision has been made."

Hartmann stood perfectly still.

"No!" Koch cried. "I won't let it happen." He stumbled forward. Hartmann braced himself. Koch went past him into the "restricted" room. "Please stop," he yelled to Hartmann.

"Not until you show me what they did. Give me control, Koch, and I'll give you life."

"It's in here, in here," Koch said, beyond coherence. Hartmann followed.

"What have they done, Koch? You have three minutes. The bomb goes off in three minutes. Do you know what that means? A nuclear explosion, a tidal wave, and hundreds of thousands of people dead, including you, Koch. For myself, it doesn't matter."

"InTelSatNav IVa," Koch stammered. He tore open the front of a panel and exposed a staggering complexity of electronic circuits. "They are steering us through inertial guidance. They can do that. They move us in London, and the command goes through a satellite to the ground station we have out there on the deck. They are moving us with hands in London!"

"Then they can release us in London."

"No, they cannot. They told the truth." He pulled out a circuit board, then another and another. "Once London overrides my control of the ship, which can be done without my knowing, only the ship can switch out the satellite command. It is used for emergencies, if the crew has to abandon the ship. In fires or spills." He snatched at another circuit board, uncertain what he was doing. "We never used it before. I don't know if I can—"

"You have two minutes."

"Mr. Hartmann, you must believe me. I don't know how. Switch off the detonator and we'll do this together."

"You'll do it, Koch, alone. You have one minute and fifty seconds."

Koch opened a second panel and again was faced with a confusion of circuits. He had to disable the links with the satellite. If he had time, he could smash the parabolic dish on the deck, but that would take hours. He looked at the diagram on the panel door. It was a circuit diagram, but it gave no indication of what it was for. He went back to the small plastic boards of integrated circuits and started to pull each one out.

"One minute thirty seconds." Hartmann's voice was calm.

"Okay, okay, okay," Koch yelled. The wires on the circuit boards cut his hands as he removed them. He turned toward the bridge, yelling to his first mate. "Try it! Do we have control?"

"Yes," the first mate said. "We have it!"

"Now disarm the bomb!" Koch pleaded with Hart-mann.

Hartmann walked onto the bridge and kneeled down in front of the bomb inset. He pressed a combination of six digits.

"RETRIEVE," appeared on the readout.

"CLEAR."

They had forty-five seconds to spare.

Hartmann stayed kneeling. They had wanted him to blow up the ship. They had made the decision to destroy *Bronze Maru,* and it wasn't difficult to know why. Now he realized that he had the Americans in check. They would now do what he wanted, everything he wanted, because he held all the cards. Of course they had wanted him to blow up the ship. Better to lose the ship and its people than the ship *and* Dar es Salaam. He meant what he had said. He would again set the three digits for the timer of the detonator in the *Dar es Salaam harbor,* if they didn't release his allies in Dar. If he didn't have a safe and welcome arrival in Dar, he would take out a whole city and a ship filled with people. Hartmann threw back his head and laughed.

He went to the microphone. "London, are you there?"

There was a muffled sound, then Gandre came on. "Yes, Mr. Hartmann."

"Good try, London. Now go to hell."

"We will negotiate, we will negotiate," Gandre chanted.

"Like I said before. When the *Bronze Maru* arrives in Dar, if our greeting isn't friendly, I will detonate the bomb. I mean what I say. You have proof of that now. So do this right. If you don't, I guarantee you will have a hole where Dar once was. The stakes now are the ship *and* the city."

25

Guilt sank in, as the tension slowly dissipated. They had gambled with the highest stakes and lost. Now they were paying in the currency of despair. Gandre was listless and wanted to sleep. It seemed almost impossible to him. Might had been thrown against *Bronze Maru* and had affected nothing.

He gazed at the screen on the wall. Every several seconds the small red dot brightened, then faded, then brightened again, as the satellite plot of *Bronze Maru* traced her progress, slowly up the coast of Africa. He pitied the person in Washington who had to make the inevitable decision. He wanted no part of it. He finally threw the toggle and opened the line.

"Washington," he said, his voice dead. When they did not reply, he guessed they also were grappling with private demons.

"Yes, Gandre, we're here," Cowles finally replied.

"I'm sorry, so very very sorry," Gandre said.

Cowles cleared his throat. "All of us are." He paused. "You did your best, Gandre . . ."

"But not good enough."

Then the President came on the line.

"Mr. Gandre, thank you. And Mr. Tikkoo, too. Will you please stay on the line? I want you involved in what we now must decide."

"Yes, sir."

The President went rapidly through the options.

"Excuse me, sir." It was Cowles again. "But why not let him think that Dar has been given back? How can he know?"

Gandre answered for the President.

"You heard him, Admiral. He is too cunning. On the one hand he has radio communications with Dar. So he'll

225

know anyway. And once he gets there he'll want assurances before he releases the trigger. The man is mad, in my opinion. He wants an excuse to blow up the ship. The slightest deception will send him off."

"Like I said," the President remarked. "Nyerere would never agree. I can't blame him. What Hartmann asks, therefore, gentlemen, is impossible to give."

Nobody refuted his logic.

"Mr. Tikkoo," the President continued. "You know the ship. Can we get commandos aboard?"

Tikkoo folded his arms, thinking of what chance the ship's design afforded.

"Maru is an all-aft ship, which means that the control sections, the bridge where Hartmann is, are located far in the rear of the ship behind about a half mile of deck. The deck is open space, except for some pipes."

"What does that mean?" the President asked.

"I'm sorry, Mr. President," Tikkoo said. "I was thinking out loud."

"Continue," the President said.

"Commandos could not board from the sea. Maru is just too large, and she is moving at around ten knots. They couldn't make the climb, and the seas are getting rough, we are told. They are entering a storm."

"Which leaves parachutes," the President said.

"If commandos land on the deck they will be seen instantly, even before they land."

"Let's say that they do get aboard, on the deck," the President offered.

"If they are seen, they will be sitting ducks. Again, the all-aft idea. Guards in the bridge tower could too easily pick them off with rifles. You would be sending men to certain death."

"What about at night?"

"The deck will be floodlit, sir. Hartmann will be expecting an attack. He will be watching night and day."

Another voice spoke up. It was Secretary of Defense Gerold Chapin. "It just won't work. Parachute commandos just won't make it."

"Why so certain?" asked Cowles.

"Because, Winfield, we're talking about a moving platform. That ship deck is a moving platform. Sure we can drop people over it. But the airplanes making the drop will have to come in low, very low. Hartmann will hear the airplanes and know what is happening. Instantly, he'll know. And we can't use jets, either, not for the accuracy we'll need. Which leads to one last factor. If we were to use C-130 Hercules, propeller airplanes, the slowness of the aircraft nearly negates their getting out to sea and near *Bronze Maru* in time."

The President interrupted. "Gentlemen, our objective is to destroy the bomb—even if it means destroying the ship. We *have* no other choice. The ship must not reach Dar es Salaam. It will be tragic for the people on the ship. But it is better to lose them alone than to lose them along with the population of Dar es Salaam."

"What is the population of Dar?" asked Chapin.

"Three quarters of a million," Cowles replied.

"And the number on the *Maru?*"

"We don't know. Anywhere from a hundred thousand to a million or more. They kept no records in Cape Town, and only Hartmann has access to the hold."

"On board one ship?"

"It's a big ship, Gerry."

"Then this is an impossible tragedy."

"So you see, gentlemen, our decision has been made for us," the President interrupted. "Can we be blamed for saving a city of nearly one million?" He paused, then said, "Gerald, where are our nearest strike aircraft?"

In London, Gandre closed his eyes. This was the decision he knew they would be forced to make all along. There was only *one* alternative.

"Nothing within range," Chapin said.

"Then available to us?" the President persisted.

"Yes, sir, in Kenya. We sold them five F-111 A/E's. Our pilots are in Nanyuki training theirs."

"And we can have them?"

"If we explain the situation, I don't see how the Kenyans can refuse."

"What's the feasibility?"

"The F-111's have a range of just under four thousand miles." He paused. "With a payload of twenty-five thousand pounds. If we strike the ship as it nears Île Juan de Nova, around twelve hundred miles from Nairobi, we can get there and back without refueling. As for munitions, they can load standard air-to-ground rockets. The Kenyans have them."

"With what *specific* objective?" Cowles asked.

"To pinpoint their target in *Maru's* stern, where the bridge is," the President said. "If we can destroy the bomb, Hartmann is neutralized. If not, we destroy the ship."

"Even so," Chapin said. "One stray rocket and the ship sinks, sir. Nobody can expect that kind of accuracy."

"Does it matter?" the President asked. "We have one chance in a million of saving those people. So we take it. Even if we fail, we succeed in saving Dar. I'm sorry, gentlemen, but that's it. Now what about timing?"

Gerold Chapin answered. "A little over one hour, once the planes are off the ground in Kenya."

"Then I'll speak now with the Kenyan President." He paused for an instant. "In an hour and a half, we'll know."

In London, Gandre watched the red light pulse on the screen, willing it to disappear. But not the way he feared.

26

Norah shifted her weight. The cold penetrated to her bones, so that she no longer could feel the bite of the wire grate on her skin. The sounds and smells of the hold were now familiar. She could discriminate among the small differences, such as when a guard patrolled one of the distant catwalks.

The hold was cavernous, beyond anything she could imagine, rising layer upon layer above and below the catwalk. She could hear the thousands of bodies rattling against sheep cages, and see, from one corner of the cage, through the dim blue light, countless hands gripping the wire edges. The prisoners whispered in a language Norah did not understand; muffled cries, coughs, and moans. She started to shake, and she felt the roll of the ship. Her senses were drenched in the smells of human waste and fear; she could not tell which was the more pungent. Her teeth chattered.

She was on her hip and side, facing David Monshoe, whose eyes were shut. He had not uttered a sound for nearly an hour, since the cage door had closed on them. The enormity of this tragedy swamped his mind with confusion and disconnected memories. He had been taken from Maseru and held as a "special" prisoner in the cells of the Bureau of State Security in Cape Town, then transferred to the docks and taken aboard *Bronze Maru* minutes before she had sailed. Without explanation he and the other "special" prisoner had been ordered to join the thousands of others in the cages; now he and the girl, Norah, were no longer "special."

"David," Norah said to him softly, "come closer." He didn't move or open his eyes. "David," she repeated. "We *must* stay warm."

He opened his eyes, then inched over until they touched. Norah put her arm through his and pressed him closer.

"There," she said, finally feeling the beginnings of warmth. She surprised herself with a smile, just a glimmer. Half the people she knew would be mortified, if they could see the two of them naked, white and black bodies hugging. They hardly knew each other, yet this experience would bind them as friends for life. What was left of life, she thought, her grin fading.

She wondered what was happening on the bridge. She had heard the engine stop, then felt the frightening roll of the ship. She had had to brace herself against the side of the cage. Then the engines had started again, and the heaving ceased. She didn't know how long they had been there. But if rescue hadn't come by now, it wasn't going to. Either people outside didn't know or, worse, they were powerless. Which was why she had to keep hope alive. If there was a way, she would find it, no matter what. She would get them out—all of them.

"Think, David," she whispered.

"I've tried, again and again," he said in a voice of defeat. "We're trapped. We have nothing."

Norah put her hand through the wire mesh. She felt the lock, smooth and cold. "Is there anything to pry it apart?" she asked.

"Nothing."

"Our hands aren't strong enough?"

"Judge for yourself."

"But if we—"

She was cut off by a high-pitched sound of a hydraulic engine, like the shrieking of brakes. She pressed herself closer to Monshoe for protection. "Oh, my God," she shouted above the noise. "What are they doing to us?"

Her question was answered by a wave of gruel that flowed through the trough just above their heads. The hydraulics stopped and she heard the sounds of people around her reaching into the trough to scoop out the food.

"We'd better eat," David said, reaching up.

"No, don't," she warned. Norah was hungry but not desperate for food, and Monshoe was the same. "For all we know, they drugged it."

David brought his hand back. Minutes later, the hydraulic motor started again, this time clearing the trough of the gruel, then filling it with murky water. David reached down with his hand and rubbed his leg. It was starting to cramp. He tried to force his mind off the knotting muscles.

Meanwhile, more minutes passed.

They heard footsteps on the catwalk. They looked and saw a guard's shadow on the opposite side of the cage. Soon, if he was methodical, he would pass them.

David whispered to Norah.

She shook her head. "No, I can't do it. I won't do it," she said.

"But you must," he said. "It's our only chance."

"I couldn't do it," she repeated, shaking her head again.

"Norah, we have one weapon, and it's you!"

Oh, *God,* she thought angrily. It was a weapon and she possessed it, and now she had no choice but to try and use it, but that made the thought no less repugnant. It was sex, and she had used it once against Hartmann. But what good had that done? It had put her in a cage and it had saved none of them. Still, it might succeed this time, and they only had one option left. No matter how horrible the thought, it was less so than the horror of the hold.

"All right," she said between her teeth. "I will try."

The footsteps got closer still. Now Norah saw the guard. He carried a rifle on his shoulder. The way he walked, he was relaxed and confident. For him the period of novelty on the ship, in the hold, had passed. He was a guard in any prison anywhere. And that was what she would exploit.

"Guard," she whispered, when he was close. "Look in here." She separated from Monshoe. "Look."

Something about the voice was different. The guard turned toward the cage and bent down. His eyes opened wide at the sight of the white woman. He had known that she was somewhere in Hold 1, but his orders were to treat her like all the others. Still, her nakedness stirred him. He ran his eyes from her hair to her face. Her eyes invited him. Then down to her breasts and stomach.

He unclipped his flashlight and shone it boldly on every part of her body. The sight of her was delicious. He switched off the light and pressed his face close. The butt of the rifle on his shoulder hit the steel cage. He reached over and leaned the rifle against the frame.

"Pretty lady, maybe you want to come out of there," he teased her.

Norah thought it was now or never. "I want you to touch me," she said. "Would you like that?" Her words aroused him, she knew by his expression. "Come closer," she cooed. He pushed against the cage door. "Give me your hand."

He reached through the cage, then pulled his hand back. "No you don't," he said. "You don't trap me so easily."

Oh, God, she thought, desperately. She had gone too fast. He was frightened. He thought that David was going to grab him or the rifle. That wasn't their plan at all. "Don't be frightened," she said, evenly. "I don't want to hurt you."

"Oh, no?"

"I want you to make me warm."

He thought for an instant. "How can I be sure?" he asked.

"You have a gun. How can I hurt you? Let me show you. Please. Open the door, just for me. I'll make you feel good."

He ran his eyes again over her body, excited by her touch. "Tell him to get back," he ordered, looking now at Monshoe. "To the back of the cage."

Monshoe turned in the cramped space and crawled to the far end of the cage.

The guard reached for the keys on his belt. With his other hand he brought the rifle nearer, placing it on the catwalk. He found the key and shone the flashlight on the lock. Slowly, now wondering if he could get away with it, he inserted it, deep into the lock, so it could go no further. For a long moment he left it there.

Norah had to keep him distracted. "None of the others will see us," she said. "They'll never know."

Almost to himself he said, "They're behind the doors. We can do it right here."

"Yes, right here, now," she coaxed.

"What was that?" he asked, his hand still on the key. He cocked his ear.

"Nothing, just a noise." She knew it wasn't. "Please open the door."

"Somebody is coming," he said. "They're coming." He withdrew his hand from the key and looked down the catwalk.

"What's going on?" a voice demanded.

The guard jumped to his feet, jerking the key from the lock. He bent down for the rifle.

"I said, what's going on?" The voice demanded angrily.

"It's the girl, sir." The guard stumbled on his words. "The white girl. She needs a blanket."

The other guard was older and in command. He took in the scene and knew what had gone on. But he said nothing about it. "Get out of here," he told the younger guard. "From now on you're to patrol Hold 2." The guard straightened up.

"You know she is to get the same treatment."

"Yes, sir, I know, but I thought—"

"You're not supposed to think. Now move it."

The younger guard walked down the catwalk until his footsteps were no longer heard. The older guard smiled at Norah. "Good try," he said. "You almost succeeded, didn't you?"

"I don't know what you mean," Norah replied.

"You know." He scowled at her. "Just don't try it again."

When the guard left, David moved forward and wrapped her in his arms.

"Oh, God," she said, relieved yet achingly disappointed.

"You almost made it," he soothed.

"But we're no closer," she said. "Now we don't even have that."

"We'll think of a way. Believe me, we will."

They said nothing for the next several minutes. Finally David broke the silence with words that came through clenched teeth.

"It's unbearable," he said, twisting his body.

"What's wrong?" Norah asked, alarmed by the stiffening of his body.

"It's the cold," he replied. "My legs are cramped."

"Can I do something?"

"No," he said, then, "Yes, please warm them."

She sensed his searing pain. "Does that help?" she asked, massaging his leg.

"A bit, yes."

She saw his body relax. "Oh, David, you fool," she said.

He was surprised that she hadn't noticed. She mustn't

have heard the guard's questions. But the same thought occurred to them in the same instant. Almost giddily, he wondered why he had not thought earlier. It was so simple, so near, yet such a part of him that he hadn't given it a thought. The degrading business for Norah with the guard had been unnecessary. They had had the key all along.

"Hurry," she said. Neither needed to explain to the other.

David reached down to the false leg and unstrapped the laces that held it on. He brought it up to his chest. "Loba would have a fit if he knew he had done me this favor," he said. But he knew that Norah could not understand. He snapped off a plastic hinge and exposed the end of one of the four steel bars in the leg that provided the support. It slipped out easily, like a knife from a sheath. The support bar was nearly a foot in length and made of an alloy for lightness and strength.

For leverage, he bent his good leg in front of the cage, then inserted the bar between the retaining pipe and the loop on the frame. He applied pressure and the tortured metal of the frame groaned.

"They'll hear," he said, releasing the bar.

Norah had an idea. "Can you speak their language?" she asked.

He nodded, then in Zulu and English told the people in the adjoining cages to make noise, any noise. Instantly, there were the sounds of fists beating against wire, hoarse voices, and screams.

David once again wedged the bar under the pipe. With all his strength he pulled, rising from the bottom of the cage. The loop started to give, then it snapped. The restraining pipe and lock clattered to the floor of the catwalk.

"All right," he said, smiling. "Now what?"

It took a minute to uncoil their bodies and crawl from the cage, and for David to replace the false leg. Stiff and sore, they moved at first with difficulty, then the blood began to flow. Soon they were limber and ready.

They heard a guard run down a nearby catwalk. He

would be phoning to tell Hartmann about the disturbance in the cages, the shouting. Keeping to the side of the cages, they crept low along the catwalk. The shouting and screaming continued. David heard many of the voices demanding also to be freed. Around the corner near the forward bulkhead, they stopped and looked left and right. David spotted the guard first and darted back one step, bumping into Norah. "Finally we're in luck," he whispered.

The guard spoke into a telephone. "Something set them off," he was saying, then, "No, I don't think any are loose. It's just one hell of a racket, like they're letting off steam." He listened, then replied, "I'll let you know if I do."

David leaped on his back just as he was hanging up the telephone. With a forearm frozen around his throat, he bent him back. Norah snatched his rifle from the floor. He struggled for an instant longer, then slumped at Monshoe's feet.

"Is he dead?" Norah asked.

"No," Monshoe said. "But he won't bother us either." He looked at the unconscious man. "Undress him and get his clothes on. Cap and all."

She tugged at his trousers, took off his shirt tunic. She got dressed. The clothes didn't fit well, but anything was better than nothing. The guard's cap covered her hair.

David was on his knees, feeling the rim of the watertight door leading to the frontmost bow section, a cavernous chain locker. There were no handles! They were now free, yet they had never been so imprisoned.

Norah tried to find a lock or latch or handle, but the door was perfectly smooth. She stepped back and gave Monshoe a helpless look. "It opens from the other side," she said. "We're trapped."

David stood with his back to the bulkhead, the guard's rifle cocked. The holds were sealed from the outside. Which meant there would be guards in the chain locker on the other side of the bulkhead. There had to be. How else would the guards get in and out of the holds? He went to the phone and pressed a button designated by a number. Anything but the bridge would bring what they wanted. "This is Hold 1," he said, urgently. "I need help."

A guard replied, "Where are you?"

"At the bow end of Hold 1!"

"What's the trouble?"

David paused. "Nothing that a couple of us can't handle," he said finally. "The white girl is acting up. We'll have to restrain her."

"We're coming through," the voice said.

The guards' speed surprised Monshoe and nearly threw him off balance as the door opened. They saw him immediately. The first guard tried to jump him, while the other one ducked back and started to close the door.

Norah swung the rifle butt at the guard struggling with David. It caught him in the back of his head, knocking him out cold. "Get in, David!" she yelled.

Monshoe threw his weight against the door. It flew open toward the guard. Monshoe was on him in that instant with a raised fist, which he slammed into the side of his face. The guard tried to kick him loose. But when he saw Norah standing with the rifle pointing at his head, he stopped struggling.

"Don't shoot," he said. "Don't shoot!"

Norah and Monshoe were breathless.

"We did it, David," she said. "We did it! Are you okay?"

"Yeah," he replied. "But we've still got a way to go." He looked around. "Keep that on him," he said, searching the locker for rope. There wasn't any. He opened a metal cabinet. "Gaffers' tape," he said, motioning for the guard to sit up. "Take off your clothes," he ordered. "And be quick. I'm cold."

The guard undressed. Monshoe put on his clothes, then wound the silver tape around the guard's legs and hands, finally lashing his arms to the chains. As an afterthought, he tore off a strip of tape and pressed it over the man's mouth.

"Much better than rope," he said. "Now, where do we go from here?"

The reply was so automatic. "To Hartmann," she said.

"What I meant was, how?"

"Back to the bridge, by any means we have."

"First, out of here."

She looked at him. "Are you sure your leg is all right?" she asked.

"Never better." He looked at the guard's clothes. "Not a bad fit," he said.

They climbed out of the locker on rungs welded into the bulkhead. The hatch on the deck was open. Monshoe took the lead, and when he reached the top, he looked around.

"More trouble," he yelled down to Norah.

"What is it?"

"The whole deck is exposed."

"But it's dark," Norah complained.

"No, it's not."

The deck was bathed in floodlight so blinding bright that Monshoe had to shade his eyes to see the bridge in the stern.

"They will see us," he said.

"It's a chance we have to take," she said.

"Here goes," David said, slipping out on the deck on his belly. He crawled behind a winch ten feet from the hatch. When he saw Norah's head appear in the opening he called out, "Over here."

"I see what you mean," she said, finally tucking herself behind David.

The deck shone brilliantly from a score of high-power beacons on stanchions. A strong wind sprayed rain through the air. The motion of the ship in the heavy sea was even more exaggerated on deck than it had seemed below. Even in total darkness, the journey to the bridge along the expanse of the deck would be hazardous.

Norah looked back toward the white bridge. Even from that distance, its height was imposing. She wondered where Hartmann was, on which deck. She felt his presence with deep foreboding. She didn't know how they could win. Everything was stacked against them, just as it had been right from the beginning. They had had one break, and they needed more.

* * *

"What are those?" Norah asked, pointing to the deck.

"They're pipes," David replied.

"Are they blocked at the ends?"

"Of course not."

The pipes lay on the deck in rows parallel to the ship's sides. Like everything else on *Bronze Maru,* they were outsized, designed for the offloading of crude oil. They lay in sections, yet they ran the ship's length into the shadow of the bridge. And they were of a diameter to fit a human.

"Okay, let's try," Monshoe said. "You go first. I'll be in the pipe beside you. Take care."

He watched her crawl around the winch and disappear into the end of a pipe, following shortly after in the one to the right. It was tight. The curve chafed his elbows. Progress was inch by inch. There was nothing to grab. And an oil film made the surface slippery. The rifle dragged behind. Finally he got to the end. He looked out and guessed that there were yet two more sections to cover to the bridge. Like a turtle, Norah poked out her head a minute later.

"Can you make it?" he asked.

"Yes," she replied, breathlessly.

They went into the next section. Monshoe crawled with persistence, each movement steady and timed so that his energy would last. There was no race; only the finish line. To cross it was to win.

Norah moved in spurts, then rested. She smelled the noxious fumes in the center of the pipe. The energy she was expending made her wonder if she had the endurance —not to get through the pipe, but to meet the obstacles beyond.

They pushed on, into the third section, then, finally, to the end. Norah's arms shook from the effort; David's body ached. But they were gladdened by the protective darkness of the bridge's shadow. Now close to their objective, they crouched near the hatch leading to the bridge elevator.

"Now listen to me, Norah," David said, his voice stern. "Here's where we separate—"

She started to protest.

"We have one rifle," he continued, "for *me* to use. These are my people and this is my responsibility."

"We can go together," she said.

"No, because if one of us is hurt, then the other will be trapped. We'll separate. I want you to go down the port side. Try to find an opening, a stairway, whatever. Just try to get to the top. I'll do the same on this side. But don't move onto the bridge, no matter what, until after you hear gunfire."

"He'll have guards with him."

"I know. But I think I can surprise them. If anything happens to me, I want you to continue the attack."

She took his hand. "Please don't let him hurt you."

"Not if I have any say. Now let's get moving." He started off, then looked back over his shoulder. "See you at the top."

Norah moved along the front of the bridge. She had nothing with which to defend herself, and she would need a weapon if Monshoe failed. She tried the handle of the port bridge door. It was locked. She turned around to see whether David had entered the bridge. He wasn't in sight. Just at the end of the bridge, where the deck curved around, she saw markings on the white paint. It was a red life buoy. Lashed beside it was an ax, which she took down and hooked into her belt. It was cumbersome, but she took it. Having *anything* now made her feel better.

Less than a minute had passed since they had parted. Norah knew that she must not follow David. He was right. It would be a waste. Somehow she had to approach from the port side. She looked up at the lights shining from the forward portholes at the deck levels of the bridge, at the very top. It seemed so high, so far. But she must *get there*.

At the side of the deck, she was steps away from the edge and the boiling ocean far below. Again she looked up. This time she saw the ladder, like the one they had used to climb from the chain locker, welded to the bridge. The question went through her mind. Could she do it? It wasn't a mental exercise now. She tried to weigh risk against advantage.

Risk: the ship was rolling. The rain made the ladder

rungs slippery. There was nothing but the ocean far below to break her fall. And what was there at the top?

Advantage: it was the only approach on the port side, away from David.

She moved fast up the lower rungs. Then she climbed with greater caution. She did not look down but concentrated on the bridge wall only inches from her face. First she released her right hand, grabbed, followed with her left. The pit of her stomach felt light. One foot found the higher rung, moved to ensure her grip, then the other. All for one rung up the ladder. Her elbows were bent when she wasn't reaching. She had to keep her chest in close to the wall. She held with her wrists. So long as they didn't tremble from fatigue, she was all right. The flat blade of the ax felt heavier on her back.

A gust of wind sliced past her, plucking the hat from her head. She instinctively reached out to catch it, then stifling a cry, returned her hand to the rung. When the ship rolled to starboard, away from her, she was at an advantageous angle, flatter to the side. But when it slowly heaved to port, she was on a flexible tower, leaning backward over the ocean. She now advanced only when the ship rolled to starboard.

She turned her face and needles of sea spray stung her skin. She had to keep her mind from what lay below. What came to her was Eli Thre. She wondered if he knew. And if he worried. And if he cared for her. And if, and if and if . . . She looked at and saw the configuration of the bridge. The ladder ended on a small platform. It connected Deck 9 to a superstructure jutting out twenty feet from the bridge. She guessed it was to hoist cargo.

There was gunfire.

She froze on the rung. Ten bursts had sounded. David had made his assault. She tried to differentiate the timbre of the gunfire. Was there one gun or several? She wanted to believe one, David's. And that meant he was safe. Yes, there had been only one. Now she climbed faster, anticipating her success.

David had done it! Suddenly the lights on deck switched off. The blackness terrified her. Alone, now in the dark, she was even more helpless. The deck now was a dull gray in a sea of black. Why had he done this, she wondered, groping up the ladder.

"Norah!" A voice on the ship's PA system, echoing and distorted by the wind. It was flat and hurt and terrible. She could hear a gurgled breathing. It was Hartmann. "I know you're there; I'm going to kill you." Then he laughed. He was hysterical and mad.

Norah hugged the ladder and cried.

He had won, just as she knew he would. All their efforts were for nothing. Eventually he would find her. She didn't know how, but he would find her and he would kill her. What was this stupid game they had played? How could they have thought of winning against *him?*

Now, uncaring if she fell, the climb was easier. She wondered if Hartmann was coming up after her or was waiting at the top, a few rungs above. It would be so easy. He could kick her into the sea. Or was that too easy? She could not conceive of the ugliness in his soul. Finally, she reached the top.

Now on the platform, Norah looked through the window. The bridge deck interior was bathed in a soft green light. David was on the floor. The guards were dead, as was the ship's captain. She stared hard again at David. She would not accept that he was dead, too.

Then she saw Hartmann.

He limped toward a steel cylinder, then kneeled down, wounded, extending one leg in front of him. He took a piece of paper from his pocket, looked at it, and put it on the floor. As though he were savoring it, he pressed three buttons.

The first activating instruction; "Enter."

Norah slipped the ax from her belt. She did not know what Hartmann was doing, but in his desperation, it could be anything with the purpose of destroying them all. She felt along the door between the platform on which she was standing and the interior of the bridge. She pushed down and it gave. Slowly and quietly she opened it.

His back was to her as she crept across the floor until she was so close that she could hear his breathing. She raised the ax high above her head and brought it down hard. The blade glanced off his shoulder and dug into his arm. He looked up. Norah stared at what she had done to his arm. She had cut through to the bone, but he seemed not to notice. He just *looked at her*. She raised the ax again, and he did nothing to stop her. He stared at her as though he were seeing her for the first time.

Their eyes met, and in that instant she knew she was defeated. Her mind was a blank.

Slowly she lowered the ax. Starting to sob, she held it at her waist. Her head bowed, she could not break his hold. She had hurt him: his arm was almost severed. But it didn't seem to matter. Now he could do anything he wanted. As though conceding to him, she threw the ax aside. Transfixed, she waited for her punishment.

He moved, but he didn't stand up. "You'll die with me," he said.

She nodded her head submissively.

Then he raised his other arm and pressed the buttons.

The second number; "Enter."

"Please, please, Ernst," she whispered.

"Yes, I promise. . . ."

Norah watched as he pressed one of the buttons. It would be over for all of them, swiftly and painlessly. This end was quiet, and she welcomed it.

Just as she shut her eyes, there was the flash of metal shining in a blurred arc; then she heard the ax blade thump into flesh.

She didn't have the courage to open her eyes, but she felt the weight of Hartmann's body against her legs and the warm wetness of his blood. A hand rested gently on her shoulder.

A second later the supersonic howl of the F-111 A/E's shattered the silence.

Fragrances from the citrus orchard, a shining blue sky, the sound of people laughing, children playing, lovers' whispers, affection, and lazy comfort, they all focused for her with unprecedented clarity. She opened her eyes and smiled with the knowledge of one who had survived. She was home and would never leave again.

Her hand quietly in his, Eli Thre sat across the table. They had come back to the café where they first had met, what seemed like decades ago, to reassure themselves. Once the madness was stamped out, they had to confirm in gradual degrees that normalcy reigned. It did here, as in no other place.

The breeze caught her hair and made it shimmer in the warm sunlight. She was more beautiful than ever. Eli wondered what that hell had done to her, inside where her real beauty lay. He could only guess. She had changed in those few horrible hours from a girl into a person of quiet strength.

She sipped at the straw, wondering if she should describe those final moments. It was something that she couldn't understand, why she had been defeated in that moment of victory. Ernst Hartmann was dead, but he had also won, as she knew he would. He had won over her in that instant of surrender. David had not been troubled. He had acted. He had swung the blade, as he would have at a log, without remorse or guilt. In the end it was David who had ensured their safety. She took the straw from her mouth and looked at Eli.

"I heard from David, you know," she said.

"Oh? What does he have to say?"

"Nothing much. He's back in Maseru, being King. He said they put his uncle in jail. This and that. He wants me to visit him. But I wrote back and told him thanks but no. He signed it, 'Fast Talker.'"

"That he was," Eli remarked.

"I still can't believe the Americans were going to bomb us."

"They had no choice. It wasn't just the Americans, either."

"Thanks," she said, grimacing. "Thanks a lot."

"You were saved by the lights. When Hartmann turned them off, the fighter pilots lost visual contact with the ship. Their orders were to be accurate."

"No, it was David. I couldn't move. But he screamed so loud into the microphone, he almost didn't need short-wave." She sipped again. "Can I have another?" she asked.

He motioned for the waiter.

"Tell me about the American again." During her debriefing by MOSSAD, she had learned about Crawford. She wished she could have known him.

"He was an amazing little guy," Thre said. "Between you and him, we stopped Hartmann. From what Egon tells me, Crawford enjoyed those last days. He felt like a participant, which he definitely was, and not the spectator he saw himself as. He was a hero, and the Americans are treating him like one."

"Do you think the South Africans will ever change?" she asked.

It took Eli a few seconds to understand what she was asking. She was switching from one thing to another. Maybe she was unable to dwell on any of it for long.

"That's what Connie Uys believes," he said, finally. "He's pushing for reforms. And that won't be easy. But even the Boers were horrified. They'll make amends. The blacks are living reminders, like Protégé—prisoners now."

Norah smiled and nodded. "Amen," she said.

ABOUT THE AUTHOR

MALCOLM MACPHERSON worked ten years as a staff correspondent for *Newsweek* before devoting himself full time to writing novels. He was based in Chicago, Los Angeles, Nairobi, Paris and London, covering news events on four continents. He now lives on Manhattan's East Side, where he is at work on another novel, his second.